Praise for Susan Froderberg's
OLD BORDER ROAD

"*Old Border Road* isn't a western by any formal definition of the term, but Susan Froderberg builds on those old tropes to tell a mournful story of men and women scraping by on America's arid frontier.... This is a western transformed by its focus on a young woman.... Katherine has a raw poetic voice that makes the tale an arresting incantation of longing and regret.... The effect is often moving and evocative.... It's good to be reminded again that this classic American form is no one-trick pony; it's still evolving, still turning those sepia myths into challenging new fiction."　　　　　—Ron Charles, *Washington Post*

"This debut novel is like a big-budget western with the set-design Oscar in the bag. Everything looks authentic, dusty. Even the narrator sounds voice-over ready, her accent baked into her words.... Ms. Froderberg isn't one to let up on the intensity; the weight of her words can feel biblical."
　　　　　—Susannah Meadows, *New York Times*

"Reminiscent of Faulkner and Stegner."　　　　　—*Elle*

"I especially like the energy and cadences of the sentences in *Old Border Road*. The book catapults forward in this fearless and honest voice. It's Katherine's life story told her way and she is one of the most engaging narrators I've come across in a long time.... And Katherine is as good a listener as she is a teller."
　　　　　—Peter Orner, *Granta Online*, "Best Books of 2010"

"Susan Froderberg's *Old Border Road* is a woman-finding-her-voice novel, but with none of the treacle or tropes of the genre. Froderberg writes with an elegance and originality that captivate.... The story has heart, perhaps because in Katherine we find a character to rally behind without feeling as if we've been manipulated into doing so.... She is spirited but humble, fallible but ultimately triumphant."

—Emily H. Freeman, *Minneapolis Star Tribune*

"In *Old Border Road,* Susan Froderberg's remarkable feat of literary ventriloquism gives us two inventive and haunting voices to remember. One is that of Katherine, the young ranch bride striving for the language to fit her predicament; the other is the author's own, a fresh dialect of talent on the fiction scene."

—Ivan Doig, author of *Work Song*

"Ms. Froderberg superbly draws on the Sonoran Desert's singular features to highlight Katherine's changing emotions. Her joyful honeymoon is set in a mountain lush with 'blue spruce, dwarf cedar, juniper'; but her marriage deteriorates as the heat wave 'drives desert rodents and millipedes to hole in the earth, singes wings of monarchs, silences chickadees, sends cacti into dormancy, has every animal panting.'... This stark and convincing portrait of Katherine's maturing from a 'love-struck girl' to a self-reliant woman is captured in a splendor of naturalistic detail. Katherine's coming-of-age story is given additional dimensions by the background drama of the drought and the need to provide water to an expanding desert population.... The hard lesson of *Old Border Road* is that there are endless enticements that lead men to dishonor." —Sam Sacks, *Wall Street Journal*

"Set against a stifling drought, events take on their own slow-burning heat.... Froderberg's writing...achieves the sublime."

—*The New Yorker*

"This remarkable debut novel, the story of a girl, begins with an adobe house and a road that runs south to north.... Susan Froderberg keeps circling back to beginnings...she starts Katherine's new life again and again, dashing hopes, revealing the meanness in Son and the difficulty of making a living from the dry earth." —Susan Salter Reynolds, *Los Angeles Times*

"This simple story is beautifully told. It takes place in a distinct landscape, alive with intense color, dense texture, and sharp sound.... Froderberg writes movingly of the haze of happiness that is the honeymoon. 'It is rapturous and ordinary, detailed and blurry, seeming to go on and on for a long time, and it is too soon over in the way all time can be.' More moving is her description of how time moves later, after the betrayals. 'Days and nights go by, regardless. The days are but a form to prop us, a stay to prevent our undoing, the nights but a measure of distance and passing.'" —Barbara Fisher, *Boston Globe*

"I read Susan Froderberg's fine and beguiling first novel a little bit, and a little bit more, and suddenly found myself in a beautiful and heartbreaking swirl of story and life and language and could not stop. The world therein is raw and urgent and yet adorned with element: burning and cooling, light and dark, droughty weather, delicate seeds greening, our perilous existence, our enduring sufferance."

—Robert Olmstead, author of *Coal Black Horse*

"Told in a vernacular that mixes biblical grandiosity and down-home grit....A southwest gothic debut that fans of Cormac McCarthy should adore."   —*Kirkus Reviews* (starred review)

"Susan Froderberg uses striking, poetic language to convey the parched landscape and internal stagnation...A conjuring of the Old West through the lens of modern times, with uncommon and wonderful landscape and flora terms...sprinkled through the narrative to bring this dreamscape to life."
—Jenny Shank, *New West*

"Employing a dreamy stream of consciousness evocative of Virginia Woolf, this debut novel conjures a seventeen-year-old newlywed from Arizona who realizes that her husband doesn't nearly live up to her expectations."   —*Ms. Magazine*

"A sunbaked exploration of love and pain in the American South-west, charts the turbulent ups and downs of a marriage."
—*Entertainment Weekly*

"The rural Arizona landscape echoes in every word of the sparse, beautiful prose....An exciting new writer to watch."
—Rebecca Shapiro, *BookPage*

"Froderberg's novel is deliciously poetic, surprisingly timeless—though set in the present day—and undeniably western."
—Julie Hunt, *Booklist*

"Froderberg's shimmering debut, set against the dusty, barren backdrop of the American Southwest, explores the joys and con-sequences of young love."   —*Publishers Weekly*

"Froderberg is truly Cormac McCarthy's literary offspring, echoing his hot, haunting brand of southwest essence, desert landscape, and gothic narrative elixir. . . . Although set in contemporary times, there is a timeless quality about *Old Border Road*. . . . I was exceptionally moved when I came to the last line of the story, a sentence that touched me with its purity, subtlety, and pith."
—Betsey Van Horn, MostlyFiction.com

"*Old Border Road* fills some gaps in the Cormac McCarthy school of writing with Froderberg's plucky young female narrator. . . . The novel's artful language is beguiling."
—Vikas Turakhia, *Cleveland Plain Dealer*

OLD BORDER ROAD

A NOVEL

SUSAN FRODERBERG

BACK BAY BOOKS

LITTLE, BROWN AND COMPANY

New York   Boston   London

Copyright © 2010 by Susan Froderberg
Reading group guide copyright © 2011 by Susan Froderberg and Little, Brown and Company

Back Bay Books / Little, Brown and Company
Hachette Book Group
237 Park Avenue, New York, NY 10017
www.hachettebookgroup.com

Originally published in hardcover by Little, Brown and Company, December 2010
First Back Bay paperback edition, December 2011

Back Bay Books is an imprint of Little, Brown and Company. The Back Bay Books name and logo are trademarks of Hachette Book Group, Inc.

The publisher is not responsible for websites (or their content) that are not owned by the publisher.

The Hachette Speakers Bureau provides a wide range of authors for speaking events. To find out more, go to www.hachettespeakersbureau.com or call (866) 376-6591.

The author gratefully acknowledges the editors of *Conjunctions* and *Prairie Schooner,* where parts of this novel first appeared, in different form.

Library of Congress Cataloging-in-Publication Data
Froderberg, Susan.
   Old Border Road : a novel / Susan Froderberg. — 1st ed.
      p. cm.
   ISBN 978-0-316-09877-9 (hc) / 978-0-316-09878-6 (pb)
   1. Teenage girls—Fiction. 2. Teenage marriage—Fiction. 3. Marital conflict—Fiction. 4. Life change events—Fiction. 5. Self-realization—Fiction. 6. Arizona—Fiction. I. Title.
   PS3606.R5827O43 2010
   813'.6—dc22   2010011403

10 9 8 7 6 5 4 3 2

RRD-C

Printed in the United States of America

For E.J.,
WHO SAID TO STAY THE COURSE

AND

FOR GORDON,
WHO POINTED THE WAY

What is that which always is and has no becoming,
and what is that which is always becoming and never is?

—Plato, *Timaeus*

CONTENTS

OLD
BORDER
ROAD

ONE

A HOME TO GO HOME TO

He has shown me the old adobe house outside and in and he has taken me riding across all the parceled acres of land that surround the house and he has told me the told-again stories born of the place and of his family and of him. And now it is me showing Son what I have come from, going south to north along the coast, from one border town to another one yet, from forests petrified to those old-conifered, from cottonwood to silver fir, diamondback to amanita, erg dune to tidal flat, and sandstone to agate, from what is to what has been, from memory to what might be.

Our start-up is done according to ritual, our send-off as to custom and trend. The town people gather in earnest and attend us bearing gifts, the golden aster is vased upon the altar, the pig turns out on the spit in offering. We say all the words supposed to be said and do all the things supposed to be done and we get all the things that one gets. We get suitcases lent to us and bills tucked into envelopes, and we get stories of people's own and advice aplenty for living our lives anew. We take all of it as given in the wholeheartedness that it is. We get wishes scribbled across the side of the pickup truck that we leave there as a kind of flourish to our pilgrimage, keeping what's written through the new moon we are in, as that moon waxes crescent and quarters to full and as it wanes gibbous and fades on toward its end. The words as they were chalked, the sand and the dust, the grime and the duff and the tar and the oil and the mud, and whatever else of the earth we collect up along the way, will all be washed away in the moon after, once we are back to here where we are, to begin another beginning.

LET ME TELL you, then, properly, from the beginning.

Let me tell you about the knocking, the way it came as a start in the hold of the night. It's a knocking that remains yet inside me—the weight, the cadence, the meter, the stop it put to the breath, the stall it got of the heart, a feeling that will always be, coming as it did at the wrong time, and so far into dark. I can still hear Son calling out to open up, and I'm trying to lie still enough not to be here, with my heartbeat beating so loud I'm afraid of it giving me away, even with him out there and with me in here in the bed. The knocking kept on.

It's me, he said. He said, I know you know who this is.

His words were slurred, but I knew who this is, was.

It was a knock on the door I had wished for. I didn't answer it. I had an old nightshirt on and pincurls in my hair and school in the morning. Son said he knew I could hear him, and I cupped my hands on my chest to quiet me down. The knocking finally stopped, and there was nothing but the sound of the wind gusting the dust up out in the empty lot. I got up from the bed and made my way in the dark to the door and opened it. He turned around on his way to his pickup when I said to him, Come back and come in.

Son had never been to my place, but I had been in his truck once. That was down in Mexico, and he had offered me a ride back over the border. He lived on this side, our side, down on Old Border Road, and he had shown me the old adobe house on the way to taking me home. That's where I live, he said, and at this he reached over and pulled the back string of my haltertop free so he could catch a peek. I told him the way to the trailer and to please keep his eyes on the road. This is where I live, I said, and he turned in and stopped the truck and let it idle in neutral. I got out and said maybe I would see him again some-day, and he shifted into gear and pulled out of the lot.

IT WAS JUST the one time on the road back from Mexico that I had seen the old adobe house. I had only otherwise heard talk of the place and the family about town, talk that had of late carried a look my way or the drop of my name. Or some remaking of my name.

My name is Katherine, same as my mother's name, same as my mother's mother's name. I've never been a Kathy, never been a Kath, not a Katie or a Kate, not a Kat, a Kitty, a Kitten, not a Kit. Katherine I have always been, as Katherine I am today. I'm Katherine to my mother—a Katherine with a given middle name added on when she's summoning me or angry and needing more span and heft to fill the call out. To my father, I am always Daughter, as maybe my other name unhappily recalls to him my mother. Daughter, he will say when I telephone him. Hello Daughter he will say. He will write it Dotter when he writes to me, thinking the spelling funny or charming in some way, as I do as well.

I am Darlin' to Son. Darlin' I always am.

I would be Girl to the old man. Just Girl to him.

Dear Girl, I would hear from the old man's old wife.

The New Girl is what I was called at school. I heard this name among the murmurs from the other girls sitting behind me during our classroom break out in the shade of the ramada. Their talk settled about in the air with the drift of their cigarettes and the pulsating clack of cicadas. There were also remarks from certain evening regulars at the coffee shop, those who had a tendency as well to keep abreast of my business. My mother was one to bring home common scraps of gabble too, just as she fueled rumors about me with comments of her own.

I tried to shut the talk out.

My mind was made to break away early.

Son would come by in his pickup to get me, as was the plan. I skipped out of astronomy, though astronomy was my favorite class of any, maybe because we lived in the midst of the land of night sky and I could do my homework just by looking upward. More so, I had hopes of one day becoming a scientist, a doctor or a researcher of some kind. Certain ways of thinking were hard for me, but other things came naturally. The body, the earth, the universe — those mysteries unseen, I could somehow most easily see. Not because I was good at finding answers to equations, but because I loved the locked rooms of the questions themselves. I could imagine the workings and the designs of things. Pictures came to me in what seemed layers and boundaries, in what they call surface and expanse, or in drift and intent — or something like this anyway, although I know no better way to explain it. There are laws to hold to as well, laws physical and universal, laws unchangeable as to truth until falsified, laws that make a person feel safe.

Today I would be safe going with Son.

We drove through a grove of groomed fruit trees with the old adobe house out ahead of us commanding attention from the podium of earth it was built on. Son pointed to an empty plot of shade, where he said the sedan was missing from. This meant it was only the old man at home, he said, that his mother, he said, would be gone shopping or to luncheon or to some function or other that she could do her hair and dress up for. I didn't ask him if our timing was planned or accident, I only wondered it.

The hill was lawned handsomely with Saint Augustine, and today automatic sprinklers sprayed watery rainbows over the slopes. Desert poppy and dusty maiden grew in the beds along the walkway, and a climbing rose laid claim over the portal. A shepherd kind of dog rose up from the welcome mat and sniffed at my fingers and slapped its dust whip of a tail against us in greeting. It leaned into Son's leg and he whumped the dog on the shoulder a couple of times in a language back. Son was about to open the door, but the old man was there to open it before us. He came out and tipped the hat back on his head and said he was pleased to meet me and he did seem so. He took my hand as if to shake it and he pulled me forward to him to where when he spoke I could feel the prickle of his breath on my face. After an uncomfortable while like this, he chuckled and let me go.

He said lunch was just about ready. We went into the old adobe house and he led us through the many cool dark rooms of it and then we moved on into the kitchen. We sat at a table in a nook next to a window where we could look out at a grove of old lemon trees, their trunks all whitewashed white and their leaves all trimmed to globes, the fruit on them hanging like holiday ornaments. The old man set aluminum plates of frozen dinners out as a lunch for us—frozen green beans and frozen fried

7

chicken and frozen mashed potatoes all steamed with heat now, and biscuits just unwrapped from their own aluminum blanketing.

I readied it all up myself, the old man said. You kids, dig in.

He put cold bottles of cola out to drink, asking me what about a glass and ice with that or why not a nip of whiskey? and I said I would pass on the whiskey, as I had homework to do after. He passed napkins around and he took a seat and we set to eating, the old man talking the whole time in story as Son and I gnawed on our wings and sucked down our cold cola drinks.

My old man came west to these borderlands, said the old man, when he was but a young man. He came out and bought him all the acres around us you see. And he hired many men and planted many trees, the trees of which bore the fruit to be sold towns and counties and states away. Thence my father's wallet got fat mighty durned fast, as you can imagine. And so he bought more land. And with his profits from all the land, he told the men to build him a hummock in the middle of all his acres. Then he had the men collect the gumbo from just over the border to mix the adobe mud up with. And he had them build the adobe house atop the hummock we sit upon. He told them to cement in the borrow pit, and so they did, and they painted a turquoise color inside it as he had said to, and they filled it in with water to the brim. He told the men to clear the land south of the old adobe house and to build him a corral there, and stables there, an arena and cow chutes and a tackhouse there as well. And lo, my father decided that fruit had been a fruitful living for him and so he would make it a bigger venture yet. He told the men to build him a melon shed out behind the old adobe house. Then all the acres around the melon shed were cleared and the soil made ready and the seed was sown in with the seed drill. And during this time he built the waterways — the mother ditches and the acequias and the regaderas. He put in the presitas, the floodgates and the watergates. And the water was pumped through the fields in these manmade capillaries of his, these valves and these shunts of his.

And so be it my father did indeed become a rich man, he said. And he became a favored man in town. And the people made him the town mayor. He had many friends and patrons and many functions and parties to attend to. He had all this but he had not a woman to share it with. Then it was at one of the many socials he did come to meet a woman from the county east. And they were married and soon after they begat me and we lived the three of us, a happy family as ever there was one, under the roof of this here adobe house. Even during the driest of spells in the heat of the days we were happy. There were nights, I remember, when it was fiercely hot and we would go to bed with wet sheets and the fans blowing on us to get through the night and the weather.

Whoo-ee, he said. And still we did all right.

And then my mother died and my father mourned her for the rest of his years. And the town people had empathy for him and elected themselves a new mayor. And I took over running the working of the land for him when he could not sleep nor could he get out of bed either.

All of this when I was yet a young man.

And so indeed, I too would need a wife. And good fortune was soon bestowed upon me when a new family came into town from back east. They were nesters who had come as many others had come, and that was to better their health and thereby their lives in this dryland habitat. They bought property just north of our land and they built themselves a fine house upon it.

They planted acres of bermuda and alfalfa and pastureland, and we paid them to let our horses and cattle graze on those acres. And lo and behold they should have a lovely daughter with the prettiest yellow hair a man might have ever seen. Anyone might have ever seen. And soon the howdy-do's were made, and yes, I was lucky indeed.

Speaking of which, the old man said. He lifted his hip an inch off the bench and took his wallet out and from his wallet he brought a dollar bill out.

How about a bit of gambling? he said.

You know this game of liar's poker?

WE LEAVE WITH the music playing, with the guests out on the dance floor in two-step and atwirl, with some filling their punch cups up from the spout of the fish mouth, with others at tables working seriously at their cake. We leave behind the bouquets of desert flowers and the decorations of papier-mâché, the piles of ribboned merchandise, all the bright and many-colored lights. We step outside the rented tent into the greater tent of a tinseled, starlit night. Above our heads is a spread of lost heroes and creatures of make-believe, a spiral of spiraling galaxies, a curtaining glow of aurora, a soffit of planets and stars. In skies to come, there will be more and different views and still but a speck of all there is, wombed inside this universe as we are, with our vision so hindered. Yet I look outward and am filled with pictures of the more and the what-there-might-be for us. What can be for me and Son. Now is only the beginning.

Hold it while ye may, yet happy pair.

We freeze in the click of the shutter.

And time is burned in, in a rupture of light.

The scene is a clumsy one, with Son in the lead and staggering on to the pickup and me behind, trying to make my way through a maze of suns that veer about and kilter off before my eyes. I gather my veil and train, hitched to a great weight of dress as I am, and climb up and in and slide over to the middle of the benchseat, pushing aside the cumulus mass of satin and tulle and organza, letting it all pillow onto the floor and pile up over the seat and spill out through the window. Son gets in beside me, halo'd as he is yet by the ghost of the flash. He is light and mass and heat and smile, and I am alive in the high spirit of him, of us, and of all that is tonight. I wish not to forget, but it is too much, this present is, all too much for the senses—like the blaze of the sun that can't be looked at too long. That potent the moment is.

We are caught in the blind spots of one last picture. We blink and rub at our eyes and wait for the world to right itself again. Then Son turns the key and starts us up, and we give our good-byes and take our good-lucks, and everyone waves, as everyone does.

There is space and time and color and sound.

How else might I tell you?

WE ARE TOO young to be thinking of doing it. But Son told me his mother told him he ought to be doing it. He said she said it is not correct to be spending nights in the same girl's bed when you are not yet wedded to her. Son's mother was hushed after our promises were made. She said no more about Son's leaving after roundup and supper each evening, and his not coming back until morning feed and watering time. When nothing was different but for this ring I've got on my finger. The ring, that too you could say is thanks to his mother, as she told the old man to give Son the sum he needed to go into town to see Mr. Gomez at the jewelry shop with. Now look at me, here at my age, wearing a diamond ring on my finger. A bright solitaire to be joined with a thin gold band meant to fit right with it.

The two of us, we too fit together perfectly.

My legs are hitched up around the crest of Son's hips and he rocks us into the bed like this, moving us as one in this way, the whole bed awave in the rhythm of us. I cinch my arms around the roll and the breadth of his shoulders. His breath and his words are buried in my hair. We move and we move without missing a beat, and we're roused and soothed by the cadence we make. I keep my eyes on the stone, the whitehot sparkle of star inside, hoping to take some kind of meaning or power in the spell of it. I let myself be carried off in watching it, in a thought that becomes no thought at all.

By the law, I am a child. I'm not legal age to be married. My mother told us she is happy to go down to the courthouse and sign for me for the license. She told us she is happy to have Son for a son. When he is around her, her movements quicken and her lashes flutter and her voice turns sweet as her cakes and her drinks can be. She will tongue the icing off the knife blade and fill tall glasses with ice cubes and iced tea for us. We will sit out in her patio of shade, and she will flush and bat a napkin at her face, as she talks about who has taken ill in the hot spell or what succulents in the beds have succumbed to it, as she talks about the modern coolness of the new stucco church at the plaza and the kinds of flowers that will hold up inside it. Styled in the Spanish style, she will say, and, inside, a fancy archway beneath which the baptisms are given and the matrimonial vows exchanged.

Son will make jokes about robbing cradles.

She will slice another slice of cake for him and lick the knife another time. He will say how nice my mother's legs are, and this gets her to throw her head back and laugh the way a young girl laughs.

I would ask her about her wedding dress.

Now you would ask me. You would say, Why go and do a thing such as getting married when you are too young to be thinking of doing it? I can only explain it like this—that whatever you believe it is that is supposed to come true for you, well, one day you think it has. Though if you were to ask me now, I couldn't tell you what the truth I believed in was, or is.

I WEAR MY mother's wedding dress and don't notice the stain on it until it's too late. Just try to smile, someone says, and carry your bouquet lower, more like this, and no one will ever know what's there. We're on our way to the church—the satin train of the dress spread across the entire backseat of the station wagon—and this feeling comes on over inside me that what I'm about to do is wrong. It's like the start and run of a stain, and I look down and see the black I've put on my eyelashes falling in drops on the lap of my dress. But there's no going home I know to go home to.

The awful unease is gone from me by the evening. It's gone before the handshakes and the laughing and the two-stepping has begun. I'm calmed during the song and the long walk down to where Son is waiting for me.

The spell, or whatever you might say it was, has passed.

Likely it was fear that started it. Or it might have been girlish habit or tendency. Or it could have been being mixed up or overwhelmed or even being just tired. Or maybe any number of things. Whatever the feeling was, it came over me like some great alter in the weather when I got into the backseat of the station wagon. My mother put her foot to the gas and we were off in a kickup of dust. She paid no heed to my abrupt quiet, as she must have been deep in some daydream of the notice that lay in store for her that day. She didn't look back at me. I didn't speak. I couldn't say anything without something inside me breaking up and coming out in a kind of strange and embarrassing sound. We moved down the road inside a cloud of whirling earth, my stomach rocking in unsettling waves, and my mouth watering up with a worrisome taste. I took long deep breaths in to make the dizzy go away and the faint stop. I sat looking out at the world as it went wheeling by outside the window, feeling undone. I was overcome by a reckoning, is what I was, a kind of knowing, a kind of something that made me hesitate, made me want to say, Wait — say, Can't I maybe stay a child for just a little time longer yet? Yet knowing too it was too late to back up and turn around now.

I cleared my throat and hoped to stop shaking.

We rode down Main Street. It seemed the longest ride I had ever taken, but we were already turning into the alameda before it seemed we should have been there. My mother parked the car in the shade of desert sycamore, and we got out and I gathered my train up and we walked out into the hot open sun of the plaza. A diamondback rattled out in front of us onto the footpath, and my mother and I cried out and shot back, watching the thing slither off into the nopal.

You'd better decide to take it as a good-luck sign, she said.

We hurried on into the courtyard and were soon inside the cool reprieve of the sanctuary. Chiseled figures hovered in the stillness above while on the ground busy women floated about with great concern for certainty, for detail and timing. I stood in the foyer, amid all this, trembling in vaulted shadow during the entire wait of the gathering, a heap of feelings welling up inside my chest and pushing my breath out in small and labored breaths. I stood alone in a thicket of confusion and the stirrings of goings-on, in the hard lope of my heart—a pounding so loud others surely could have heard it as well. Finally the building up of who knows what it was broke apart inside the hold of my throat. It spilled out when my mother—dressed for this occasion in a prom dress of mine, one that I would never wear now—came up to me and spoke a few sentimental and commonly said words right before the step and assemble of the ceremonial party started.

I couldn't keep it reined in anymore. The dark poured forth from my eyes and splotched up the bodice of the already stained dress. The mascara matted my lashes together and rolled down my cheeks, turning the world a bog and my face and dress a mess. Dark blotches would mark all the photographs of us that were made in testament to the day. I would later see me standing upright and smiling in the biddings to be fertile as the earth and happy until death.

You are pale as a ghost, my mother said.

There were all the people there. There were all the names that had been written in the book. There were the words we had been told to speak. There was the thin gold band ready to be fitted against the bright solitaire meant for it. There were all the wishes prepared for us, all the gifts set out on the table, a feast on display, a great fiesta awaiting. The band was ready to play.

Son stood at the far other end from where I was, dressed up in a dark and stiff formal outfit not his, tugging at his shirtcuffs.

But I cannot here recall having seen his face enough, as my mother was suddenly walking off ahead of me and blotting him out, coupled and arm in arm as she was with her young escort. There was a humming commotion among the guests, a resonance as of insects. A soprano'd voice cued me to move, and all the many heads turned back to watch as I walked toward them. I thought right then but too late that the song that had hooked me once was the wrong one to choose for today.

I tried to let the melody calm me.

The bridesmaids started out ahead, their gowns proudly homemade, their hair done up and laced with heliotrope and adam-and-eve. Then it was me. I walked alone. It was my way of doing things. I had said I wanted to walk it alone, as I had written but never heard back, though I held to the chance that my father might show at the last minute. Yet knowing I was born only a daughter and not a son—an old and piddling story, too many times told.

So I walked alone now in the weight of that dress and in parched afternoon light, the dress so heavy and the air so dense it seemed I moved in slow motion, as though there were something from sleep I was harnessed to and trying to make my way forward in. I walked down that long aisleway, past all the town people who had come for the show and that I mostly didn't know, their faces looking to me all one and a single blur of questioning. I walked on and on for what seemed a long time. I walked along to that wrong song. Pillars of dusty light filtered in through the tall windows and settled on the heads of the attending, bestowing them with a kind of otherworldliness. You should have seen everyone, the way they had come dressed up in their finery and niceties and frills. The women had come powdered and feathered and gloved, their hair twisted and braided and coiled, and there were pillboxes and bonnets and mantillas among them. The men wore their best-yoked jackets and leather vests, their silver bolo ties and turquoise studs, their tooled belts and rodeo buckles, their dress boots of lizard or snakeskin. They scratched at their starchy collets. They covered their crotches over with the flat of their felt hats.

All were upstanding now.

It was time to go on and do what we had decided.

What I had decided.

MY MOTHER CALLED the sheriff the first go-round. He showed up at the trailer and told me to get into his car, and I argued that I would not, and he said, You had better or else, and he said a few words more added to all this too. So I got in, mad as I was, and the sheriff delivered me back to her.

This is some months before Son.

Let me thank you personally, my mother said to the sheriff.

Why tack a personally on for, I said, not asking a question.

My mother's way of keeping me with her was to say she was grounding me. She said I was to take the bus straight to campus, and after classes I was to go directly to the coffee shop for evening shift where she would come pick me up. It was home only after that, and that was it every night after work, no matter what. Her dictum lasted about a week before my anger at her began to stir about from where it was seated not so deeply. It spiraled up and out of me like a dustdevil. My mother was one great spouting horn of her own, coming at me with threats the way she did, with a potlid in her one hand and a spatula raised above her head with the other. I fired some words at her, hoping to knock her back, and this must have worked, as she was stopped in her fury and her face went suddenly deadpan. She wiped the froth off her chin with the back of a hand and she drove a cold hard look into my eyes that I won't soon forget. She put the potlid and the spatula down and turned away.

Just go, she said.

The trailer I later found was on the far edge of town, parked on desert pavement out on a deserted lot. The earth was barren and hard, having been winnowed over the years by the sand and the wind. A gasoline station sat next to the lot, and with a telephone booth there if I would have needed it.

I believed I wouldn't need it.

It was hot in the trailer on hot days out. It was hot in the trailer even on not hot days. I sat on the front stoop with a hand saluted to my forehead to keep the burn of the sun off my face. I listened to a fiery wind huffing through the bitterbrush and mesquite. The repeat of cicadas came from everywhere and who knows where, going on and on as they will in their constant song and trill of courtship and territory. I sat in thought of better days to come as hot gusts of wind scarved dust across the lot. I imagined lush woodlands and wild rivers and grassy fields. I thought of boys who played guitars and sang to me. I thought of all there was that had been left or lost or simply tossed away and forgotten.

There was a dumpster that sat out across the lot. There would be picked-over bones and blackened peels and soiled diapers and such toppled out, no matter if the garbage had just been emptied from it or not. There was not much else around. Just a billboard at the side of the road with a cowboy pictured on it who held a coiled rope in his fist and a cigarette between his teeth. I thought about someday getting braces for my teeth, thinking how that might change everything for me in the right direction. I added money to come and counted up the weeks. I thought about the days and the places and the people gone and now far away.

I picked a stick up. I tossed it to shoo a raggedy crowbird off the strewn garbage, and it kwok'd and lifted and paced. I swatted the flies away from my head. I looked for shade, a cool place. A truckload of fieldhands passed and there were those hisses and clucks you get, and I picked a rock up and pitched it at their wake of hopeless noise, choking on the choking cloud of dust they left behind.

I was thirsty.

I got up and wandered over to the gasoline station to buy a soft drink. There was an old card-table and some half-broken fold-down chairs under a single pecan tree there, and I sat and would drink my drink in the shade of it. I used the sweat of the cold bottle to wipe the dust off my face, and then I might rest my eyes on the empty phonebooth ahead of me, at the lovers' names painted and scratched on the glass, at the book of pages yellowed and hanging abandoned inside on the chain, thinking how often I mistakenly heard the telephone in it ringing. Thinking how I would be sickened by someone feeling as sorry for herself as I was feeling sorry for me.

WE MAKE THE first stop the trailer where the clothes I left are waiting arranged for me on the bed. It's almost too small a space in this aluminum alleyway, not space enough for me and all this dress I'm fettered in. It takes a long time for Son to unbutton all the hundred tiny buttons down the back of it. Such frippery, he says. He's drunk on wedding punch and he stumbles back and forth and the whole trailer rocks from side to side with us. His tongue is thick in his mouth and his fingers none too nimble and he mumbles and knits along the length of my spine, tail to nape, impatiently. He undoes the last button and holds up the heft of the dress, and I free myself from within and climb out and under from inside it. There is a whoosh of fabric to the floor, the tent of it collapsing in release, a great rush of breath as of a wind gust through desert brush.

Son takes hold of me. He says, C'mon, Darlin', we should let's do it here, but I tell him I want to do it as these things are done on such a day as this. What we do will be held in memory, I say. For always, I say. So? he says. That's good any way it goes, isn't it? But he shrugs and lets me go and picks the borrowed suitcase of my things up and carries it out to the truck. I put my new travel dress on and follow after him, closing the door of the trailer the one last time.

The night sky is filled brimful as a night sky can be, lit brightly as it is with clusters of planets and pulsating stars and marriages of galaxies, all of it within a wobble of dust and gas and debris unseen. There are the Dippers Little and Big tonight, a lovely Pleiades, and a throbbing red star out like a tiny heart. This is the stuff of which we are made, I say to Son, all that is of us is above us. We stand together looking upward, our mouths hung open as if to swallow what's above down and into us. Looking out at the past in its far distance, where from there, here we are not.

Let's get a get-go, he says.

He lets the truckbed down in a screech of metal and hinge. There's a thump of a suitcase tossed in, a jingling ring of ringed keys, Son humming that wrong song the wrong way. He opens the door and acts to doff a hat, and I take the keys away, telling him he has too much punch in him to be driving out on the highway, and when the fun is just beginning for us. He says, Okeydokey, you are the wifey, Darlin'. We hop up and into the pickup and I pull us out of that empty lot, leaving the trailer behind, the dumpster, the billboard, the gas station, the card-table, and the fold-down chairs, leaving the lot of it behind.

We drive out past the outskirts with the lights veiled upon the town and atwinkle in the distance. We take the highway west and come soon into a great arenal of sand, an arena of darkness, a kind of nothingness that goes on and on for miles and miles, making a person uncomfortable, distrustful. It is darker than dark in the night. Our headlights begin to flood saguaro and organ pipe and ocotillo. Bright coyote eyes wink like stars along the roadside, and startles of jackrabbits take cover in the brush. Desert rats dart to and fro in a rush to their middens — twig, bone, teeth, shell, toy and cob and fur, and whatever else they may be home to. Creeping things unnamed go every which way in a dash to sand hole or desert nest — timid creatures fright-ened by the rouse of our engine and the ricochet of our lights.

Son jumps into a story about rabbit hunting with boyhood chums. He laughs about getting drunk and shooting twenty-twos from the windows of pickup trucks.

My father always said to keep your eyes out the window on the broken line ahead if you're feeling carsick and queasy, I say.

Son slaps some kind of drum routine out on the dashboard.

Why do guys always do that? I say.

Do what? he says.

He rolls his window down and lets the cool desert air in and we sit in silence for a while. In not too long a time we come into a sea of rippled dunes that crest and pyramid at our sides and attend us like guests for miles ahead. On the foreland in the distance lie the curved spines of the foothills, seeming to be beasts fallen to extinction at the earth line. We make bets on how far away we are in minutes from here to the pass, and our game carries us along for a good stretch of highway. After a time we go to naming the names of places to come that we have seen on the map, names such as Spring Valley and Torrey Pines, Oceanside and Riverside, Santa Clarita, Santa Rosa, Santa Jacinta, and Santa Whatnot, remembering Petaluma and Fortuna and Ventura, Red Bluff and Coos Bay, and not to forget Lincoln City or Fall City, Tumwater or Winslow, nor Astoria. We will move through names. We will move through valley and mesa, playa and canyon, grazing field and urban park, through shrubland and grassland and woodland, past chaparral and fumarole and peninsula, old-growth and clear-cut slopes, and we will move onward into so much of the world out in front of us we don't know yet. Who might possibly be as happy as we are?

A scratching of melody comes from the radio, chords rising open as the land that carries us, rhythm mimicking our passage down the road, harmony making this life seem it should be only that. We sing along to what songs have always been about — beginning, going on, breaking up, forgiving. We sing in missed words and broken phrases as glints of tiger moths fly at us like snow, streaking the windshield over.

In time we begin to climb. We come to the top of the pass and into blue spruce, dwarf cedar, juniper. Just off the highway, lit up among a hush of trees, is the small lodge we have heard of and have chosen to stay at, for this our first night betrothed, a place that is just the beginning of all the places we have yet to get to. Yet believing there is no more joy in the getting there than there is in the going.

Hold it while ye may.

We get out of the pickup and breathe in the incense of pine

air and woodsmoke. Our breath pales the dark and goes ghosting off between us. Above us is a canopy of trees, and through
the tree holes there shines a luminous star. The stillness is certain here, compared to nights upon nights glutted with the high-
pitched shrill of crickets—that hum in the ears that can buzz
up the nerves. Except for the riffling of the creek alongside us
now, the quiet is like something from out of a dream, making us
want to whisper at one another in the dark to hold to the silence
better, as if not to be waked from the time and the place we are
in. A desire path cuts through the grass, and I point to it that we
should take this shortcut way instead of the steps laid out ahead.
There, the way through the trees, I say. Son takes off on the
path into the dark ahead of me, and I turn to run and catch him
when then comes a *thwok,* like the sound of a softball hit against
a bat, and Son has run smack into the overhanging branch of a
rambling tree. He's laid out flat on the ground. Even sober he
could not have seen it coming. I cover my mouth to mute my
laughing and I wait for Son to get up. But he doesn't. Don't be
kidding around, I say. Still he's quiet. C'mon, I say, you have had
your fun. But he's quiet yet and now you see I'm not laughing
anymore. I bend down and Son is cold silent. I touch his face,
feeling the wet trickle of blood, and my heart tumbles inside my
chest like a stack of children's blocks toppled to the floor.

Son, I say. I shake him.

Another light inside the lodge goes on.

He opens his eyes and smiles.

WHAT ARE YOU doing just staring there, Girl? the old man
says. He finds me standing in the afternoon ticking of the grandfather clock, in the cool dark parlor of the old adobe house, in

front of a fireplace meant more for fancy than for function. I stand at the mantel, handling the knickknacks placed just so and studying the pictures there in front of me, and I tell you, I could stay standing here this way the entire rest of the day and on into the evening, throughout the night even. I could do it all over the very next day for the entire day again. That's how much in awe I am of Son's growing-up days I see before me in the pictures, how in awe of the ways of his family I am, so foreign as they are to me. I'm taken by the history of him. I'm taken by the flesh and the hair and the teeth of him, of all that I see.

But I don't tell the old man any of this.

That boy sure knows how to set a horse, don't he? he says.

He picks one of the pictures up and puts his nose to it, with his eyes asquint as if he were seeing something in it for the very first time. Then he puts it back down.

You kids, he says, and he chuckles the way he does.

Anyways, I need to skedaddle into town to see a man about a new saddle for the bay, if you maybe want to ride along, he says.

Son says for me to wait for him, I say, and the old man okeydokeys me and leaves me standing at the mantel. I go back to looking at the pictures, all handsomely framed as they are and carefully arranged between candlesticks and Navajo bowls and pottery vases and those kinds of things set there by the old man's wife. There's a photo of Son when he was at the age of still being a Sonny, a small boy in cowboy hat and boots, holding a rope coiled in his kid-gloved hand. There's a picture of him as a 4-H'er, standing proud beside his show cow, and next to it the purple ribbon won and hung in another frame. There's a picture of Son grown some, in uniform with numbers on his chest and a ball in the hook of his arm, and I'm struck with a worry now about others that might have loved him before me, girls' names I've heard from him that come back to me, visions that give me this sinking feeling.

I want to shake the crazy thoughts away.

I look at the picture of him most recently, on horseback and dressed in vest and hat and badge, his chest out and held proud as a dancer does it, with the old man at his side and with the rest of the posse back in the background. I look all the photographs over again, who knows how many times. Until I notice something about the look on Son's face, how the look is the same, no matter what age or situation, in each of the pictures.

There is something that is off in him.

What is it I see? Is it boredom? Or seriousness? Or conceit? Is it impatience I see? Is it Son's being posed to be what's right in the eyes of others? Is it his trying to fit with certain attitudes and virtues they find most redeeming?

Will that look be changed in photographs of us to come?

How could I doubt it?

I will myself not to doubt it.

I am so much in love these days, I take pity on anyone who isn't us. I look at everyone throughout the day, couples young and old, people here and there, alone or with others, smiling or talking or whatnot, and I cannot see a single face of anyone who could possibly be as happy as I am. It is only us who really know love, me and Son.

THE WOUND ON his head adds to the sanctity of this night, to the ritual of it, as if the clout were a sacrifice to powers unseen to ensure the blessings of our marriage. Son laughs when I tell him this, says I'm loco, says I'm loony in my cabeza, is what I am.

But I tell him I will treasure whatever scar might likely be there to remind me for the rest of our days. I say I will cherish each day I am graced to see it. I'm looking at Son and staying my eyes on him, trying to embrace what I see. From this moment on, I will myself to hang on to everything here, this night, our beginning. I wonder about the reel of time we are in and how it will spill out into memory someday, and how it will all be lost or be changed. I want what is now to be always what it is. I cling to the words of every song that plays on the radio. I study the arrangement of the bed in the room we are in, where the door is, where the bathroom is, how the suitcase rests open, how the shoes are kicked off, the way the keys splay from the toss, the way the flower in the lapel begins to fail. I press at my temples to stay all that's before me inside my head. The smell of the perfume on me, on him, I savor it to save it. The feel of the silk of this nightgown that slips from my shoulders and down past my hips, the way the fabric of it puddles as it does to the floor, I will the imprint in. I want Son's chest in my keeping, his mouth, his hands on me, always to feel it all as I feel it now. I want always this happiness of wanting. This happiness of having.

Remember this moment, I say.

I WONDERED TOO late about the luck of the dress.

It was my mother's, the one she had worn with my father, the one she had on just the one time on that one day, before all the bulk of it got packed up into my grandmother's hope chest, where it would stay boxed and wrapped and mysterious until there was serious enough claim for it to be brought out to life again. I had seen the dress only in the photograph, the one my mother had kept for whatever reason, as it was my father in the picture with her, and not any man of hers recent. The photograph is also kept inside a hope chest, this being my mother's, one of the few items of furniture she will drag along with her from place to place. On slow afternoons I would open the chest to study that picture of my father and my mother, thinking if I had been my mother I would have lived a different story, given that dress.

Given my father.

It's a white satin dress with a long train. There's a pale stain my mother left beneath the layer of tulle on the lap of it, but we don't see this until it's too late to get another dress, and so I wear it the way it is, stain or no stain. I cover the stain over with a manner of moving my hands or with the gather of the organza or with the collar and flower of bouquet.

My mother's most recent bouquet was a small one compared to mine, more a nosegay or a posy, you might say, as though her hopes or her enthusiasm or her something or other had waned along with the size of her blossomed arrangement. Of course she wore no gown or fancy dress this time, nor any kind of altered rendering of one as she had with some of the men at the nuptials in between. She even left the posing out, as far as you could see from the snapshot she sent from the gambling town farther north. There she was, with a new man in hand, with him trailing a couple of steps behind her and her turning in a hurry to go, as if she had to get out of that chapel before someone up in the blue told her no, told her you can't be going out running around and getting married this many times, over and over again.

WE LEAVE THE lodge with mist rising like smoke from the dew and with sunrise embering in pink through the trees.

Flycatchers chitter and pip and acrobat about in the branches of broadleafs and pines. The wind sways boughs and rustles bracken and skitters twigs and leaves, and it slaps a cold wake-up at our faces.

We are day one married.

We're restless with readiness to get back onto the highway. We get going and are soon moving westward to the coast, where we will from there make a turn right and go straight the rest of the way up toward the northern border. Our holiday lasts half a moon's phase and it is rapturous and ordinary, detailed and blurry, seeming to go on and on for a long time, and it is too soon over, the way all time can be. Just as in my telling this, present tense to past, just as long and quick as that.

We do many things in many places. We sit atop a marine terrace eating abalone and vinegared chips, with breakers striking at the cliffs and Son speaking of the old man's infidelities. We stop at a famous place in Angels City, and I'm lucky they don't card me, and we drink whiskey and dance a-go-go at a disco, confident as if we should be locals in the place, even with Son dressed in cowboy boots and with the faded ring of snuff tin on the hip pocket of his dungarees. We take rides to the moon and we startle at alligators and we climb up into tree houses and we spin about in teacups, all in a fantasyland, spending day until night there, as if we were young kids again. We pass through clots of dust and sheets of chaff and we pass through cloud and fog and hail and rain and we travel through warm fronts and humidity, choke points and wind shear. We drive over golden and stone and floating bridges, over river and channel and bay. We chug the truck up to the top of a silent volcano and we throw snowballs and pee yellow holes and get cold too soon, not knowing proper coats. We take to the beach, the truck curmurring through scour and berm, and we stop to dig razor clams and geoduck and the tires out. We pick blue mussels and dogwinkles off rocks and we collect sea stars and sand dollars in jars. Each night we stop at a motel with the same something-dollar name — all the motels pinned along the interstate — and each day we start at one of the breakfast places in a coffee shop chain. We drink our coffee sugared and creamy and we eat our bacon crispy and our eggs over easy. Every day is filled with the smell of a beginning, with the sweet wet smell of just-washed skin and hair and the old-spicey smell of Son's aftershave, and sometimes the air is gritty with windblow, or it is minerally with seaweed or is resinous of pine. There are lingering tastes of salt air in the fog or cut hay in the heat, and some days there is a bitter carbon on the lips from the diesel that rises off the highway, and at times a taste of metal, like car parts, or some days there is a taste of rain cloud or artichokes or burnt leaves, and even a taste of wet dog somehow. There is on and on the thrill of a song that comes over the radio and marks our days to be remembered in that way. There is the harmony of our voices in the to and the fro of our words, as we tell of places we have been and of places we would someday like to go, as we talk of accidents that have happened to us — good and bad and neither — as we speak of the still-few people we have been through or those we would like to know, and we take all of what's said each to the other and shape it into something new to put inside a place that fits right and holds inside us.

Our journey turns a great blessing in its perfection. Within each day upon day there is suppleness and reflex, as in the movement of our youth, all within the changing and the staying the same. That knowing, or whatever it was it was — the thing that had risen from inside me on the way to the church — it must have been leftover matter of some kind, like a comet, you could say, that just got rocketed out and away.

Why should I have been so afraid?

Yes, we are yet the happy pair, we are, with not a thing to mar any day of all the days on the road for us. Save for a comment about my not eating all the breakfast on my plate. Save for the fall and the lump on Son's head.

WE COME TO my father's place, arriving in a terrain of mountain and waterway and evergreen, a wilderness that was a beginning for me — a childhood place and so of innocence, a paradise that way. We come to my father's house just outside the borderline of town, an old log abode built close to the shores of the sound and buried deeply in forest. A great western hemlock stands at the edge of the woodlot and serves as witness tree, its coned crown and fluted trunk and drooping leader bearing claim through generations to this family's parcel of land. The hemlock has been witness too to my imaginings, as I played hero or captured or saved in the woods for the countless hours of lost days. There are still the worn paths where in the past I have ambled alongside my father, picking wild blackberries or Indian plum with him, or I have stooped with him to brush the duff off chanterelles and fiddleheads, to know them and so to pick them too.

To be safe, my father would say, and he would blow on the underside of the mushroom. Look here, he would say, these split gills will always tell you. Then we might fill our coffee cans full to the top with berries, him reminding me to pick only the tiny wild ones, leaving the fat himalayas for the bear and the deer behind. He might tell me other things that would stay inside my head. He might say, Let the clams you dig sit in a bucket of their water overnight until they have spit the sand out of their shells. Or he would say, Carry a stick when walking down a lonely road so if you should come upon a mean dog, all you need do is shake the stick in the dog's face, and mean it, to keep him away. Or he would say, Walk fast when there are other people around and they will leave you be, because they will think you are busy.

There's a light in the cabin window on, and we knock and find my father there with his wife. My father opens the door and puts a face of welcome surprise on. Well, hello, Daughter, he says. He has a scruffy beard as has always been his habit. He has a bigger, rounder belly now. He smells like just-chopped wood. He shakes Son's hand and gives me a pat on the back and he offers us drinks and we follow him into the kitchen. His wife is pale and thin of hair and flesh, and her smile is cool and thin too. She says her name and flutters her arms and then she pivots and disappears somewhere.

My father makes a joke about marriage and the bump and the gash on Son's head. Son says he hates to say it, but he's had a headache ever since the wedding day. I say I hope that a husband isn't like wearing reading glasses, where after a time you get so to rely on them you can't manage without. Son says something clichéd about love being blind, which doesn't make much sense or fit right with what's said, and my father seems embarrassed for him but laughs anyway and goes on quickly to one-up Son with another joke of his own. I look at Son, who looks smaller now than I had before seen him, even though he rises a good half foot over my father.

My father takes a bottle of wine from the refrigerator and screws the top off. He puts the screw top to his nose and sniffs it.

Good week, he says.

I breathe in the home smell of maple bacon and cherry tobacco and woodsmoke. I leave my father and Son in the midst of their polite talk and I go to stand over at the sink and look out the window. I can see the smokehouse outside my father built for the curing and drying of fish and meat. Next to it is a large vegetable garden, neatly rowed and tended, with bulging heads of lettuces and lazing squashes and beans vining their way up tepee'd poles. There's the swing still hung from the alder, and I can see me there now on the wood seat of it, swinging high and hanging on tightly for life. There's the thick dark wilderness out there surrounding it all—the swing, the garden, the smoke-house, the house. The wild of all that wilderness out there, the dark and the hush in it, the surprise in it, the hide, the seek, the find in it.

Go play, I can hear my father say, prodding me out.

From here where I stand at the window, I also see the add-on my father built as his family grew. I can see out and into the window to the bedroom across the way there. There where my father's wife stands looking in the mirror, brushing her pale thin hair and putting lipstick on her pale thin lips. She stands in the bedroom that used to be my room. She looks in the mirror that used to be mine.

Yet it was me who left my father's house, after all.

Wasn't it?

THE RAIN COMES and the rain ends and the woods are left gauzed in pockets of mist. We walk out into air soft as baby hair, air that has a weight to it too, air that makes ferns and leaves and needles shimmer in droplets that tick wet to the earth. We say our farewells and get settled back up into the pickup, sitting quietly with the truck warming and humming, and then Son wipers the windshield and U-turns us around. I rub the vapor off the glass with a sleeve and through the blur I see a door close and the lights go out inside the house. Take it slow, I say, and Son does, moving slowly along the rooted-over driveway to keep the rattle of us down. He pulls us out onto the road and toward the way we have come, taking a left at the crossroad, where we will head down along the coast highway to the interstate and so back to Old Border Road, a place to be called home, a place to begin another beginning.

TWO

ROSE'S DADDY

We move into the hold of a ministering day, with dawn smoking up in color off the horizon, with foothills behind dimmed in hour and distance. We pass through outcrops of rocks and stands of cactus, pass through miles of sand and scrub beyond that, and finally we enter a broad flat valley of watered and tended land, a vega of plowed and pastured earth girdled by trench and by flume and by ditch. The air of the lowland is heavy with the aroma of manure and chemicals for growing, nitrogens and ammonias and whatever other compounds and minerals there are that bite the nose. Brown-skinned people are scattered about in the fields at the start of their day, stooped amid the rows and dressed in colorful clothes, hoeing and picking, some lifting and packing, others walking with burdens loaded atop their heads.

This great trench was nothing but tamarisk and pedregal before it was turned watershed, Son says. He says, We'll get the old man to tell you some of the stories, about the might put into the making of this place. Open your ears and it'll open your eyes. You don't know that we're driving through gold.

He reaches over and gives a squeeze to the back of my neck and turns us off the highway onto a long straight two-lane. If we keep along this route, it would take us all the way to Mexico, down to the headwaters of the Gulf, down to a delta of mud, is what Son says, a desert of salt cedar and iodine bush and pickleweed. But some miles before the border we come to a crossway and go a different way, making a hard turn onto a gravel section-line road, driving by ditches and siphons and headgates, moving now straight ahead toward home. We cross over the cattle guard, and metal strakes zip through the tires and the shocks of the truck, sending a quivering that rises into the bones and vibrates out through the molars. Soon enough the old adobe house comes into view, perched atop the hillock as it is, moated by emerald groves and all aglow in pale light. We see the old man and the old man's wife out on the porch of the house, the morning sun sainting their heads, the two looking as if they had been standing there waiting for us the whole time we had been away.

The old man comes out to the pickup to greet us.

Son, he says, and he claps his son on the back.

Girl, he says, and he reaches for the suitcase in my hand.

WE SETTLE INTO living as a family in the old adobe house.

Who ever would have thought this would be? I say, thinking of the day I first saw the place, riding along Old Border Road in Son's truck on his way to taking me home, both of us sunburnt from having camped out for the weekend on a beach down in Mexico with people we had in overlap, and both still feeling the pain relief of the tequila in us. He pointed and told me to look through the grove of old lemon trees, and that's when he reached over and pulled loose the back string of my haltertop.

That's how it all started, and so we will tell our children someday.

Today we start out our being married and being at home by washing the honeymoon off the pickup. We hose and we sponge all the earth that we've collected up along the way, rubbing off what's left of the chalked and faded sentences that someone intended for us to live by, words we had ridden with as the moon rode full circle about us. We soap and we rinse and we chamois, shrugging at the etchings in the side panel that don't go away, though knowing what remains of the saying will soon enough fade in the scour of dust and the bleach of sun of this place.

Hold it while ye may, yet happy pair.

Light strikes the metal. Bursts of stars trick the eyes.

Victuals is hot and about on the table, the old man calls out.

We leave the pickup to sparkle clean in the shade of a honey mesquite, and then go inside the house to bathe ourselves before the noon meal. We're used to being the two of us all these recent weeks, whether inside a cabfront or a motel room or a café, and now we're loath to let the one of us go too far away from the other. So we go into the bathroom and strip our clothes off together, and we climb into the tub and turn the valve full open and start the spray over us as one. We huddle together and turn in circles, the shower drape cocooning about us, lathering each the other, the slipperiness of skin between us stirring our yearnings again.

We come out garbed in fresh clothes and clean and decent as a new home.

The old man's wife has put a fresh linen dress on and has her long braid done up in a knot and she has called us in to sit. She has the table set with fiesta-colored china and flowery napkins and a marigold bouquet. A tiny yellow bird picks at the seeds in a bowl in the cage by the window. I stand behind a chair and compliment the fancy arranging, and that's when I see there are places for only three people set at the table. She looks at me and puts a hand to a cheek. The little bird flitters about and upsets its water dish. Old habits, the old man's wife says, and she shakes her head and goes into the kitchen and comes back with a knife and a fork and a plate, and she fills the empty place.

You ought to call me Rose, she says.

Rose, I say.

Rose is all right. She is kind as a mother could be. She tells me about writing thank-yous to those who gave us candleholders and electric mixers and butter dishes and all the rest of what Son and I got just for getting married. She tells me I might want to give some of the many vases and candy bowls to the hired man's wife or to the church ladies running the rummages. She says there will always be a certain trend in gifts, which only tends to make for excess. But we are not the kind of people who believe in being wasteful, she says, no matter that we can amply afford to be. We do not throw away, she tells me, sitting up all the straighter and tucking stray hairs back into the knot of her braid.

Rose will tell me many things. After a time she shows me a lot of what to do, too, like how to hide a stitch when taking a proper hem up, and the way you make a chili roast and a casserole and a lemon pie, stiff whites and all. She teaches me what to use and what to do to nourish the earth so as to make a garden sprout and bud and green from seed. All of what I learn about being a wife I learn from the old man's wife. I learn from Rose.

Rose calls the old man Daddy.

The old man, Rose's Daddy, talks about how blessed he is

with his Rose, how hopeful he is when it comes to Son, how proud he is of what he has and what he has cared for, how thankful he is to have been given the old adobe house and all that has come with it. It is my old man that I praise above all, Rose's Daddy says, for the house and the thrave of acres surrounding it, all handed down to me, as you see before you now. And for the melon shed and the toolhouse out behind the house, he says, I am thankful again. And praise too for the tackroom and the corral, the pasture and the shoots, the swimming pool, and all the rest that adds to the bounty. We have mare and we have bay, we have pinto and sorrel and paint, he says, and we have livestock enough to sell or to trade. We have a good batch of hunter cats, to keep gophers and snakes from making holes and breaks in the field rows. We have rabbits aplenty to eat, which may feed and fatten in the alfalfa. We have all the implements and equipment needed to furrow and harrow, to till and to seed and to mow, to comb and to bale, all of what will take root and rise from the earth. We have the watertruck to water the roads with. We have a good hired man and a steady cadre of Mexicans. We have all of what we need to live and to work and to be as a family. Yessirree, indeedy, he says. And so be it.

IT STARTS TOO early, the disturbance of weather.

With all of everything aplentiful about us, and the homecoming fiestas still ongoing, we're come hard into a dry spell. We're come into day after stifling day of roaring heat and burning dust and not a hint of rain to be seen or rumored. We're caught in thermal pockets of hot that lock us in from above, air without dew point or humits or millibars of vapor, the aridity allowing barely sweat enough to cool the skin with. You should feel it here. You should see it. The hot ground bores through boot soles like an electric heater, and the hot air burns in the nostrils when you breathe it. The sere drives desert rodents and millipedes to hole in the earth, it singes wings of monarchs, silences chickadees, sends cacti into dormancy, has every animal panting. People who claim to have come to this place for their health are speaking of leaving for the same reason. The spike on the gauge has everybody talking and restless and seeking water and breeze and shade, has all of us seeking any anecdote or what facts there might be to reveal some end to the hex of this weather.

Whoo-ee! Rose's Daddy says. We have got to keep ahead of the pulverulence come down upon us. We have got to keep the dust down and the animals watered as best we can, so we and all the stock shall not be succumbing to the coughing pneumonia. We know the hardships, he says. We have been through them before. We have gnashed our teeth, yet we have not been beaten back. It is a fallen land that we survive in, yet it is a land reclaimed and so redeemed.

He hitches his britches up with a thumb.

Yet pray, he says, this heat shan't be making any new history.

For the time being, he says, we start with the watering.

Now morning and evening Son and I go out back to the melon shed and climb into the watertruck as a team. We ride down the road and head toward the canal, our mouths and our noses covered over with bandannas. We step out into the burn of the sun and drop the hose into the harnessed water and stand and wait for the tank to suck its fill up. We watch the water rush past, just the sight of it pouring a cooling into us. The old man says the river capture is an inheritance set into history, a history that has come with the land. The water is a measure we've come to depend on and have paid for, for a time, and the watermaster must divert and deliver every bit of acre-feet to us for wetting down the fields and the animals and the roads.

Yet even with the water allotted, we're still surrounded by dirt rectangles of fallow land that lie between lessening acres of green. And despite all the time spent spreading cargo loads of channeled water out to still the road dust, the road dust still gets everywhere. It coats all of everything both inside and outside the old adobe house. We brush it off our clothes, brush it from our hair, even from our teeth. We blow it out our noses, spit it onto the ground, into the sink. Dust pelts the animals, the flowers and the trees, Rose's old roses. It drifts in through the chimney, sneaks between the screens, gets in beneath the doorframes. It powders the shelves, the dishes, the bedding, settles onto the pillows and between the sheets. Every day we try to keep ahead of it, just as every day we watch it settle back in again and onto everything. Still, we keep on with the watertruck, soaking the roads load after load, washing down the dust before the dust swallows us. We keep on going, believing, I suppose, only in the going-on in us.

THERE WERE TIMES ago it was as walloping hot as it may worry me about now, Rose's Daddy said. It was a dry spell that came on before I was set into this world, when life here relied solely upon the favor of the river and of whatever gods there were thereof. So the story had been told to my father, and he to me, he said. You kids want to listen? he said. Or what?

Son dragged a bench over to the work desk and Rose's Daddy went back to the story.

All of life depended upon the river, Rose's Daddy said. Thus this place was sprung from it, as life was risen up from the dust and given succor by the waters. And hither a settling was born at the crossing, he said, opening the lid of a tin box and taking a pouch of full aroma out. A crossing, he said, that has homed some tough-minded tribes. Sun worshippers, they were, which I guess a one would have to be to live in such a cloudless and sudorific land as this. Yet it was place enough for what handful of them and their needs there were for a mighty lengthy reach of years. Yes, indeedy, he said, reaching for his pipe. The waters back then, they did run swiftly. Yet as the earth was multiplied with people, so did men begin to wander in need and curiosity. They went looking for what had been heard tell of from other passing nomads. They went looking for what had been seen by themselves in the depths of their nights.

He put the cold pipe to his lips and blew into it unlit.

The first recorded explorers that arrived to this place came up from what was yet New Spain. They traveled up the Gulf under the command of de Ulloa, so it was written, on a flotilla of royal ships. They sought a fabled people within a fabled landscape. They sought a promised life. They sought gold. They imagined finding silken-haired women with pearl combs in their hair and precious stones and corals in their noses, pouring wine from golden vessels. They heard tell of men here wearing tiny golden shovels clasped on braided chains about their necks, shovels that were used to scrape the sweat off the flesh of their bodies. The explorers hoped to find a golden life hither within a grand fertile valley of wild palms surrounded by snowy mountaintops. And lo, they sailed out of the Gulf and on into the yawn of the river and were sucked into waters reddened thick with mudstone sediment. And their hopes and fanciful notions were soon doused out. For upon the shore they found nothing but barren land and blazing heat and whirlwinding dust. They walked across sandbanks of hot ash, the ground on which they walked trembling like paper sheeting, as if it were a fiery lake bubbling and steaming right beneath them. At night their ships pitched and swayed at anchor within the darkness of the mouth of the river. In the seething heat of the day they worked their way upward into the waters in search of a channel, turning the sterns of the smaller boats now this way and now that, yet they made no progress against the swift currents and the weight of the river. And they toiled and they sweat and they thirsted. And they baked inside their armor and their sap was boiled away. And there was no relief come to them. Indeed, many of those men perished and the wearied rest of them did turn back the way they came toward New Spain.

We'll get soon to the point of the story, Rose's Daddy said. He packed a wad of tobacco into the bowl and tamped it in with a thumb.

Yet again the people would come to this place some years later, this time not for gold but for souls. The colonists would come, and with them the missionaries with their books and their crosses and their what-such would come. And as you well know, New Spain became Mexico, and in time our country would deal and steal and take this northern piece of southern land away for its keeping.

Rose's Daddy struck a match to the desktop and lifted the flame to his face.

And just like that, he said, blowing the fire out. In a quick swish of a horsetail a great head of settlers came out from the east. The drovers came with their cavayards, the shepherds with their herds and yokes and flocks, the nesters came with their households, the miners with their mules and implements, the merchants with their wares, and the hustlers came and the losers came and the whole lot of them came. And they inhabited the missions and the presidios and they built up more settlements. And these damned many people demanded more of the land. And what they needed most was water for it. A lot of it. In a place where there was never much of it, save for the river. Water was as gold was. Is.

Pretty loco when you think about it, he said, choking smoke. He reached for the waterjar and took a drink, then held the waterjar out toward me and I nodded it on to Son.

Henceforth, Rose's Daddy said, the world entered upon modern times and man came to believe in the power of himself, rather than believing in that of which he was made and of what made him—that nature or what you might call the maker in him or the something or other in him. Man believed in the power of science to deliver—a science that could conquer all, even conquer nature herself. Modern man did believe that all of everything was in his command.

And I say to you, how be it that some yet do?

Rose's Daddy looked at me. He looked at Son.

He took a long deep pull on the pipe.

WE'RE SETTLED INTO the old adobe house not yet the full length of another whole moon together. That moon of ours, seeming only a rumor lately, rubbed out of the night sky in the dust as it is, but swinging all the while above and gently as a ball, as the laws will tell us. Maybe its being hidden is what brings the changes on, as nights come now and Son will rise from the bed and go off into town without me, without a word, even after my questioning, as if he has given in to a kind of lunacy. He will leave the old shotgun loaded by the door and ready to shoot, though I'm not sure how to use it or even what to use it for. He leaves with the old dog lying atwitch in the spook of her dreams on the porch, with the hired man gone home hours before the dark should fall, with Rose gone to the coast for a rest at the sea, with the old man sleeping alone.

It's another night darker than dark most nights.

I stare at the wall and listen for Son. I listen for the miss in the sound of the engine, for the rattle of loose metal or the squeaking of a hinge. I wait for the crackle of gravel under tires, for a glimmer of headlight through the blinds. I see the places where Son might be, the lots his pickup might be slotted in, the barstool he might sit on, leaning over his drink, the way he will look around searchingly, the sofa he might be sprawled on by this time with some other. I see the faces of the women he could be with, hearing their laughter, hearing his. I close my eyes in the silence. I listen for voices through the adobe, listen to the wind scouring roof and bending limb, swirling the hot dust up. I lie awake a long time, through the long night, eyes open, eyes closed, and on it goes like this until nearly morning. Finally there comes a stumble of boot steps on the front porch, a fumbling of keys, a crick in the wood, the clap of a door. I keep my back facing the empty place where Son should be, keeping still enough to be sleeping. He comes into the bedroom, cricket shells popping beneath his feet. He sits at the edge of the bed, huffing in his struggle to get a boot off, then the other one, the bedsprings whining beneath us, the ticking of the parlor clock creeping in to settle between. I can hear Son's tongue moving thickly in his mouth when he curses. I can smell the drinking on him, smell the women he's been with. I can feel my heart pounding loudly enough to give me away.

Son flops out full length onto the bed, still with all his dusty clothes on, with the loose hairs of other women clinging to the weave. He coughs the dust from his lungs. He licks his cankered lips. He settles into a labored slumbering breathing.

Outside, the night vibrates.

The crickets ring on of courtship and warning.

The watertruck settles and pings.

THE KNOWING HAD been waiting for me the whole time Son and I were gone away up the coast. It showed itself as soon as we were back to town, to Old Border Road, to the old adobe house. The knowing I should have known better. The sense I should have had better sense. The terrible unease or forewarning, the in-the-bones or in-the-gut or in-the-whatever-it-might-be-called feeling, the premonition that hit me in the backseat of the station wagon on the way to the church that day—it was that that was right here homing in on me not long since returning from our journey.

We are too young to be doing what we're doing.

Maybe I just didn't want to see it right away. I wish there were a way to fool myself into telling the story differently. But the reckoning is here, likely has been all the while. It's as true in me as the weather is, and there is no way to sleep it off or will it gone. The knowing has settled in with the heat. It has settled in as we do our living here in the old adobe house. It's put into place as with housekeeping. It's seen in the common and routine. It's everywhere and in everything, resting like some warp in the climate between us. It billows in with the grit through the windows, making us as separate as the imprints we leave on the truck seats. You can see what the matter is in

45

our habits, in our manner of dressing, in our ways of moving and being. What's wrong sits with us at dinner, gets chewed in with our biscuits and stew, gets swallowed down with gulps of our buttermilk. It hangs about in the silence. It shows up in our talk. I stock the pantry, feed the dog, launder a load of denims, stake the failing roses up, write a letter to my father or send a card my mother's way, chat with Rose and Rose's Daddy, do my reading, wake from a daydream, try to sleep, always in the knowing it. I look out the window and see Son in the yard watering dying patches of grass, the burden showing in him in the way he furrows his brow, the way he drops his shoulders over, the way he stoops to put feed out for the cats and the rabbits. I see it in the way he licks his canker-blistered lips or rubs the scar on his forehead, see it in the way he sits, in the way he can't sit.

Still we will dream side by side in it.

We will dance with it at the Saturday night dance.

As my reckoning moves through the swelter of our hours, making me desperate, always a little too afraid.

What I know is not forgotten, only breathed aside, when Son reaches over for me in the night. Just as the knowing will be slighted on those days when he comes in from the scorching fields midday. When he kerchiefs his brow and takes a long drink from the waterjar and looks to find that his folks are out of the house for a time. When he comes over and reaches for me. When he takes the cloth out of my hand and the bandanna from off my head. He leads me by the shirtsleeve out of the kitchen and on through the cool dark parlor. He takes me into the bedroom and I fall back onto the bed and what I know becomes no more than what I don't. Whatever the matter is, it falls away for this time, as our shirts and our belts and our dungarees drop to the floor at our feet. And I will close my eyes to it. And I will forget what it is I have seen.

There is a spell of relief, and then it is over.

Oh, what could it be that is so much the matter?

Just nothing.

Just everything is.

NOW THE MANMADE lakes were made—Havasu and Powell and Mead, Rose's Daddy said. And the dams were built—Glen Canyon and Hoover, Parker and Laguna, Imperial and Morelos and Davis. Yet modern man can be naive, not only about nature, but about politics too and the inherent greed that is bred among his fellow human beings, he said. He can be naive as to his history.

You kids know your Homer, don't you?

Son and I shifted in our seats in the drift of afternoon and sweet tobacco smoke.

What happened next was of nature, a disaster of weather, a torrent of hot as anyone had heard tell of or seen. And what happened was of property matters, water rights, greed and pride, what money could and could not buy. And the life and the death of one's brethren—yet that was considered lastly.

Rose's Daddy sucked the flame down into the pipebowl.

Yessirree-bob, it was hot, he said, drawing on the pipe. It was a dry spell that had only been known by the Indians here. For the newcomers, as I said, it was a spate of heat as they had never felt it before nor seen. People lost count of the number of days they had been without rain. People who had no habit of praying began to do it. Others cursed God aloud. Some went to visit the Cocopah or the Quechan or the Mohave to consult with their medicine men. Lo, but what suffering did befall them all. People became heatstraked and sunblistered and out-and-out exhausted. They cramped and they fainted and they sweat. They stopped sweating and started vomiting. They got delirious. And the afflicted breathed shallow and quiet. And their skin turned clammy and gray. In worst cases, hearts fluttered and brains shook and kidneys quit, eyeballs dilated, clumps of hair fell out of scalps, tongues cleaved to the roofs of mouths. In all cases, everybody was scared.

Have I scared you kids yet? he said.

Son brought the waterjar to his lips and took a good long draw from it.

These old-timers lived in infernal heat, Rose's Daddy said. Or so they tried to live, within what had become a suffocating epidemic. They singed their fingers on metal implements and took to eating with their fingers. Flesh was seared, cloth scorched atop backs, outlooks shriveled. Many wore masks to protect their lungs from the dust and yet many choked to death. And those of the suffering who went down to the river to immerse themselves found the water above blood heat and unbearable to the touch. Like a hot hot-spring it was, and with the sun boiling down above them. And what water there was, was too muddy to drink. And the water was thick and red as what it was named to be.

All suffered, man and beast alike, Rose's Daddy said.

Yes, indeedy. You want me to go on?

He looked at us and did.

The fierce heat did so bake acres upon acres of grassland and pastureland down to nothing but soot. The sun's rays devoured the stubble, even consumed the chaff. It was said that fowl stopped scratching and laying and they simply toppled in heaps.

Horses collapsed to the ground in kickups of dust. Cattle were blinded. Livestock were fed a mix of pricklypear cactus and molasses for lack of proper feed. Still, they died. All the animals died. Their scaly carcasses were dried to bleached piles of bones in the sun. Not even prey birds showed up to pick the dead clean, for they could not have flown in such waves of dust and gusts of heat. What birds there were fell like withered fruit from the trees. Dried-up lizards skittered like old leaves in the wind. Rodents and bats petrified between rock slabs and dried pipes. Fish were simmered belly-up in the river. Hot cracks appeared in the earth and life was lost into the depths of them. Dust clouds concealed the sun for days on end. Lo, people were stunned within a haze of dirt, in weltering tons of it. They met with darkness in the daylight in the midst of black blizzards. They groped in the noonday as in the nighttime. And within the blackness of the days, humankind was terrified.

I'M ON MY way back to my father's place, is where I am, but the road is rough and full of potholes. I'm routed through a part of town I can't recollect, a place of concrete and steel, a place of no more open spaces, no kite hills or boat docks or flower parks to mark where I might be, no lakeshore drive or waterfront walk, no terrace of benches. There's only the pandemonium of tearing what was up down. There's only the chaos of making way for the new to rise. I park in an alleyway and walk to make it easier to find my way through the detours and the boarded-off and one-way streets. All around is nothing but broken ground and brownfield, a lot of abandoned lots. The school is gone, the playground, the garden store, the dollar store, the movie house, the tent shop, the bakery, the millinery, the library — all of it gone as if to vapor and floated away. I look at people I don't know on the street, their faces blank and with not a glance or a nod in their passing. Seabirds flap their wings at my head and careen and shriek about for what's guttered in the street. I cringe and cover my ears as a wailing hospital vehicle hurtles by in a flash of red lights. I look into the windows to see who might be inside when a burst of light erupts from I don't know where. I look out at the water, dark and churning on the bay, at the nimbus veil that hovers above. A boat of some kind lets out a mournful bellow, and I feel the hollow echo of it rolling beneath the shell of my rib bones. Then I awake to the deep harsh sound of myself, more a pitiful groaning than the loud cry I'm trying to cry out.

THE OLD MAN'S stories are good but not always the whole truth, Son says.

I filter through a pile of new mail, just arrived and already collecting dust on the sideboard. Bills, bills, bills, I say, mimicking my mother talking.

The old man tends to leave pieces out in his telling, he says.

What pieces of what? I say.

Like why he's let some of our fields go fallow.

What for in this heat?

Money's to be made selling water to those on the coast.

Won't the place blow away on us?

Dry years make you even more money.

Is that how you think?

Don't matter what I think, when the old man won't listen.

He listens to somebody, I say. Everybody listens to somebody.

Sure, he says. He listens to Pearl Hart.

Pearl Hart. Why have I heard that name before?

Because she made sure to make one for herself, he says.

She must have money or something.

She does all right.

Rose's Daddy comes in and sees you in his chair, he will raise some Cain, I say.

Yes, indeed, Pearl Hart's done all right all her life, Son says. He swivels about in the old man's chair. She's got plenty of acreage, he says, both of the wet and the dry kind. Always had it. She's come from an early family of desert homesteaders that proved up their land. They got in on water rights from the get-go, he says. She's got her a little empire here. She's talking of running for county water commissioner. You bet, he says. She's got all a that and a face and body to go with it, he says.

She could be your mother, I say.

Don't I wish, he says.

Here, I say. Your posse dues are due.

I leave Son aswivel in Rose's Daddy's chair and go into the kitchen to show Rose the postcard. Pictured on it is a watery landscape with white breakers rolling into sea cliffs that lie along a wrackline of seaweed. There are several people dressed in foul-weather gear and huddled over the body of what appears to be some beached sea mammal. Drawn onto the picture is a penned message that reads, *we are here,* with two stick figures arrowed in red that stand hand in hand in the sand on the card, one of the stick figures with curlicues of hair around the round of the head.

That one would be my mother, I guess.

Lordy, where is she run off to now? Rose says.

She and this new husband she's got are working their way up along the coast. She says they're planning on driving as far north as Alaska.

Alaska? Rose says.

Who knows? I say.

It's cold in Alaska, she says.

I know.

And I know too, Rose says.

She looks at me and I see she sees everything.

My face does things I don't want it to.

I know my son, she says. Always going out and running around and staying out late. I know his ways. Verily, verily, verily. He just doesn't think about it, is all, she says. Listen, Dear Girl, what men think and do—and all of them think it and do it—well, it doesn't need to mean a thing. What means something is the way a man and a wife are living a life together otherwise.

I put a hand to my chin to make the quivering stop.

Now don't go being a crybaby, Rose says. She fishes the tea bags out of the tea jar and gives each a squeeze. After a time, she says, you learn to not care so much. You'll see, she says. It'll all be all right. Believe me. Don't waste any precious day given to you worrying yourself about matters that don't really matter. You'll just end up at the end of your life shaking your head at the meaninglessness of what you fretted over. At the futility of your worry.

She splits the bags open and throws the sodden tea leaves out the window. Then she opens the freezer door and puts ice in a glass and pours tea over the ice.

You want lemon? she says.

I nod, feeling better and feeling worse, relieved and saddened by Rose's words. I wonder if growing up feels like growing old.

IT IS HIS leaving that clings to me like the dust on me, his leaving that follows me into my sleep, the words and the images distorted, and always worse at night. His leaving moves into my waking. It settles into memory of what couldn't have been, but will be because I have heard it and seen it.

I grab him by the beltloops and say anything I can to make him stay, and with my eyes I say all there is that can't be said. He takes my grip apart and turns away, my pleas thrown aside and set adrift to settle about the room as the dust does. He says a man can't be roped down or harnessed up or led around, says that a guy has got to get out with the guys, says that he can't be stuck home with a wife all the time, says all those too-often-said kinds of things to me. Then he swings the door wide and goes out, not looking back to keep from having to see what he might see. I follow him out to the porch and get a handful of his shirt, beseeching him not to leave, to please take me along, and he shrugs me off and I grab him again and he throws me aside, harder this time. The old man's old dog runs over and starts nipping at Son in the confusion. I sink to the porch step and hug my knees to my chest and drop my head, hearing Son's boots scuff in the gravel, hearing the whine of the hinge, a slam of metal to metal, the opening roar of the engine. I lift my head and see him drive away, watching until the body of earth he leaves floating behind him disappears and is gone.

The old man's old dog settles beside me and licks the wet salty drops off my fingers. Right, I say, out with the guys. I look into her milky old eyes and she looks at me. What guys? I say. I never met any of those guys, I say. She pants. I let out a breath. We sit out on the porch step, sit a long time as the night comes on, in the click and the shrill of katydids and crickets, the old dog chewing on her ticks, my legs getting all chigger bit. The ashy sky darkens. Behind the thick scrim of dust there's a ballet of planets and stars that can't be seen, hidden bands of constellations, zodiacs, and galaxies, cosmic debris, swarms and belts and arcs, all of everything forever hovering. I wonder at the celestial skin above, thinking of it as what might lie between people, the what can't be seen but is known—the pulls and stays and gives, the drives, the barriers, the distances. There's comfort in the order of the universe, I remind myself of this, knowing there are constants in the chaos, knowing there's a given in the eternal, knowing there are reasons to believe.

The old dog nudges me to get up from our stoop and move.

Where is it you want to go? I say. The old dog cocks her ears back. Maybe we'll stay and wait it out? The way the Indians did, I say. The old dog winces. Things will always change, I say. The old dog gets up and shakes and I get up and follow in the wake of her dust. She wanders out back to the melon shed, where she will use the cool of the concrete floor as a bed ground as is her way. But here, I say, up, I say, and I open the door of the watertruck. Good dog, I say, and I give her a boost in and she settles on the benchseat in front of the steering wheel. I roll the windows down. Then I settle my head on her haunches, finding this bed a better one than our own half-empty bed to be in for the night.

ALL TOO SOON another night arrives with Son gone to town, and in the morning he's not home and next to me in the bed. Instead it's the old man's old voice that rises from the depths of my slumber and brings me back to here where I am, back from a home that wasn't or isn't anymore — the same old and told-again dream that has made its way into me. Awake now to the talk outside, I roll out of bed and go to the window and look out into the haze of the day, blinking away the fragments of what has welled up in my head during sleep.

The sheriff is out on the porch, standing and waving a hat as he's talking to the old man. I pick the clothes up off the floor from the night before, giving them a shake before climbing back into them.

Settle yourself, Rose's Daddy says when he sees me come out the door. Everything is all right, he says. I study Rose's Daddy's face for the truth. I look over to the sheriff, not able to read his face for much of anything, but seeing it as pockmarked as the moon would be.

They had to keep him for the night, is all, the sheriff says.

Run in and curry a comb through your hair, Rose's Daddy says. And put your inside-out shirt right side on so we can get an ándale, he says.

He's standing by the door of the watertruck when I come back out of the house. Slide over, he says. You are yet faster than I am, he says. I want to rocket off in a blast of dust but it's not in the nature of the vehicle. I drop the water load out of it to lessen our weight, and it leaves the road steaming behind us, as if some tremendous beast had stopped to mark the trail. I get our speed up and pass every tractor and truck and car that's out in front of us, working the gears and transmission as they might never have been pushed to work, and we lunge on ahead. I drive without a stop through every stop sign we come to in town. We chug and we grind and we rattle and we buck, and like this we get to the place in no time, in a no time that stretches on forever.

We get to what's not much of a hospital really, what they call here the Centro Médico, but really it's more a hold for keeping a few tired and bent-over old people tied into wheeled chairs and railed beds. We find Son in an empty waiting room, waiting for us with a bandaged head, smoking under a sign that says not to. A man in loose, pastel-colored clothes—a doctor's assistant or a special nurse or a specific someone of some kind—calls Son Lucky and takes Son's cigarette away. He gives Son a piece of paper and tells him to come back in a couple of weeks for the stitches out.

They say he did more damage to the trunk of the old madrone tree, and what a pity to put to waste good shade like that, the man says, talking now to Rose's Daddy and me. We'd've had to race Lucky here out of town if he'd've been hurt worse.

The sheriff tells Rose's Daddy he should have taken Son's driver's license away from him for driving as drunk as he was. But the sheriff says he didn't because he knew Rose's Daddy needed Son out on the place to work. First thing you'll want to have that kid do is pull his pickup truck out of the bar ditch, the sheriff says. I'm relying on you to keep an eye on him, he says. And then some.

We shall bosal him by the nose and lead him straight on home, Rose's Daddy says.

By the way, the sheriff says, turning to face me as we leave. How's your mother? he says.

I LEAVE SON in the bed, leave him breathing as if he were laboring in his sleep, muttering as if he were struggling to find his way out of the tangle of a bad dream. I grope my way forward in the dark, arms held out, reaching for the hand of a helpful unseen being if there be one. Floorboards creak beneath my feet. The cool dark parlor is cooler and darker yet and filled with the tocking of the old clock. The stars that fill the sky above are still blanketed in nightdust, and no one is out of bed but me, even Rose, who says she can't sleep till morning anymore. I'm up in the small numbers of the day to beat Son to the ready for the morning water run. I'm up to get a pot of coffee on and flask it up for the ride, and I will tie some buttered biscuits in a tea towel for later, to take the burn away from our stomachs that the brew leaves inside. I will fix myself up too, hoping Son might take notice of my just-washed hair before the dusty air sucks the sheen from the sunburnt strands of it. Hoping he might take notice of my skin smelling of primrose soap and soft yet from the water and not yet dripping and sticky with sweat as it will get too soon into the day. Hoping the shirt he loved to see me in in our beginning will catch his eye again, before the weave goes from crisp to wilted as the day sets in. Wanting him to see me as the girl I am, as the woman I am, the woman that rides beside him, wanting and strong and never-dying I am, just as during our honeymoon time. To have those days again, days that had the feeling of running away in them, with our movement weight-less, our course brought to us seamless and easy, melodious, effortless, unthinking. What we had. Those nights and those days. That time. I want it back. I want him to want it back.

I want to say, Why not make our time the way we want it?

What is it that keeps us from that?

Son cuts the headlights, with the sun breaching the horizon and the moon floating pale over the earth on the other side of the sky. Dawn birds scatter and lift in the field like a toss of dark seeds. The watertruck fags along, the old dog trailing all the while behind. We jounce about and buck and sway over the ridges and ruts and holes of the road. The cabfront smells of metal dashboard and leather seating, old pipe smoke and coffee spills. Dials waggle in their casings. The wing windows are flared for a draft. The squared puppet jaw of the ashtray juts full open waiting for an offering. I take comfort in the watertruck's carry as we move over the curves and dips and straights of the road. Maybe it's the hard and gray interior, the order and scatter of instruments, the simplicity and complications of the mechanisms, the laws of gravity and motion and speed, all of what will unfold in intention — maybe it's all of this that is pleasing.

Son takes the tin from his hip pocket and fills his lip with a chew, seeming to tame the bumpy ride in his manner. I try to make talk but my words are eclipsed by his silence. He's quiet as the morning is. He takes his cap off and rubs at the fresh scar on his forehead. Scar over scar. He adjusts the sideview mirror. He doesn't turn his head my way. When he does look over, he looks not at me but at something that must be past me, over my shoulder, or out the window, or across the field and out toward the mesa somewhere, or off into the ether, or the nether, or the whatever.

We drive with the dust trailing behind us, and it spirals into our pull and is billowing in through our windows before we can get them rolled closed fast enough. We come to the zanja madre, the mother ditch, flowing with its allotment of channeled upper river water diverted in. Son lowers the hose and I switch the pump switch and we stand in the haze of the start of the day. Even in the morning air, my skin will freckle over and Son's scar will redden up, both of us not so slowly on our way to leathering together. We move into the shade of the tank and fan ourselves with our hats. We drink our water from gallon waterjugs, swallowing the dust, breathing it into our lungs, where it dissolves into our bloodstreams, this dust of which we are all of us made.

We dump the water load over the canalbanks, taming the loose dirt for another day. We take the corduroyed road back home, driving past the old adobe house on the way back to the melon shed. Rose's shadowy figure appears out of a sway of screendoor. She had been talking of taking another visit to the coast, telling us the sea air and salt breezes would be a salve for what ails her. But this time she didn't go. I had asked her what it is that could be ailing her. She laughed. Age, she said. Will and age.

Son shifts down so as to lessen the wake of our clamor. He pulls us up onto the concrete slab of the melon shed, where we leave the watertruck steaming with relief in the shade. The dust motes of morning are afloat above, already beginning to settle onto the metal hood and the top of the tank of the watertruck, ready to lay claim to the day again, ready to lay claim to everything.

The old dog gets up and shakes a burst of dirt off her fur. She comes over to us wagging her dusty shag of a tail and swags on up the front porch steps of the house ahead of us. Git, Son says, and he hazes the dog away with his hat.

There's a swing chair stayed by chains hung from the tesota beam of the porch ceiling, a double seat put there for Rose some years ago, and she is alone and asway in it now, fanning the start of the day away from her face with a fan of Mexican lace. In the other hand, her skeleton-thin fingers cling to a delicate china cup.

He is a new one come to town, Rose says.

She bats the fan wearily in front of her.

Lovely morning it is, Dear Girl, she says, and nods to me.

If only the day wouldn't get any hotter, I say.

A new one what? Son says.

He is to take the place of the Padre of many years here.

What Padre's this? Son says.

The one that of a sudden went and gave up the ghost on us, she says. Standing there right up at the pulpit, he was, and in the middle of Job. He stops reading and we think he is about to add something come to him from heaven on his own for a change, maybe speak some words of divine inspiration, you might say, as his eyes they were rolled upward and his mouth was hung open as if to give us something of a prophecy. But no, instead he just folds up and goes down to the floor in a crumple and heap. He goes and expires on us, is what he does, she says.

She folds her fan closed and puts it into the pocket of her housecoat.

Huh, Son says.

It seems all to have worked out for the best, she says, but I know a person shouldn't say such a thing as this.

She turns her head and looks out at the sunrise coming through the grove, as though there were forgiveness within the old lemon trees. She takes a sip of coffee and sets the cup back to tock in the saucer on the table beside her.

It worked out well for us parishioners, she says, talking into the dawning morning. That is, as this new man has at least a knack for words. And maybe he'll be able to work some kind of divine miracle to break this plague of heat that's been cast upon us. As if this were the Wilderness of Sin we are living in. As if some brujo somewhere cast a pyretic spell on us. Or bruja, could be.

Good. Why not you just go and have him take care of it for us, Son says.

Why not you two kids come and take a listen to him for yourselves?

I'm no churchgoer, Son says. Why'm I even telling you what you already know?

Just give it a try, she says. You'll like the new Padre. He's different.

She looks at me as she says this.

I'll get the bacon on and the smell of home going, I say.

This man's not your ordinary Padre, she says.

We got any more aspirins anywheres? Son says.

He opens the screendoor and I catch it before it slaps closed.

The man can sing, Rose says.

I'll put more coffee on, I say.

And he's a healer, she says.

Her words are whooshed away in a gust-up of dust.

Dear Dotter,

Greetings from the Northwest Territories! We have had a good spring, having gotten our firewood in while the weather was dry for a time. We have put much game away for the coming seasons, including a large grizzly from which we rendered much fat. The Indians have proved friendly lately but somewhat short tempered when given spirits. We are planning a feast for the upcoming holiday and it is our plan to invite them to participate. They will no doubt entertain us with one of their quaint dances that would likely involve two or more of the group going at each other with broken whiskey bottles. I hope you are enjoying your new life in the Southwest. Please do not show this letter to any of your in-laws as they may take me seriously, finding me somehow incorrect in humor and opinion. I would like to visit someday but the weather would likely be too much for me. I would like to have you come too for a visit, but the wife's kids seem to be filling the place up here, and as you surely know, there are jealous tendencies aplenty.

Good luck, and remember never to take yourself too seriously,

Love, Yr. Paw

HAVE YOU NOT ridden alone atop a horse before? Rose's Daddy says to me. I tell him not really, nothing more than a pony tethered to a pole at an age I was hardly walking at yet. He says to me that is a scantling better than nothing, and do I have some boots. No boots, I say, adding that I care little about taking the habit of riding up so not to worry himself about it anyway. Rose's boots will do you, he says, and as I'm saying no, I don't want to go, Rose's Daddy goes into a closet and retrieves the boots for me. Go on, he says, put these on. I beg him not to make me ride, plead the whole time he's leading me out to the corral, telling him as I'm following him that I want to go back to the house.

Lo, the mare is already hitched at the post, he says. She is bridled and saddled and waiting for you. At the very least, he says, you need to come have a look. Here, just come stand next to her. Come put a hand to her withers, he says. But when I get to the horse and take a close look at her, she looks at me and stamps a hoof and whorls her head and snorts.

She doesn't like me, I say.

Girl, he says, you do not in a glance know what the horse does or does not like.

Well, that might be right, I say. And right to the point, I say, as I don't like not knowing what might be in the mind of an animal, especially when it's one I've got to be up and staying seated on. Besides, I tell him, maybe I've not ridden alone, but I've been around the place with Son on the back of his horse a couple of times. That was fine, I say. That was enough.

Girl, Rose's Daddy says to me, if you do not ride, do you not know you shall not fit rightly into the family? And how be it, he says, that you think your leaning back on the cantle of a saddle with a hold on Son's belt is in any manner riding at all?

So I get up on the horse the way Rose's Daddy tells me to, afraid anyway, just exactly as he says not to be. He pets the horse on the neck to steady her and he gives me a pat on the back to steady me. He gowpens his hands for my boot sole and I step into his handhold, pulling myself up with the pommel as he tells me to, lifting my backside into the saddle, and sliding my feet into the stirrups. He keeps hold of the bridle until I settle, and he waits until the horse settles as well. He keeps a grip on my reins as he mounts the bay, and he leads me out of the corral until we're partway down the canalbank.

Now take the reins in your hands thiswise, Girl, he says.

Like so?

That would be right. You are doing fine, he says. He keeps his horse in a slow walk ahead, turning around and telling me to keep my heels down and to sit deeper into my saddle. But his words are hopeless, as I'm aware of nothing but the awful weakening now in my knees, of the tremoring in my legs, of the numbing and tingling in my fingers, of the sickening rolling within my belly. Rose's Daddy breaks into a trot and my horse follows his lead and now my heart races full out. Without my doing a thing, aside from trembling violently, my horse decides to go from a walk to a lope, and why is she rearing her head back? What do I do now? I call out. But the reins are lost from my hands, and the mare breaks pace and moves from a lope to a fast gallop with me holding tight on to the horn in a pound down the ditchbank in nothing but a whip-up of dust all about and the hollers of the old man fading behind.

I catch the ground hard. I lie with all my breath punched out, splayed in a welter of dust with a mouth full of dirt, waiting for my breathing to right itself, trying to see what I can see through the curdles of light and pockets of grit I'm caught in. I gasp and I cough and I spit. My ears ring loud as the locust shrill. Rose's Daddy is upon me, tugging me up from under the arms and getting me up to my feet, but the boots are too big and slipping off my heels, and I wobble and fall back down to the ground. He squats down and shoves my boots back on. He handkerchiefs the dirt and the blood from my mouth. He stands me up again and puts the reins back right away into my hands. Ataway, he says, and he lifts my boot into a stirrup and I'm set back into place in the saddle. I yawn to make the ringing stop. I finger for the broken tooth chunk cutting into my tongue.

After that, we ride every day. I ride the way Rose's Daddy teaches me to ride. I know that he knows. In time, I will ride Rose's thoroughbred mare, Son's cutting horse, the sorrel, the pinto, the old man's bay. He will teach me dressage and gymkhana and he will have Rose show me the ways of dressing to go riding out in for each. He says I will dress western for the barrels, and I will dress English for the jumps, and I will be ruffled and glittered on rodeo days. You will be holding trophies and showing ribbons of your own. Just wait, he says, someday you shall be waving a white-gloved hand in the parade. And Son will ride behind you in the posse. And he will love you all the better for it all, just you wait and see, Girl. Riding will give you kids something to have in common together, something aside from the common drudgery of what a married life can bring, he says. It will help keep him home some.

That will keep you happy, will it not?

THREE

PEARL HART

Devil's rope, Rose's Daddy says. So such barriers were known, he says, back in the heyday of the open range. Today we ride out to check on the fencing, the barbed wiring having been strung in place by a nearby rancher, a man whose pastures have all but turned to dust on him. He has not the waterways nor the means to bring the water in, Rose's Daddy says, thus we have sublet and shall let the shepherd girt it.

The horses' nostrils flare at the pungent smell of the herd.

Right there before you, wild grass turns living flesh, the old man says.

They're like humps of fleecy clouds sunk to the ground, some of them drifting, nibbling, and bleating. The sheep rise and shy at our approach, but for a couple of rutting males that follow a female at the heels and mind us less. She skitters about as the males stop to joust over her, their heads knocking loudly with a thick wooden sound.

Thereby be the drives that drive us, he says.

Why doesn't she run?

He answers with a kindly laugh.

Lo, the comedy, he says, nudging his horse ahead.

Lo, the tragedy, I say, following after.

You shall remind me to tell the herders when they be ready to pull stakes and take leave that they best pick up every scantling of the poison meat they put out for those annoying coyotes, Rose's Daddy says. Lest the dog should run out there after and wolf any of it down, he says. We lost a good heeler that way once and the incident wrought quite an upset. Son was thrown hard when it happened, attached as he was to that animal.

I twist about in the saddle and see the old dog fagging behind us, her tongue aloll, her paws stirruped in dust, good as she is for neither heel nor head. Up ahead is a ditch that holds a rivulet of water, and I know she will jump down in and lap up what she can and then roll around in what's left before scrabbling back out.

Does that dog have a proper name? I say.

Her name was Shebah when we picked her from the litter.

How come everyone just calls her Dog?

What would be wrong with Dog?

The mare blows, making the sound of bird wings aflutter.

We fall into the even plod of the horses and the hum of tractor engine in the distance. We're soon come to the first of the burnt-out patches of newly planted pastureland, and here Rose's Daddy pulls the reins back. He rests his eyes for a time on the ruin, as if he might bring the grass back into being if he stares at it long enough.

I should have futured those acres to idle as well, he says.

He gives a hitch of the shoulder and pivots the bay, and the mare follows. We pass stands of withered grass and crops of failing hay and acres of thirsted and yet-to-be-seeded land as the hum becomes more a roar. Son sits high atop a cultivator in the field ahead, running a disc through the loam. You can see how sullen he is even from here, see it in the way he sits or, more like it, slumps, see it in the way he won't look over at us though he likely sees us closing in.

Behold that dandy machine he rides upon, the old man says.

The lull of it must have put him to daydreaming, I say.

Son doesn't turn his head to look our way. He just tractors on. Between the din of the machine and the haze of the day, it's easy enough to conjure visions up. You can look out and blot the cultivator out and picture instead a yoke of oxen and a single man behind, doing the work by leg and by hand, by muscle and by heart, by need and by will. And you can imagine times before that, back with the Pima and the Quechan and the Cocopah, you can see them here carrying sticks and punching holes into the earth, see the way they will stoop to drop a seed and pat a cover over, the way they will pray the crop up the rest of the way.

'Tis not the individual, the old man says, but only the species nature cares for. It be none but she who so declares the truth.

We ride side by side, the horses settling into their gaits, sky and land and all forms before us undulating in the kindle of the day. The low growl of the tractor fades away in the distance. Aside from the soft pounding of hooves beneath us, it's back to a simmering quiet again.

Whooo-ee! he says.

I look at the old man as the mare slows and the bay takes the lead. He rides over his spread with an attitude of pride and vitality, even in times hard as these. He sits deep and relaxed in the saddle, reins held in a refined manner, with a bit of air under the armpits to give his arms a proper lift, his chest held open and high. Whenever he's out of doors he wears atop his head of gunpowder-colored hair a high-crowned straw hat of legendary name, and within doors he wears the imprint of the hat ringstraked about his forehead and hair the rest of the day. He wears a white-yoked shirt with pearl snap buttons and he wears sturdy tan canvas pants, western boots with roper heels and more a rounded toe, a belt hand-stamped and engraved with his initials, a great silver buckle won in a long-ago rodeo that looks to keep his belly alift. The outfit is fresh laundered and polished every day and it varies little in style and color. His face is creased with squinting lines, variegated with weather and time. He turns to look back at me, his blue-as-blue-sky eyes lit bright in the shadow of his hat brim.

Never cluck at your horse, he says.

When have I?

Never giddyap a horse either.

I never thought to.

Then hereby you are on the right page.

He takes his handkerchief out and honks his nose into it.

He passes me the canteen and I take a good long drink, not stopping to breathe to lessen the taste of iron and dust, feeling the liquid funnel down the parch of my throat. The water sploshes about inside my belly as we ride along, sounding like water does inside the tank of the watertruck. I pass the canteen back to Rose's Daddy. The wind picks up and rustles past, like the sound of gossipy women.

There's something in yesterday's *Star* about a woman by the name of Hart.

Pearl Hart, Rose's Daddy says.

Yes, that was the one, I say.

What one is the one? he says.

IT WOULD MAKE it seem a new start of things. It was our bedroom anyway, wasn't it? The one room of our own in the old adobe house we could lay total claim to. Rose agreed and went into town with me and helped me buy some things—paint and wallpaper and colorful bedding and drapery—and then we came back to the house and I right away started peeling and scraping. You should have seen me, brushing, covering, hanging, tacking, changing the shades so as to let the light come into the room in a different way, setting lamps to glow warm at the bedside for nighttime, and putting a radio on the nightstand to let the music in for loving. I rugged the floor over with a Navajo weave, hoping to cover the groans and the cricks in the wood. I perfumed the bedding, the sheeting and pillows, the cases and coverlets all, and then opened drawers and sprayed the scent inside there too. I covered the bureau over with a lacy cloth and put photos of us atop it in frames and I nailed pictures of exotic places on the wall, hoping we might someday, in the not-too-faraway, even be able to get to them.

And the old dog nudges the door open with her nose and comes into the bedroom. She stands there wagging her dusty old tail and looking at me with her kindly milky old eyes. Then she squats on the Navajo and right away just goes and pees on it.

WE WOULD ALL of us fit right into being a family. Despite the spate of heat, or those hints of parts of the past gone bad, or what animals have died, or what people have left, or whatever other troubles there have been to roughen the days, we would each one of us try to show we were living with our spirits mostly high. Rose would tie her hair up in a headcloth each day and join in with the housekeeper to keep up with the dusting and the scrubbing of the old adobe house, despite you could see she was weary. She would have all our breakfasts and lunches prepared so we could come together as a family and sit at the booth in the kitchen to eat when we were called in. She would be sure to have a proper supper for us, her diningroom every time set with the bright fiesta-ware and fresh linen, her flower arrangements now dried, but lively yet. She would fuss about, usually humming some church hymn. The little bird would flutter about in its cage. She would sit at the head of the table, erect as a caryatid, her pale skin coppered by the evening light coming in through the window, expecting some effort out of us at talking. And this she would get. Son would rally to entertain with reports on the running of the cultivator or the watertruck, or he would tell stories of spill-off from a gopher hole or how a cow died or a horse foaled, livening his telling with accents and voices of different people and a humor that was deadpan. After supper, he might get up and lead us outside to show us one of the new fancy rope tricks he had been working on, which would often as not get a soft applause out of Rose and a hoot and a whistle out of the old man. Son would coil his rope up after and stand there licking at his lips, as if he were trying to tame the smile of pride down with his tongue.

Some nights, we would sit out poolside. We would be sipping one of Rose's cordial drinks, all of us aglow in a fluorescenty aquamarine, the light surely making us appear some gathering of alien beings. On one of these nights, Rose brought up the subject of going to church, a suggestion that brought all talk to an abrupt halt. There even seemed to be a sudden lull in the cricket shrill.

What I mean is, Rose says, is all of us going to church and showing up as a family does.

Her face is lit green, and pools of dark goggle her eyes.

Rose's Daddy stirs in his chair. He clears his throat. He says she ought not go on about a subject that never took any of us anywhere, as a manner of speaking, and that churchgoing was to him strictly a matter of society and the show that goes along with it.

Son rises from his chair and excuses himself for the evening.

No, Rose says, and she reaches out and hooks a finger into Son's beltloop. You'll not be excused until you promise me, she says. Promise me for my birthday. That's the one and only gift I want. All of your attendance is all that I am asking for.

Rose's Daddy sits there staring at the rise and fall of his belly, not saying yet another word, his nostrils too telling noticeably of his breathing. Then he looks over to his wife and says, You want that for your birthday, Mother, then we shall do as you bid us. All of us shall give you your wish. Is that not right, Son? Rose's Daddy waits for no response and gets up from his chair. Hence, it is settled, he says. He goes over to Rose and lifts her hand and kisses her spidery thin fingers. Come along hither and take a walk about the place with me, Mother, he says, so that we might enjoy an evening survey of our holdings.

No, leave me alone, Rose says. I'm tuckered, she says.

Rose's Daddy turns Rose's hand in his and kisses the palm of it this time. Then he gives his britches a hitch-up with a thumb, as is his habit, and walks away humming some *dee-dee-la-da-dee-dee-la* tune, as is but another one of his ways.

Sometimes there would even be words to these melodies.

> *Oh! lay my spurs upon my breast,*
> *My rope and my piggin' string,*
> *And when ye boys have got me laid to rest,*
> *Go set my horses free.*

A NEW ROPE will be stiff at the gather until it gets good and broke in, Son says. You got to work it over with a rolling motion of the wrist like this, he says, and then to make it curl with the right kinda bend in it, do it thisaways. When you loop it, you loop it high over your head and with an even swing, see.

The gyrating lasso makes a thwerping noise above, like some great insect homing in on us.

Now you need to throw your aim sharp and lay the rope on quick, he says. He licks his lips, throws the toss, and catches the fencepost. He knocks the toss off with a jerk and upswing of the rope, then draws it back in and shakes the loop out.

Here, he says.

The rope keeps wanting to bend in the wrong direction, I say.

No, he says. Gimme it. I didn't teach you it thataways, he says.

He takes the rope back and loops it elbow to fist, showing me once again the way to do it. You watching? he says. This is how you make it work easy for you, he says, and he whips the lariat aloft into great whirling circles. Now up over and pull for the head, he says, like this. He casts the rope over the horns of the sawhorse, then undoes the rope and drags it back to coil it up and start working it another time. You want to loop down and time for the feet, he says. He throws and lands the rope under the splayed legs of the sawhorse. Just let the calf run right into the dropped loop, he says, then go for the tug. All in the timing, he says. All in the wrist.

Here, he says, your turn, Darlin'.

IS THAT THE same Hart of the early pioneers here? I said. The one with the daughter near my age?

Naysirree, that would be yet another, Rose's Daddy said. The Pearl Hart scrived about in yesterday's *Star* is a flowery piece of history that passed through these parts, he says, she being a woman from a different family entirely and famed for different reasons. The Hart in the *Star* is the Hart that made her name as a lady bandit, as she was the first woman to rob a stagecoach and one of the last persons ever to do so. Or so such facts have been documented.

Rose's Daddy stood in his saddle and resettled his sit in it.

Indeed, the Pearl Hart in the *Star* was quite a damsel, he said. She was famous for being a lady desperado and famous as well for being a looker. And I can bear record to this, as I have seen many of the many pictures of her as a young woman. And she was yet alive and looking fine when I was a boy, he said, even waxing older as she was. People in town stood aside when they saw Pearl Hart coming down the street. A mighty beauty was she, even dressed as a man, which somehow only enhanced her appeal. She was of French descent, dark-haired and almond-eyed, with a shapely figure. Born into a fine and well-to-do family from the Canadian northeast. It was told she had been admirably schooled, at least until the age of six-teen, when the family's hopes for Pearl's future were disrupted in the stead of by a man named Frederick Hart, a man said to have been her father's age at the time of their meeting. It is known that Hart was a gambler and a borracho and an overall ne'er-do-well of scrofulous character. And yet it came to pass that she would gallop off with this fellow, to the great dismay of the family.

Rose's Daddy gave a cock of the head in the direction of the old dog over alongside the road, tug-of-warring with one of the hunter cats, a pocket gopher stretched longways between their teeth. Ataway, he said.

Gallop off to where?

As it is told, Pearl and Hart went first as far as Chicago, where the legendary Buffalo Bill was staging his Wild West show. There was a famous western horsewoman performed in that show, and it was said Pearl was thereby so inspired by what she saw that she convinced Hart they should make a life betwixt them for good out west. They would raise horses. They would rodeo. They would open a hotel and a saloon and entertain guests by staging floorshows. They would strike it rich in mining, finding turquoise and silver and gold. Lo, they would do all the things young minds think of putting their minds to, getting rich in the meanwhile, of course, as goes every hopeful story. But it was too soon brought to pass that Pearl conceived, as it is with women, and she did come to bear a girl child. Yet their lives lacked contentment, nor were they healthy, and Pearl sent their baby daughter back east to live thither with her mother. And soon enough after, Frederick Hart would leave Pearl to join in with a pack of Rough Riders and head south with the gang. And that would be the end of the romance between the two of them.

Watch it on your right side, Rose's Daddy said. Horse cripplers, he said, nodding at the pricklypear.

Pearl did what she could do. She found work in the mining camps, cooking, cleaning, and meeting other of men's needs. Thence she met up with Joe Boot, and she would become his helpmeet from then on. And he for she.

Joe Boot who? I said.

Joseph Whipple Boot, another fellow yet inclined to borrow trouble. It was sore times, and she and Boot needed money, as did most everybody. But they wanted to come by it easy. Thus it was their idea to rob the stagecoach that traveled Florence to Globe. And they did so manage to stop the stage and empty the pockets and purses of all the passengers and take what they could take. They rode off after into the dunes with their saddlebags full, whereby the two of them became lost and they wearied too for lack of food and water and shade. The end of their adventure came when the posse found them a few days later, clothed in coats of skins and sleeping on bed ground in a drycamp around the remains of a cookfire.

Give me a swig from your canteen, the old man said.

Drink the rest, I said.

Boot was given thirty years in the territorial prison, served about one before escaping, then likely making his way over the border and where he too may have stayed. Pearl was sentenced to several years, served a few months of the punishment, and was released to make her life over again. She had by then gained fame and was called the Bandit Queen and thus was able to live for a while by such notoriety, hence her interviews in magazines and acting roles in plays, and entering entanglements, as was her way, with men, and women too, I have heard tell. Then as quickly she disappeared, likely having remade herself in another place, using a different name entirely.

Then what?

That would be as far as the story goes, far as I know, he said.

So what does all this have to do with the Pearl Hart that lives here in town?

None of it does, Rose's Daddy said. This here Pearl Hart of settler days was not the Pearl Hart of bandit fame. The Pearl Hart we know today was a Charmayne Newby, originally, and born to a family whose power was gained during the era of early claims, some generations ago. They turned water barons, he said. She just took the name Pearl Hart, as the name Newby had been tainted by some low-down wheeling and dealing during the time of water-law changes and huge water-stock trades. And by then the name Pearl Hart had become glamorous and thus catchy, I guess. If she were going to be associated with bandits, she wanted one of her own choosing. Charmayne, you could say, took a new name and made herself into what she wanted to be. Indeed, quite like Pearl Hart did herself, when you ponder it some.

IT APPEARS FROM out in the distance, like some indomitable biblical creature lumbering down the road and aripple in the heat, with the sun a great ball aflame and sinking into the mesa behind it. The watertruck moves from silhouette into body and frame, from silence into sloshing cargo load, from looming beast to beneficent being, and it sways and it pitches and chugs on through the open gates and into the arena. Son empties a full waterload out of the tank of it, the water pouring out the tail end like torn rags, and the hired man tractors behind, pulling a harrow through the dirt to level the wetted ground out. Then they drive the equipment out of the arena and come back rolling the barrels in, setting them up into a measured isosceles. The sky begins to cool from dust-colored into dusky blue as the two mark the cubits out, the dampness and cooling dimming air cuing a colony of mouse-eared bats out to dance about our heads. The flying rodents move from their roosts of rocky outcroppings and out from the hollows of cactus and cavities of trees, out from under parapets, bridges of canals, footholds of ditches, or wherever it is their middens may be. They swim about and spiral in the sky, the wingbeats like the sound of flapping lips, their sonar'd mouthparts and noseleaves divining the next meal before them — the moths and the gnats and the midges and the other vulnerable insects their tiny canines make ready to clamp down on. And they will somersault at the catch, and some will feed on the wing while others alight to dine.

Those itty creatures sure do like to bat about after a water spill, Rose's Daddy says.

They're especially pesky when I'm irrigating, Son says.

They are good for many things.

Maybe giving you rabies, Son says.

They are important predators. Nature needs them.

They should have a better appetite for gophers, Son says.

Here, Girl, Rose's Daddy says, take these.

He hands me a pair of spurs.

Herein you need to get some time in so you can beat the clock, he says. You need to practice wholeheartedly. So you can beat Pearl Hart's girl Pearl, he says. Daughter Pearl has taken the purples for too many years now, and the big win money that follows, he says. Money, I am not ashamed to say, we could use these days. Put these blunt rowels on, he says, and get upon the paint there.

I've never ridden the paint before, I say.

You are riding him today, he says. He is a good-paying horse for the barrels, he says. Trust me, he says. Now make haste and get upon him.

Son comes out of the tackroom with a new rope. He holds on to the home end, looping what's paid out elbow to fist, working the stiff of the coil from the braid of it. Hey, Darlin', he says when he sees me sitting in the saddle atop the paint. His voice and smile are full of expecting something from me. I feel my posture give, thinking of what his disappointment could be.

This is how it shall be done, the old man says. When I call it, lift up, sink in, and let the head go. Let the horse run like all get-out. Fear not knocking a barrel over just now, as you will in the stead of improve and learn nor to do it. Use your spurs if you must, and do not make a fuss about hurting the horse, as they will nudge him on but not poke into the hide any. Your spurs will prompt the horse to do what he should do. Unless you get to where you can cue him with but your knees or a word. That would be up to you and the paint, and fine indeed if that is how you should do it. But if after a time the horse has not come to give to your touch or listen to your words, or he is yet too stubborn to quicken to your spur, then we need to think about getting you a whip for him. And do not worry either about that causing injury, as it will not. The paint is too costly an animal to be beating damage on him. Meantime, we shall see how you do without the quirt for now.

What do I do? I say.

You just let him run. Pick your favorite side to make your

eight. Be sure to lean into the horse on the turns. Run the bar-rels tight. Hold on to the pommel if you need to. That is what it is there and good for. And hold on to your hat too, as some of the old boys may dock you some dollars for losing it.

How do I not lose my hat? I say.

You will figure it out, he says. Now gird up your loins and get out there and warm up in a lope around the barrels. Soon enough you and the paint ought to come to understand each other, he says. That should be the main thing. Whereupon we will start the stopwatch.

What if we don't understand each other? I say.

Then we need to sit you upon another horse, Rose's Daddy says. And listen, he says. Try not to be gaining any weight. Not that it would not suit you any. I talk here for the horse's sake. I talk for winning's sake.

Now SUNDAY EVENING comes, and Son takes the sorrel and I take the paint, and together we ride out in the reprieve of the cooldown and the calm of the seventh day. We ride with the dust rising up from the earth like mist does, ride over a stretch of dry pan and on through a pitch of tillage, going on into the blaze of day's end. We come to the cement trenches and skirt along the dirt bank that keeps acequia from plow-land, braking the horses into a slow walk along the conduits and pipes, all meant to bring life to the pallid valley. We check all the many gates that divide the water into smaller waterways, wanting the presitas full open, wanting no flow to be stanched by weed or clogged by rock, plugged by stob of wood or bunch of plastic or litter of animal, or by what other loose and useless refuse there might be to cause a drawdown.

We scan the fields over for gopher holes, punctures that let the water spill from the furrow, wastage that cannot be afforded in the swelter of the days we've been pinioned in. We look for water rustled off from us, look for breaks and cutoffs that auger the water away from our acres, turning it instead toward the way of our neighbors. We look at the foothills off in the distance lying aquiver within a drapery of scatter and swell and chafe. In the start of the twilight above lies a canopy of stars, all hidden by the curse of dust that grips us, and those planets and galaxies and otherworlds will yet another night remain unseen. Just as the talk between us is clouded in what we both know, anything near truth not openly spoken.

Son reaches over to the back of my jockey and uncoils the leather cord from around the bud of the saddlebag. We draw the horses close to pass a drink and we rest the horses and let them drink too. The fill in the ditch rushes by in stellates of water and light, the glints and flecks like a flow of gold before us.

Son says, Button, you look good in the saddle.

What's with Button? I say.

It's what you call all cowboys just starting up, he says.

Maybe cowgirl, I say.

Perky as, he says.

What happened to Darlin'?

You're still my Darlin'.

I like Darlin' better.

Okeydokey, Button. Let's get on. Hey, just kidding, he says.

He fixes a pinch to his underlip, nudges the sorrel, and walks out ahead of me, and we go back to riding single-file and silently, as I wonder whatever happened to my given name. Whatever happened to Katherine?

A military jet sonic-booms above in the waking arc of the aircraft's passing, the contrails shielded in the dulled metal light of the sky. We settle into our paces, into the lull and the pull of our shadows and the weight of the day we are fated to. The horses snuffle. Son rubs at his forehead. I wonder if he might be pained by one of the headaches again, yet I know my asking would rankle him all the more. I wonder maybe too if quiet is something that simply comes naturally to Son. Or if speaking is something he never learned to do all that well from the beginning.

IT WAS ROSE who told the rest of the story, Rose who told the part hardest for me to believe. It was Rose who ran a comb through her once flaxen and now gone-to-fine-white hair. Rose who said, This town's Pearl Hart was, and still is, a mighty beauty. Everyone around who knows of her knows it to be true, Rose said.

The little bird flitted about in its cage.

Lord above us, Rose said. This heat. And my, this hair. How I would love to cut the lot of it off. It's like having to wear a fur wrap inside a steambath. What a burden in such an infernal place. Just who in her right mind would have it? But Daddy, he'd have a fit if I went and cut it, she said.

They say Pearl Hart isn't her real name, I said.

True, Rose said. She was born a Newby. The Newbys have been around these parts since horse-and-buggy days, she said. The grandfather, Jedediah Newby, was one of the original engineers come out here and put this country under ditch. It was Jedediah and his team planned the early waterways of the place. They built the canals and the overflow channels and diversions and the headgates. They built a town. And it was his son, Jeremiah Newby, who became head of Land and Irrigation Company. And along with it, he had a nice sideline in pigs. Indeed, he did quite well in pigs.

Rose freed the caught hair from the teeth of the comb and let the filaments wift from fingertip to wastebasket in morning strands of light.

The family lived a life of plenty, she said. Charmayne—Pearl, that is—was well kept and well nourished and well jewelry'd for all of her growing-up days. Her father quit pigs at a middle age and took his family and his wealth and moved over close to the river on a big piece of land that had belonged to his father, and with the riparian rights attached to it, you see, which made the family wealthier and more powerful yet. He moved into cattle then, thinking he was going to clear himself of any linkage to swine and the life that went with it, I suppose you could say. Though to my mind, a pig is a highly intelligent and respectable creature.

Rose put her comb down and stared at the bird gone quiet inside the cage.

Anyway, but Newby moved, she said. He built a stucco house in a mission style in the midst of a stand of date palms and olive trees alongside a tender stretch of the river. He schooled his daughter in the East and she came back west knowing how to talk and how to dress even better than she did before she left. She had studied acting and singing and danc-ing, all of the classical types—your drama and your opera and your ballet. And she had too in the meantime gone and changed her name so that Charmayne Newby would now be Pearl Hart, is what she insisted she be called. Charmayne, turned Pearl, had a way about her, Rose said, a way with mostly the male of the species. It was something that seemed to come naturally to her, just as with the Pearl Hart of legend, you could say, as the both of them always had a passel of fellows about. Maybe being this way made it more difficult for her, as she had a time of it settling down, so I've heard tell, that she had trouble knowing which of several men she ought to marry and make a home and bear children with. After a considerable while, she decided upon this man name of Ham. But the condition was that Pearl could have her liberty when it came to other men, and her husband should do the same if he be as inclined. Pearl is married yet these many decades to the same man. She and Ham have done fine together all their lives. They are dueños in the Water Association today, and yet too are steady in the business of stock contracting and the raising of fine thoroughbreds on the side.

Now I can see, Dear Girl, why your eyes are so wide, because I myself say, My oh my, Lordy, Lordy who can live a life like out of some French story? Of course, everyone around says the same thing, especially when they see Pearl about town. But the fact is they cannot admit to admiring Pearl for what is but a straightforward manner. I admire her for the kind of courage she has. Don't you? For her willingness to ask for whatever it is she wants. Because you never know when asking might just lead to getting. Well, Pearl is a strong woman, no doubt about it. It is not only her comeliness, and her money, and the power of family history, which has indeed helped a lot as well, but that she has had a need for sexual excess, which has only added to her attractions.

How could you know all this? I said.

Daddy told me, Rose said. And Daddy's facts come firsthand. Why would he be telling you?

He tells me a lot of things. Always has. Tells me every-thing, ever since our wedding day. Rose gathered her length of hair up and draped it over a shoulder, then began to knead her fingers through it, as if she were playing a reed instrument.

Yes, I truly believe it is best to tell the truth, she said. That is, if it can be taken. Not everybody can take the truth. Daddy and me, we made an agreement before we were married. And we carried it through all these years together, with the great-est amount of mutual respect. It is not such an easy way, but I tell you, two people can gain a mighty lot with honesty. And I have come to know what I could never have known, simply by listening. And Daddy surely learned a lot from Pearl Hart, learned about being a free spirit of sorts, learned about being more attentive to women and to their needs, and learned too about the water business. You could say I learned a lot from her as well. Though I am no beauty and have never had any money to speak of and I would rather sex be left to the ani-mals. Those are surely the big differences between Pearl and me, Rose said.

What animals?

That's a big part of why I don't mind much what Daddy does, she said. Easier on me, if you take my point. Though I must say, I do enjoy the stories quite a lot.

How do you know the stories are true?

It's surely difficult to think they would be true, she said. I don't see how any story like Pearl's could possibly be. I only know it is Daddy who tells me so. And his testimony, it never has changed.

Rose finished braiding her waist-length braid and she coiled it up atop her head and pinned it up into place to stay.

Lord, she said. This heat has got teeth in it. It's about to eat right into me. It's about to chew me up and swallow me right down. Reminds me, she said, throw a little bit of seed into the feeder cup for the bird while you're standing there.

It still got water? she said.

DID YOU SEE her?

Did I see who?

You know who. Who could have missed her, I say, dressed as she was in that getup. I could see her dabbing at her eyes, even under the big fancy hat she had on. I could see the handkerchief dangling in her hand the whole last half of the sermon.

What? You think she's been converted? Son says. Not her.

Maybe not converted. But what the Padre was saying seemed to be having an effect on a lot of people. You could see it on everybody's faces. What he said even got to me some. What he said about love.

Yeah, but Pearl's girl's like Pearl. She's no fool, he says.

To question the existence of God, he said, is to question the existence of love. Where is it that comes from? I say.

Son grinds the gears in the downshift and hard-turns the pickup, listing me over into my door side. He jars us to a stop in front of the restaurant and cuts the engine. The hood of the truck steams in the heat.

Didn't he say it was out of the book of something? I say.

Smell them fresh corn tortillas in the air, he says.

Not that I'm saying what he said fits right with the facts.

He said a lot of superstitious hooey, Son says.

It wouldn't be science, I say. But the way he described

the why of our being here. And talking about what he called the light, and becoming the light. It was poetical, didn't you think?

The ratchety tight noise of the pullback of the handbrake puts a stop to my talk. Son spits his chew out the window. He says he hadn't really heard a thing. He says he was too busy thinking about getting back before the water order was set to come in. Says he was just there and having to listen for the sake of his mother, as it is, after all, her birthday. There's work to do later in the day. The work piles up, he says. And the water doesn't wait.

But I know too that the water is not scheduled until tomorrow, as Rose's Daddy had mentioned it at the stove this morning when he was showing me the proper technique for milk gravy. Telling me, Let the butter melt real good, and add your flour and let the flour brown some before you start adding the milk, and add the milk in slow—no, slower than that—slow, real slow, here, let me show you. And Rose's Daddy takes the fork out of my hand and says, Work your fork into the mix like this so it should not clump up any, so we don't have any lumps in our gravy, he says. Thou shalt not have lumps. No man wants lumps, he says. There you go, now you have got it. Praise be we have got time for cooking lessons today, he says, as the water shan't be coming till mañana. I planned it that way because of Rose's birthday today.

Now I turn to Son and say, Why can't you be a better liar? Are you mean? I say. Or are you just dumb?

Don't ever call me that, he says.

And he jabs a hard forefinger right into my breastbone.

The sedan pulls up beside us at just this time, and Rose's Daddy rolls his window down and thumbs his hat back.

What foolishness is wrought between you two? he says. They will kick you out of the posse, Son, if people see you behaving in the way just witnessed. That bump on the head must have done something, he says. Or are you weakened by the heat? He looks past Son and sets his eyes on me, studies my face as if to find the rest of the story there.

You children ready for some patty enchiladas? he says.

The old man looks at Son. He looks at me.

Put your party faces on, he says, and let us get to our meal.

I open the door and slide out of the truck, the poke from Son's finger burning right into where my heart is.

THE MAN LEAVES a mark, Rose's Daddy says. I found out by having him to ride the buckskin yesterday and taking him out onto the mesa. He sat a horse rightly, yet you can see the old boy is not seeded from horse people. Rose's Daddy chuckles and pushes his menu aside. Lo, you should have seen him arrayed in his vestures of camelhair, and with shirt and suspenders and a tie on of the city kind, not your bolo. Camelhair! In this heat. *Whoo-eee!* I put a hat on his head and what a Buffalo Bill he looked to be, what with that long hippie wild hair of his.

Rose's Daddy sops into the tomatillo sauce with a piece of tortilla.

A teacher back east would have taught him the basics, as he handled the horse with skill to suffice, he says. The buckskin was a fine match with his camelhair, mind you, so he was properly suited. Though he did not ride straight-backed, but with that cultivated slump you see in some of those ivy-schooled easterners. Whatever the cultivated slump is supposed to mean.

Yet he and I had a pleasant ride. The Padre has got a bit of wirecutter spirit in him. He minds his ways by a different set of rules, his rules, if you know what I mean. Something you would not expect in some bible'd personality such as his. He would be rather more in keeping with a few of the old-timers we have got around here. You could say the Padre is more what they call, these days, new-agey, rather than old-timey.

Pass me over some of the avocado mush, he says.

Therein we are riding along and the Padre said to me how I ought to be meditating. I said to him, said, I am meat eating. Always have I been meat eating. A good meat eater am I, I said. No, he said — said meditating, as in pondering, is what I mean. And I told him I am without doubt well-practiced at pondering. Riding is the very best thing for pondering. He said he means something more like finding peace, or finding a quiet stillness inside. And I said, Surely, I do that all the time, right in the middle of the night. Said, That is what I love best about sleep, all that magnificent peace and quiet and stillness I find inside. And I think he might have thought my laughing impertinent, as he dropped the entire matter of pondering and meat eating after that.

I shall have a machaca burrito, deep-fried, Rose's Daddy says, handing his menu to the waitress. Make it swimming in green sauce today, he says, not red.

Then we got somehow upon the topic of Pearl Hart, a name that seems to be cropping up in every conversation these days of a sudden, he says. The Padre tells me she has tithed a plenteous sum of money to his church or to his congregation or to his whatever body the money will go to. Maybe to the Padre himself, who knows? And the Padre said to me, What a good-hearted woman Pearl Hart is. Said she has donated not only her money but also her time lately to the service of the church. Said Pearl Hart is generous indeed. And I said, Yes, indeedy, Pearl is that. She is giving in many ways, she certainly is. Who would say she has not been truly giving?

Rose napkins the corners of her mouth.

Oh, Daddy! she says. You would not have said that.

I kindled no wrath, Mother.

Pass the bottle a hot sauce, Ma, Son says, all the while keeping his eyes on the waitress standing over at the register.

I take a swallow of my cold cola drink, taking mouthfuls of ice chunks in and crunching them up with my teeth. Feeling that burning spot over my heart turning to a numbing. Thinking reasoning doesn't do a bit of good when you think it should.

What else? Rose says.

What else? Herein I can tell you I was honest with the Padre. Said to him, You might call me a Christian man, certainly, sir, with a good deal of respect for other people's way of thinking, yet nay, I do not believe most religious talk to be very near any truth. Said, I myself find most of it a hard thing to reckon with when it comes to intelligence.

Those are rude words to say to such a man, Rose says.

He did not wax sore as to what I had to say, Rose's Daddy says. The Padre seemed to take my opinion just fine. He is not the closed-minded kind, as some hombres are — as though they be afraid of their brains spilling out. Do you not think he has heard all the arguments before? The Padre is a listening man, the reflective type, he says. He may go quiet on you, but I believe that be a trick among their profession to try to get you to think about what it is you went and said. Yet much as I have already thought plentifully over the years about the delicate subject matter of which I have spoken, I have not come to any change of mind about any of it. So I told him.

I give Son a kick in the leg under the table. This gets him to turn his head away from the register, away from the waitress, who is by this time regarding Son in the same way he is regarding her. He gives me a look. I give him a look back, the unspoken words turning to stones and arrows between us.

Before we bid our good-byes, Rose's Daddy says, We were the two of us laughing about this and that and the other, who knows what subject we had got on to by then. And the Padre had his camelhair jacket shoggling over the cantle of the saddle. And he was using his straw hat like a fan and Lord forbid he would not have had it to fan with.

Lo, would you behold what has arrived?

The waitress comes to the table carrying a flaming cake.

You kids like the pretty new jinglebobs Rose is wearing for her birthday? he says.

Rose closes her eyes and blows, and the candles sputter out.

I leave my eyes open and make a wish of my own.

THE RIG COMES jouncing and fishtailing by the old adobe house, trailing a funnel of dust in its wake. The commotion gets the old dog to stop the mad chew she has going at a tick on her haunches, and she gets up and shakes and trots down the porch steps to go after the ruckus. Rose's Daddy comes out of the house and lets the screendoor slam, ignoring Rose's protests for the noise of it, and he heads out to the corral after the trotting dog. I follow behind too, getting there in time to see the man that's driving the horse trailer get out of the truck and square the hat atop his head afresh. Then I see the woman get out the door on the other side. See the woman dressed in a pearl-buttoned silk western blouse and slender-fitting cowboy denims, her riding boots drawn up to the calves with the britches tucked into the ostrich shaft, her concha belt studded with turquoise and silver and aglitter in the sun. See Rose's Daddy turn his head to the woman and tip his hat. Then he goes over to the man and reaches a hand out.

How you, Ham? the old man says.

Pree' good, Ham says.

Holding up in this godamighty weather?

Pree' much, Ham says.

How you, Pearl?

Can't complain, she says.

How be your girl? he says.

Pearl's fine too, Pearl says.

She places a wide-brimmed, pencil-rolled black Montana on top of her head and turns and walks over to the pasture fence, looking about as if she were expecting something coming. The man called Ham goes around to the back of the horse trailer and unlatches the slidelatch, and he swings the doors of the horse trailer open. There before us are the powerful hindquarters of the horse. There's the oilslick shine of hide, the plaited hang of tail, the stocking of hockjoint and fetlock, all those parts of the horse the old man has taught me to regard. He and Ham stand one on each side of the stallion, and Ham gives the horse an easy slap on the flank and the horse backsteps until it is backed out of the trailer. Ham clips the reins to the hackamore and Rose's Daddy takes the reins and leads the animal to the post and tethers him. The horse is thoroughbred and magnificent, above sixteen hands, must be, and well muscled in the shoulders, the withers high and sharply defined, the neck long, and the eyes intelligent. I go over and put my hand to the blaze on the flat of its forehead. I look right into the large, dark, glossy eyes, seeing facets of my reflection inside. The horse looks right back at me, flares its nose, knowing, I tell you, seeming wise beyond belief.

I see you've been taken in, Pearl says.

She leans against the post in the shade of the paddock, tapping the ashes off the end of a slender cigar. The skin of her heart-shaped face and long slender neck is pale as milk, seeming never to have seen sun before — amazing, given this place — and her black hair is gathered into a knot at the nape. She smiles at me, showing perfectly even white teeth.

Rose's Daddy has promised me the foal, I tell her.

Has he? she says, smiling bigger.

I wait for her to say something more, but she doesn't. She just looks at me and puffs on the little cigar, with the paddock, the pasture, the fencepost, the pecan tree, the ground, and the sky behind her all awaver, everything today seeming to be dissolving in the heat. There's something intimidating about her that makes me feel trembly too, something about her that silences me, makes me want to fade quietly away, makes me want to overturn my words and hide. Maybe her knowing so much more than me, having gone off to a fancy college. That, and too, her having the courage to name herself her own name, and being brave enough not to care about what people say. Or maybe none of any of this. Maybe it's not what I've heard about her, but instead what I see before me now — the way she holds herself, or the smell of her foreign-smelling perfume, or some aspect of her person I just can't explain that makes me uneasy, too uneasy to speak.

Holy Roller's the name, Ham says.

You take good care of our Holy Roller, Pearl says.

It shall be, Rose's Daddy says.

We best be going, Ham says.

You give our best to Rose now, Pearl says.

That shall be too, Rose's Daddy says.

Tell her I hope to see her soon in church, Pearl says. You've heard about the Padre, haven't you, the new one come to town?

I heard about him and rode with him, he says.

Yes, and I had a look and a listen for myself, she says. Let me tell you, that man is one hot gun.

When you want that herd of ropin' cattle here? Ham says.

Anytime soon. And you shall be sure to cut any muleys out of the bunch. Muleys won't do.

You bet, Ham says. No muleys it'll be.

Ham backs the empty horse trailer up and pivots it around. Pearl gives a flutter of gloved hand and quickly rolls her window up before the boil of dust begins to roll inside the cabfront. I wave good-bye and turn to see the thoroughbred standing at the post and looking at me. I go over and hold my hand out to the animal, bursting with a feeling I have been struck dumb with of a sudden.

Mornings and evenings now I go out to the pasture and wait for Holy Roller to spot me. When he does, he whickers and comes up to the fence. Sometimes I'll have a pocketful of hay or a handful of grain to feed him, and I'll let his violet-soft muzzle and nostrils graze the cup of my hand in the offering. Other times I give him nothing but mouthfuls of my words and strokes across the nose and the blaze. I want to have him for my own, want to own him and keep him, but the old man says that Pearl would never part with such a fine-paying horse. He is worth more than the affection of some lovestruck girl, he says.

So I'm banking on the foal.

I go into the tackroom and sit at Rose's Daddy's old wooden swivel chair, the afternoon light caging in through the barred window. I take a match from the box and strike it atop the metal desk. Then I make a wish, not waiting for any birthday, and lovestruck girl that I am, I blow the flame out.

⌒

FOUR

THE PADRE

What we drink we get from the well, the same water hole dug out years ago by Rose's Daddy's daddy. What comes out of the pipes and the faucets is brackish and rust colored, the leech of ore or iron, of sulfur and selenium, and the other salts and elements drawn into it, people have said. Rose's Daddy said no well dug anyplace else on the property would suit any of us any better. He said you had to learn to drink water differently around here, taking it down quickly and not taking breath in when you're swallowing, even biting into a lemon wedge after the water is down, the way you would do it drinking tequila. He said you had to get used to the iron coloring staining everything too—the sinks and the tubs, the food you cook, the clothes you wear, the taint it leaves in your hair, on your fingernails, even your teeth. Still, the alchemy of the water in its mix with other liquids would catch the eye every time, the way the iron turned the old man's bourbon dark as ink, and watching as he would drink his drink this way anyway, no matter the color or the odor or the taste of it. I would find him sitting out by the pool at night, his face reflected fluorescent, drinking his tall black cocktail, iced with iron-colored ice.

Come sit and keep me company, Girl.

I went over and took a seat next to him, pointing out the waterline, dropped feet below the paint of aquamarine.

It's turning into a wading pool, I said.

Will be soon. Unless this fit of weather should go on forever.

The ice tinkled in his glass like the tiny voices of frightened people.

Girl, would you not be surprised to know that we sit atop an aquifer here? There is a pool lying right hither below where we recline tonight. At one time there were miles and miles of rivers and streams running underneath us. There were lakes. I would bet, a sea.

Then there must be plenty of water.

Heaven knows there was, he said. That is, before some of the bigger irrigators around here turned to groundwater supplies and began pumping with great intensity, and even more during the dry spells, with the river giving so little. The practice had our county and town near to exhausting its reserves, thereby putting the water-bearing stratum that upholds us close to collapse. If not for a double-hundred-mile-long aqueduct built and tapped into the river earlier dammed, such a catastrophe might have occurred. But the water was delivered, and life was brought back to the land. And we went on with our ways of plenty, our ways of wastefulness. Yet what we have now is groundwater dwindling in quality, as surely is our due. For our practices of feeding and planting are spoiling the aquifer below, mixed as it is with tail-water, with the seepage and runoff from the irrigate—an over-load of pesticides and chemicals, and the metabolites and dregs that come from them. We need to bring the drainage up from the ground below our crop zones just so that it may be carried away from the very soil we want left fertile and of benefit.

Yea, these be complicated matters, the old man said. If only it could be a simple case of pray and wait for the rain gods to replenish us.

A giant striped mesquite bug sculled to and fro in a struggle for a way out of the pool. I thought about going over and scooping the thing up and putting it to the concrete to free it, but didn't, figuring it too long a reach down to the water. Besides, my trying might have put a stop to the old man's talk.

There have been steel flumes and pipe siphons put into effect to draw the water up, he said. And there are concrete bypass drains thus laid to trough the water away. The reject water has been pumped out of the earth by the acre-foot and routed into the river, the river mix then channeled to a slough down in Mexico. But with a drought cast upon us, and our river water become so diminished, the undilute of saline and the undilute of all the rest of what ought not to be in the water is all that much the greater.

Rose's Daddy took a sip of his icy black drink.

Lo, man was born unto trouble, he said. For indeed Mexico protests, as surely anyone could predict the way that story would go, as her need is for water, not waste. And as we wait to come to some new accordance, all the while the ribs and the veins of the earth are being sucked of the nutrients so needed for nourishment. Perhaps our harvest days are past.

He brought the glass to his lips and drank again.

There is talk these days of building a desalting plant, he said. Seems there be ever more devices of the crafty. Yet such a fix is as costly as it is cumbersome, near impossible in times tough as these. All the meanwhile, the thirst of the cities on the coast becomes more difficult to quench, what with the ever-growing number of people in need of a drink and a wash. As that mass of people increases, so will the power of their dollar and the demand for their share. And such tender becomes ever more enticing.

The mesquite bug reached the side of the pool and finally began to climb.

So how be it we are to give what we have so little of to give? he said. Do we go on breaking treaties? Or do we do what a man does best, and just go out and get? What do you think, Girl, are we truly our brother's keeper?

Rose's Daddy put the glass to his lips, drawing this time but a long draw of air.

IT'S THE KNOCKING of a pecker bird that spurs me to morning, a drum call that opens my eyes to the light spilling in through the cuts of the blinds. Son is already up and gone to town — I can hear him telling me this now, hear him telling me he is leaving as I'm already drifting back under a cover of sleep. I resist the ought-to's, the should-be's, the prods of duty that would make me throw the sheet off and get up out of bed. It's not until the knocking stops, in the loud silence that follows, that I'm roused to the other side and waked to the day. I'm waked again to yes, waked to those hopes that are a pull forward, whatever it is that gets dawned upon us — some kind of betterment or remaking we come to believe in, what it might be that makes us try. For if not striving, what might there be but tedium?

I rub the crust from my eyes, trying to arrange the pieces of the night I've just risen from, remembering now the manila envelope arrived in yesterday's mail, remembering the sentences of intent to be written out, the many pages to be inked in, the categories and the summaries of me needing ordering, and all the questions answered properly and sealed up and sent for judgment by a soon-to-come date.

Answer: To make something of myself.

Answer: For myself.

Answer: Not applicable.

I reach for the cord and pull the blinds open more and full light breaches in. Objects are drawn forward—lampshade, bureau, armchair, mounds of clothes from the night prior, toppled boots, balls of socks, a snaking of belt, a glinting of silver, islets of underthings, a daddy longlegs coursing daintily over a pair of denims. A glass sits on the table next to the bed, but the water left in it is too scummed with dust to drink. I lick my parched lips, swallow dry spittle. I yawn to make the ringing stop, now in the already rising timbaling of cicada—those mightily vocal tiny invertebrates in some great state of proclaim.

The cool tiles send the blood running upward. Lost parts of what came to me in sleep crop up—a skitter of images, fragments of sentences, strands of nonsense, the whole of it as hopeless as trying to hold on to a handful of water. Memory breaks away from the dream as I hear Rose's Daddy talking yesterday about breakfasting out today and see the look on his face of being somewhere else, the way he bit at his lower lip and put his hat on and walked away in a direction not intended, the way he stopped and muttered something before turning around. He and Son are by this hour at the coffee shop, likely settled into the middle booth of their regular choosing, ordering their eggs and their biscuits and gravy, their bacon crispy, their oranges squeezed at the asking. A starchy light will flood in through the window where they sit blowing the hot off just-poured cups of coffee. The old man will put his cup down and begin to explain the aims and the means of selling blocks of the property off, selling land attached to water rights that so up the sum of the profits. They will nod, one to the other. They will chew their food slowly, deliberately, turning occasionally to look out the window, noting each pickup truck that pulls up in front, knowing every man that gets out, suspicious of every man they don't.

Reach some more of that hot sauce over, one of them will say.

I splash the rust-colored water over my face, holding my breath as I do to shut the sulfur odor of it out. I brush the brush through, and my hair crackles and sparks in the starving-for-water air here.

The hour strikes late morning time.

I ready myself with a different breath for the pouring scorch that awaits. Then to add startle to startle, opening the door to step out, I find a diamondback laid choked on the welcome mat, and there alongside it, trails of guts and dust prints trailing off the porch, sure marks of a hunter cat. I scoot to the side of the catch, my eyeballs constricting in their adjusting to the sun's rays, my shadow creeping over the remains. I head down the steps and around back toward the tackroom, on into a morning like every morning here is, one hard to tell from any other one, in what's become a consistent and cloudless lack of variation, in a land of forever seeming but one season, where everything is the same and still, where the stretch from here to the outlines of foothills is as bleak and empty and colorless as any loneliness would be. The sun rings above like an alarm in the heat. I can already feel it eating through the weave of my hat. I head for shade, finding the shelter of the melon shed along the way to be an oasis, the old dog there splayed out on the concrete floor, apant in her sleep. She lumbers up and shakes when she knows me near, and I squeeze my eyes shut at the dust that floats up from her coat. Again pieces of the night arise — a lake it was, woods, a stream, back from where I was from, and I'm trying to find the true place I know to get the feelings right that I had had there once. Why do those people keep getting in my way? I know I must know them. But who could they be? And why do they keep me from getting close to the shore?

A pair of boots waggle out from beneath the watertruck. A chafing of rough cloth sounds against the cement, and the hired man comes crawling out from the underbelly, crablike, on his back. He reaches for his cap and doffs it at me. Mornin', Missus, he says. I good-morning him back, feeling it alien to hear me as Missus when I am just turned eighteen.

The hired man gets up and lifts the hood of the watertruck, and thick folds of dust sift out of the nooks and the cracks of it when he does. You should see the way the sun has burned through the paint of the thing, the way it has worn the tank and cabtop down to sand prime, eaten right through to the metal core in places. The sun bakes through everything, and with it comes a heat that brings the smells out, the smells of motor grease and diesel oil, of pumps and valves, weldings and fittings.

I fan myself with my hat and go on.

A military jet moves past in a thunder overhead, leaving behind a contrail that furrows the sky. I try picturing what the pilot might see from up in the cockpit — the warp and scar of burnt earth below — and how it will be to arrive soon to the blue of the sea in the distance, landing to rollicking calls of seabirds and cooling wind bursts, squinting into the glitter of water, tasting the taste of salt on the lips.

The pecker bird rattles on a hollowed-out old saguaro, waking me back again to here where I am. Here where I am, you should see it: the pastureland within desertland, the ballenas of fields and broken ground, the alkali and creosote flats beyond that, and the slopes we know as angles of repose—those places of hanging on while falling apart, places of perfect tension and friction.

I get to the pasture gate and give a kick to a post to shoo away the crowbirds rowed along the fencerail, and they scatter and caw, their cries angry and rising like razors from their gulars. One swoops down and strikes the hat off my head and I quick pick it up and hurry on into the tackroom, the blood running prickly through my veins, my thoughts running through causes for punishment.

The tackroom is dim and musty inside. Bars of sunlight filter in with the dust through the little iron-guarded window. I sit at Rose's Daddy's old gun-colored metal desk, old as one of the world wars would be, with the fan in a slow whir overhead. I pull one of the drawers open, hoping to find something hopeful I suppose, or maybe a thing intended to settle mystery, though what would I be looking for? All there are, are locks and buckles and screws inside, a box of toothpicks, books of matches, scatters of coins. I close the drawer and lean back in the chair and look about the room, at the nailed and studded walls covered over, as they are, with an assortment of montura and tack. The place is everywhere draped with stiff ropes and stirrups, bridles and reins, harnesses and spurs, flourishes of headstalls and straps, peggings of leather riggings, worn old chaps, cracked hames, unknowable leather things. A row of sawhorses holds the saddles up, each seat perched atop a beam of its own, the stirrups penduled in the strew and dredge of dirt and straw that cover the boarded floor over, the cinches sagged in the nubble and scatter of droppings from mouse and verdin and squirrel. Along the shelves are saddle soaps and leather balms, ointments and liniments, and other kinds of creams and potions that promise to heal and mend. A bottle of whiskey is empty but for a swig. I pick it up and see the current list of rodeo events that were weighted beneath—the dates and the fees, the sums of the prizes, how to qualify to ride.

So the old man wasn't kidding.

I had come running into the tackroom day before yesterday to escape the racket of target practice and to ask the old man why Son was so often at it lately with this game. Son had been out blowing tin cans off the fencepost again, and I stood behind him awhile, watching the way he cleared the lineup. He spent a round of bullets on a row of empty cola bottles he had set up in the dirt. He reloaded and looked about him, as if for what would be next. He looked at me. Then he turned and started shooting at almost everything. He shot at a desert weasel slinking field hole to field hole. He shot at a chuckwalla dropped from the jaws of one of the hunter cats, and then he spun around and started shooting at the cat. He kept on like a crazy man, firing at just about anything—at a birdrunner running along the road, at a spiny berry noded to a cholla, at a sandspout funneling along a bar ditch. He had smoke pockets drifting off into the forenoon above us like a hover of blue doves.

I hurried into the cool refuge of the tackroom. Rose's Daddy sat with his feet atop the old gun-colored desk, the whiskey bottle near him uncorked and near full, the ceiling fan whirlybirding overhead. He opened a red pouch of full aroma, tamped a wad into his pipebowl, struck a match, and lit the amphora, watching me through the flame as he toked. I stood there catching my breath and getting my awares, the ceiling fan whorling the blossom of chocolate-and-cherry tobacco about the room. You could smell a parched-earth smell just below the layer of sweet cavendish—dirt that had been whisked in by the wind and tramped in by bootsole, air that carried the aroma of the manure of animals and the sweat of men, the pungency of creosote, the spiciness of sage and rue. The heat held too the odor of worn horse blankets, the hemp of rope, the tannin of leather, and the soaps and waxes and creams used to clean and polish and nourish the hides—smells that would seep into wood and adobe and memory.

You've not ridden the paint lately, the old man had said.

I was on him just the other day.

You need to be working him around those barrels every day.

I suppose.

You suppose.

A hot wind came through the iron bars of the window like a furnace on.

What's with Son and that gun? I said.

Nervous tension it seems, he said, shaking his head.

He's making me nervous.

Don't be, Girl, he said. And too, do not weary yourself to brood over not having that foal. I can see you have been let down. We may give it another go-round, but a man can only promise as best he can.

It's not that.

What be it, then?

Rose's Daddy's words were stirred up with the buzz of horseflies overhead. He would go on with his talk. My mind would go off toward other things. I probably thought about how the hot would blow at least until twilight. I probably saw a darkness thick with dust settling in as usual, leaving the sky moonless and without stars. I probably thought about Son, where he went and hid at night, what he did. There was never a day anymore I wouldn't get a queasiness in my stomach about this.

Girl, if you be dismayed at not having the stallion here of late you can surely head yonder to Pearl and Ham's habitation, Rose's Daddy said. I doubt they would mind a lick if you were to go over there and visit Holy Roller. He raised his eyebrows and looked at me, the smoke of his pipe drifting in ropy loops about the room. I keep forgetting you are yet hardly grown from a child, he said. Nonetheless, you ought to stop sulking. We do not go in for mollycoddling of any kind around here.

I swatted at the tangle and drone of pests above my head and turned to head out the door just as Son was coming in. He ducked some to keep his hat from hitting the lintel and wielded his weapon ahead of him, his silver belt buckle aglitter like a shield and the dust pluming from his bootheels, as if he were some kind of hero from ancient times, one of those men of Greek or Roman myths that would leave imprints in the sky. He settled the gun atop the rack on the wall and turned to me.

Hey, he said.

Hey what? I said.

Enough fooling around out there, Rose's Daddy said. Hereafter we need to be in league and get to working at getting after that rodeo dough. Before we cannot afford to bring any more groceries in. Before we cannot afford to bring nor anything in. Before we cannot keep on with what is important. Before we are lost of all substance. He knocked the pipe against the desk and a dottle of burnt tobacco fell out of the bowl to the floor. He stamped on the smoldering plug and booted it across the room. We shall not be smote by the heat, he said. Now let us get a get-go.

I went out and watched Son that day, watched the way he uncoiled the rope and laid it out, working the loop over his head easy and loose so to warm his arm up. He threw the first toss out, snagging the bull's horn by a single. He drew the rope back, coiled it up, and lofted it once more, getting both horns this time. He went through all the moves again and again, his face worked into a twisted manner of concentration, roping until he was doubling consistently. After a while he changed his aim and pitched the lariat over a parceled-up bale of hay. When he had had enough of this, he started going for whatever he might have been able to get the noose around. He lasso'd the fenceposts, the legs of a table, a rusted-out barrel and keg, the mailbox and toolbox, the watertruck bumper, a tractor seat. He had me run from him so he could run after me, going for my head and reeling me in by the waist after the catch. He let me loose only to go after both my feet, all but tripping me, and I hollered at him to stop while he was bent over laughing. Then he turned and threw a loop over the head of the old dog, choking back on the rope and making her struggle and rasp.

Just horsin', he said.

A LONESOME DAMSELFLY danced about in search of a way out. I walked through a room of looping morning glories and latticed fencing papering the walls. A pot of beans simmered atop the stove, and over on the sill of the window, a jar of suntea steeped. There were vitamin and iron pills on the countertop, a water glass half-filled, a tube of handcream, a pile of grocery receipts, recipe clippings, shopping lists, doctor bills, gas and electric bills, telephone bills, other kinds of bills. A large mason jar held something dried and crumbled inside, an odd concoction of things—spurs of bursage, wool of horsebrush, hairs of wormwood, florets of snakeweed, is what the handwriting on the label said—fixings meant for a bruja's stew, you would think. I looked through the window and saw Rose, stooped in the dirt in what was left of the garden. There was her broad-brimmed straw yet hung on the peg on the wall on my way out. I reached for the hat and opened the door, the damselfly flying past in its droning escape.

The sere of the day hit like the slap the door made. Rose startled and looked back at the noise and at me coming out. Then she went back to busying herself with what she had been doing, tending to what she said was a onetime prizewinning and now dying polyantha. Rose was slender and silvery and delicate as a kit fox would be. Her hair was sprung from its coil of braid and caught in a fuzzy halo of light about her scalp. The sun burned straight above, through a gauzing of dust.

You forgot your hat, I said.

She touched her head to check. I forgot I was only going to be out here for a minute, she said. She took the big-brimmed straw from me and put it on.

I used a salute held to my forehead to keep the sun in check.

Where's yours? she said.

I'm only out for a minute too, I said.

Rose tapped at a dried stalk with her pruning shears. An old garden rose, she said, meant more for hardiness than for showiness, though no less the beautiful because of it. Yet now look at the fallen clusters. Look here at the shriveled petals. Deary me, all the many scorched leaves. These cankered stems, she said.

She reached a hand out, the skin lichened and thinned, and

I pulled her up, light as a sack full of dried mesquite beans would be. I asked her if she might like to make a visit with me out to Pearl Hart's place today, uneasy as I was going alone, but Rose complained of being weary. You go on, she said, and give Pearl my betters. She brushed the dirt from her skirt and her knees and she blew the loose hairs away from her face. She straightened her back up, rolled the hunch from her shoulders out, then rearranged the broad straw hat. And I wondered if it was forgiving or forgetting that allowed Rose her generosity, if it was one or the other or both that gave her such uprightness, such fineness, such grace.

THE HOUSE IS a two-story pink stucco built in the mission style, with quatrefoil windows and arched dormers and roof parapets, set amid acres of mixed irrigated and riparian land that runs alongside the dwindling river. The grounds that surround it are a place of shade, a refuge of desert olive and eucalyptus and paloverde, with light strobing through the masses of branches and shoots and through the crowns and the blades of leaves, light so pale and flickering it's hard to tell sky from sand from what water there is yet in the river. The watertruck chugs along through the trees, down a long drive-way rowed with date palms, the drooping thatches scratching pleadingly at the tank roof. I clutch and brake at the gatehouse, where a Mexican man in a khaki uniform of sorts stops me to question me. He picks a receiver up and speaks my name into it. He nods his head and comes out of the gatehouse and slides the latch back. He wings the wrought-iron gates apart, drawing one open, then going over across to the other side to draw the other back. He raises a hand in gesture and lets me drive through and on past.

It's Pearl's daughter who answers the front door of the pink stucco house, Pearl's daughter who does not smile in her hello, nor does she look at my eyes to invite me in—the daughter who says no word to me as she leads me through the long dark entryway, moving as if she were bored by this chore, moving as if she is aware of her prettiness too, with her mother's fine skin and straight even teeth, with breasts full beneath her sheer camisa as any man would want them, her hair styled exactly right as to the style of the times, and her legs lean and fine and tanned for the sake of fashion and others' eyes. She takes me out to an inner courtyard where her mother is sipping tea with the Padre in the spiny shade of an ocotillo. A large fountain sits dry in the middle of the courtyard—a cherub holding an urn between its hands, any water that should be flowing out from it now only in imagining. Brittle leaves and tiny lizards skitter over the pebbles at the fountain's base and over the stone toes of the cherub. A bowl of tangelos sits brimful on the table. Pearl's daughter reaches for the fruit, sticks a thumb into the skin of one, letting the juice of it run down her wrist. She licks the trickle to a finish.

I'm going into town for a while, she says.

Back by suppertime, her mother says.

The daughter holds a peg of tangelo up to her lips, either to hide her smile or maybe to be silly, thinking it charming. She says her good-byes to the Padre and says how she's glad to see him and will he come back soon again for another visit. She speaks with her back to me, leaves without a further good-bye of any kind.

Pearl gestures a hand to the empty chair next to her and says, Please. I take a seat, my heart fluttering like the hummingbird does about the phlox potted at our sides. She opens a nacre-inlaid box and takes a slender cigar out, and when she offers me one, I thank her, no. The Padre reaches for the upright silver lighter on the table and he thumbs a flame and extends the light toward Pearl's face. She looks him directly in the eye as she draws the fire in. She takes her time, as if drawing the Padre in too. She inhales and turns to me, offers me a glass of iced tea, and as I'm declining she's filling the tumbler up anyway. I tell her I had come by not to waste any of her time but to pay a visit to Holy Roller. She tells me I've come none too soon, as tomorrow all the thoroughbreds will be trailered up to mountain country and they won't be brought back again until the drought comes to an end.

If it ever comes to an end, she says.

Where is your faith? the Padre says.

I'm counting on you, she says.

I defer to higher powers, he says. But you will be helping me draw upon these powers along with the others at the next prayer meeting. He stands and places a hand on Pearl's shoulder. Please, don't get up. I can see myself to the door. He turns my way and says he would be happy to escort me out to the stables.

Pearl draws on her cigarillo and nods.

The Padre leads me back through the long entryway of thick stucco walls and out the double wooden doors, as if he already knew the place well. The way to the stables takes us through a grove of tangerine trees, along a path shilled with sunlight and dapples of shadow, the fruit on the trees ripe and gleaming like jewelry, so tempting the picking. We walk in silence, and I wait for words to surface, hoping for the right something to say.

Won't you get dirty? I'm already wishing away what I said.

He stops and looks himself over, dressed as he is all in white linen—a long shirt that hangs about to his knees, and underneath, white linen pajama-like pants. His toes protrude from the hem, and the nakedness of his feet is embarrassing, too out of place as they are in this place, or something.

This is Indian garb, he says. Desert wear. Indian men wear such clothes every day and everywhere, and surely they don't worry much about getting dirty, he says, as such items are properly washed. As are feet, he says.

Not the Yumas or the Pimas, I say. Not the Quechans either. I've not seen them dressed in white cotton pajamas, young or old, no matter the fashion or the tribe.

His eyes. There are glints of light in the violet of the irises.

No, he says. India's Indians.

I feel the heat rise in my face.

He laughs softly, graciously, tossing his head back.

You'll need shoes. Or a tetanus shot, either one, I say, thinking this not funny enough after I've said it.

He lifts his cuffs to show me his sandals.

Those should do, but they'll raise eyebrows in town, I say.

You're probably right, he says. Anyway, I'm not going all the way to the stables. I just thought to walk you partway. Pearl would have had me at the house with her the rest of the afternoon. And I've got a sermon needing to be written before morning.

That's something, writing a sermon.

I could use some inspiration today, he says. He tilts his head back and looks up toward the sun. The rage of heaven's eye, he says. This weather would put any soul to the test.

Maybe you've got a few Indian chants to bring on the rain?

Come to our prayer meeting next week and find out.

I would. But I'm not a religious person.

I see you otherwise.

The idea of a man up in the sky doesn't really fit right with me.

Nor with me, he says.

But I liked what you talked about in church the day I came, I say. It didn't sound like the usual, you know, the usual stuff. Though I don't know how I would know what the usual is.

Come by my office and we can talk more, he says. Come some morning. Or afternoon. Come anytime. Would you?

The Padre reaches a hand out and I take it, thinking it like the first time I had shaken his hand, that time in line with the others on the way out of the church, when we said our hellos and he looked right into me the way he looks right into me today.

There's a buffet of wind as we say our so-longs.

You hear that? he says.

Hear what?

The fretful weather, he says, it may be about to change.

WE LOPED THE horses for a stretch down the canalbank, breaking them down to a trot before they had a chance to froth or begin to wheeze. By the time we were back to the stables, they were ribboned with sweat, even walking them back easily and coming into the lessening heat of evening. We watered them well and led them into the arena, where the hired man had already gotten the pens filled with the cows. Now he used a hotshot to filter the bunch through the chutes, most of them being too hot and too stubborn to move. But when he prodded the rumps and let the current buzz through, this jumped each, one by one, ahead and quick.

The horses waited in ready at the end gate.

My eyes were on Son. I waited for him to give me the nod, and when he did I opened the gate latch and leapt back and let the cow burst out. Son took off across the line on the sorrel, and Rose's Daddy came pounding out but seconds behind. The sorrel ran strong as Son looped the rope high overhead and caught up just the right distance from the calf. He swung the rope and dropped it on over the horns, then jerked it back and dallied, choking the rope up on the cow's neck, the sorrel knowing to backstep to keep the rope stretched tight. The cow bawled and snotted as the bay came up for the heels, Rose's Daddy swinging his lariat but snagging just the one hoof. The old man tied on hard and fast, and the horses pranced backward both ways— both good working horses, stretching the ropes out and bringing the calf down, pulling it out long and taut, stiffening it the way it will hang after butchering, with the tongue and the eyes bulged out. Son dropped from his saddle and loosened the heel rope, then took his own rope from the horns. Get both of 'em next time, he said to the old man. And they roweled their horses around and trotted back to the chutes and got ready to rope another cow down, one more time and then another time and over and over again.

ROSE'S DADDY WILL talk often of the days of water aplenty. He will talk of the team of hired men he once had, telling of their numbers and abilities, their eating habits and their drinking ways, their women and dogs, their children. He will talk about the foreman he had to do most of the work for him, another man he had hired to care just for the horses, a woman who would come to teach Rose to ride English each morning and evening. There was a new swimming pool put in, and a coach hired to teach Son how to high-dive and win medals. There were cooks hired to feed everyone kept hungry because of the lemon picking and the melon loading and the riding and the diving that was done. There was a driver hired to drive the cars for the old man and Rose on bridge nights and on going-out-to-dinner nights and on bright-lit rodeo nights.

There were stars out brilliant and beyond reckoning, he will say.

Rose will talk of the days there was water enough for all the roses she had planted and trained and proudly shown.

We had water enough for a prizewinning garden of roses, she will say, all of them bordered and bedded and pruned to bloom one to follow yet after another. We had flushes of ramblers rambling out over the fencepost and wild climbers reaching up over the portico. There were whites and creams shrubbed along the walkway and particolors in clay pots to add cheer out by the poolside. There were sweetbriars and hybrid teas that made a picture of the kitchen window. There were weepers clinging to the porch beams.

Now Rose wipes the dust from her eyes. She has just come home after having been a few days at the coast. She has parked the sedan under the dying branches of an old pecan tree and left the car clacking and pinging in a state of overheating. A road-runner clucks from the bitterbrush. The sun hangs at its zenith.

Another hotter-than-hot one today, she says. The old dog and a stream of dust have followed her into the house and she shoos the dog away with the back of a hand and waves the dust away from her face with a handkerchief. She puts her purse and her keys on the sideboard and walks through the cool and dark of the parlor. She goes into the kitchen and pours herself a long drink of cold tea from the pitcher and she stands with the glass in her hand, looking out the picture window, the roses gone, the stalks turned skeletal, the leaves blown out across the field. She puts her glass down and goes into the bedroom in the middle of the day. She shuts the door behind her and takes to months in her bed until death.

And she will die in the month of brides.

We would all of us do what we could do.

Rose's Daddy tended to her devotedly. Each day he went into Rose's room with another rose. He went into town to buy all the roses the old florist had yet to sell. He bought a solo rose and put it in a tall vase for her. He bought her one of the last damasks and placed it open cupped in a cut-glass bowl. He rowed china cups of dried buds along the sill of the window. He held a sweet floribunda up to her nose, known as a Dearest.

My Dear Rose, he said.

I would go into the room and roll Rose onto her side for her to see what was left of the roses the old man had brought in. I stayed her with pillows behind the splintery bones of her neck, propped them into the brittled hollow of her low backbone, used them as padding between the bonejuts of her wasted legs. In the afternoon I would go into her room and roll her to face the other way.

Son would sit quiet at the bedside watching Rose in her uneven breathing. He would sit a long time. Mama, he would say.

At night, we could hear Rose. We would lie still in our bed hearing Rose's Daddy in the room with her, in the bed with her, hear him in his whispering, in the whine and plead of the bedsprings, hear him crushing her bones with all of his needs on her.

WE DROVE TO the bridge, to the once great crossing where an infamous man, name of Abel, ferried settlers and Indians, soldiers, renegades, anything, from one side of the then bursting waters to the next. We got to the peak of the span and the old man had Son stop the pickup and flag the driver behind to move around and on ahead of us. Son opened the bed of the truck and the old man took the box and set it down on the hot pavement. The sound of him opening the hard foam of it made me shudder, the way the lid rubbed against the sides, making a thin, sickening cry rise out of it. I covered my ears to make my eyes stop tearing and my mouth stop watering. But too late — the lump of something moved up in me faster than I could control, and in a sudden came a splattering of frothy spill over the side of the guardrail and down into the ribbons of river. Son pulled a handkerchief out of his hip pocket and nudged me. The old man stood holding the styrofoam lid and looking over the guardrail down to the river. Pools of water, thin and still as shards of mirror, were aglare below, biting at the eyes hard enough to water them again.

No, Rose's Daddy said, whatever are we thinking.

She always said she wanted this to be her place, Son said.

Not if she had seen it become the dribble it now is, Rose's Daddy said. Lo, where do you suppose any thirsty coyote or bobcat will come to get what there is left to drink around here?

I don't know what difference it makes anyways, Son said. Ashes are ashes, whether they be carried around in the bowels of some animal or laid to rest with the rest of the silt at the bottom of a riverbed.

Surely, Rose's Daddy said. And well said. Yet those were not her wishes. The river was her wish. And this is no longer a river. He put the lid atop the box and carried the thing back to the truck. Get in, he said. We need to get home.

We left a boil of dust behind us, arriving back to the house and parking in a plot of shade with the truck steaming, like a cooking thing. Son reached out to take the load away from the old man, but he was shoved aside. Son let him have his way, let him heft the box straight out to the garden where he rested it in a desiccated and rooted-over bed. It took both his hands and the strength he would use to pull the horns of a calf back to get the plastic bag to come out of its coffer. I had imagined the weight of Rose's bones to be light as a sack of petals, not as heavy as it now seemed to be. Unless Rose's Daddy was of a sudden so greatly weakened.

He scooped a handful of ash out of the sack and we followed his lead, the sun ringing like an alarm in its seethe above. We sprinkled the ash about the garden the way the old man did it, the way we would scatter grain and seed to pullets or chickens. We were careful to scatter evenly among the rows and the mounds of the dead and the dying roses. We spread the bone-dust out among the wilds and the teas and the climbers, among the twisted stalks and the burnt thorns. The ash fell to earth chalk-heavy from the cling of our fingers. We blew the last of it from the palms of our hands.

Rose's Daddy opened the pages and read aloud from a book of psalms. Son and I watered the ground of Rose's garden with watering cans. Then we left the old man. We left him sitting out by the rose garden in the sere of the day. He sat with his shotgun flat across his lap, the rod of hot light of the metal sparking and glinting in the sun. He fired into the sky, shooing a clutch of little pecking birds away. But he would not shoo any spirit of Rose away.

DAYS AND NIGHTS go by, regardless. The days are but a form to prop us, a stay to prevent our undoing, the nights but a measure of distance and passing. We go through the hours, the weeks, a month now, see one or the other of us here or there, always in silence and avoiding the other's eye so as not to see, or not to be seen, as we move from one act or event, until we are somehow moved into another yet, gone on to the next thing as regularly as the clock is changed. We move present to future, within a kind of oblivion and intensity, in the time and the tide that keeps us, in a strange register of passing and continuing— instant to minute, interval to episode, season to eon, sudden ending to everlasting—doing what we must do to go on. We move through the rituals and the labors of our days, in stubbornness and resilience, the days accumulating all the same and so becoming one. We tend to what land isn't yet sold or let to go fallow. We disc and we till. We keep the horses groomed and ridden and shod, we feed and doctor the animals, we water the roads with the watertruck. We wind the old clock in the cool dark parlor. We sit together each meal, eat and drink, averting our eyes from the empty place. We sleep and we rise. We draw breath. We carry. We bear.

Within the plod of the days comes an evening when the Padre makes a visit. He comes to say things about being sorry about Rose. He says things about how a soul never ends, about the blessing of the hereafter, about how people never really leave us, about how they are always with us, if not in flesh, then in spirit. Son clenches his jaw and rises abruptly from his chair, his fists balled and his breathing caught, and the Padre stops talking.

How can you come here and talk to us like this? Son says. How can you talk about being sad for us? If you truly believed in all the hogwash you talk, with your bliss and your life-everlasting business—if all of this is so, then why would you or anyone be sorry? Why be sorry if death is the blessing you say it is? Son shakes his head. He contorts his mouth. Because it's all a load of horseshit, is what it is, he says.

He stands over the Padre. The Padre is looking at Son the whole time and without a flinch—the Padre's face calm, without a tell of anything. This seems to rile Son all the more.

You fake, Son says. You go to hell, he says. He reaches for his hat on the rack and walks out the front door. Rose's Daddy sits silently and stares emptily at the floor the whole time, moving but to take sips of his ink-colored drink.

I think of what to say to make the Padre not leave.

Please stay, I say.

We leave the old man in the cool dark parlor, in the ticking of the old clock, in the endless shrill of the crickets. We take our glasses of tea out to the porch and sit out on the steps, where the stars above are covered over in their carapace of dust. An elf owl throws a hollow toot from the hole of an old saguaro. The old dog comes over and settles in at my one side, panting her sharp animal breath at me. The Padre, at my other side, smells like the mint chewing gum he's chewing.

Those crickets never stop, I say.

I like their harmonious sound, the Padre says.

It seems more like monotonous to me, I say.

Try to think of it as breath, he says.

Huh-huh, huh-huh, huh-huh, huh-huh, the old dog pants.

Huh? I say.

Think of it as a cosmic humming, he says. A unifying *om.*

An *om?*

Yes, he says. An elongated amen, you could call it.

Crickets? I say.

Life, he says.

That any life thrives here as it does is a miracle, I say.

The old dog whines.

You ever think about the drives in nature? I say.

For example?

For example, the way striving comes out in everything. The way it does in gravity and electricity, in cosmic energy. In hunger and in thirst.

The Padre offers me a stick of chewing gum. Even in sexual desire, he says. As well as jealousy.

The old dog nudges me.

I take the stick of gum and sit looking at it.

The place is not the same without Rose, I say.

When is anything the same?

Something is wrong with Son, I say. But I suppose that's been.

Tell me.

He's a tough one to explain. He's changed. He's not the person I thought he was—though who did I think he was? You would think a wife should know her husband better. But I'm not one who does.

Many do not, he says. I see it all the time. A wife cannot know her husband if her husband does not know himself, he says. As it may too be otherwise, a man may not know his wife.

Something is worse off with the old man, I say.

That I can see, he says. Give him time to recover.

Will he?

Why shouldn't he?

He's been doing strange things.

Such as?

Talking oddly. Like he's reading from the Bible half the time.

Could be he is reading the Bible.

It's the way he treats me as well as talks to me. He has me ride with him every day, but riding the mare now instead of the paint. He has me in Rose's saddle too, has me in her riding suit and in her hand-tooled boots. We'll be riding down the canal-bank and he'll be talking to me the way he does, reminding me to use my knees and to sit tall in my saddle, telling me there will be no clucking or giddyapping, telling me as if he's never said these things to me before. And sometimes now he calls me by her name.

Rose, he says.

I REIN AWAY from the water edge of the canalbank, speaking calmly to keep the horse from spooking at the approach of the watertruck. With the animal steadied, I can sit watching the water spilling out in broken streams from the back of the tank as the truck passes, knowing Son will drop wet tons of cargo loads over the roads before the day is come to an end. I put my bandanna up over my nose and close my eyes as he drives on, listening to the sound of the tank slosh, hearing the river moving in it.

I put the horse forward with my knees and gallop out into the open dry valley, through a haze of quartz and gypsum and clay and silt. Hot dirt gusts about us in ropes and swirls on the ground. Tumbled-up weeds spring and roll in the wind, a wind that sings the sand past in soprano. I break the horse into a walk at its falter and meander on through a maze of saltbush and cactus, my thoughts drifting to Rose. I'm stuck wondering about my promise to Rose not to give up on Son, wondering what it is that holds us to the oaths we've pledged to the dead.

I'm thinking about the Padre's sermon on love again, about what he said about devotion, what he said about forgiving. Thinking about what I'll say to him when I talk to him, about how I should devote myself more fully to my husband, how I ought to forgive Son for what he's done if we're to go on living a life as husband and wife do. It's the only way to rescue all that we've had and should have between us, is what I'll say to the Padre.

I think too of what Pearl said to me the day she came out of the pink stucco house and found me out at the corral with Holy Roller. She could have seen some kind of fluster in me, from having just been with the Padre. Or maybe what she was going on was what she knew of Son, the way he is, for she spoke directly as to the problems of marriage.

A piece of advice? she said. Don't go trying to hobble a man. Not a single one takes well to the rope, and if he does and you're able to keep him from straying, you'll find yourself with a tamed and lifeless animal. I'll tell you a secret, Girl, she said. It's the trick of the cowpuncher—those wranglers that bossed many a steer up the trail in the old days—and that is, never let any of the herd know they are under restraint, she said.

I wonder what the Padre would have to say.

FIVE

THE SERMON

We swing in the lull of a little eternity, in the spell that comes near evening, in a stall of hours that bears the day's most weight. The sun bows at its summons and is fat with brimming as it dips and it seeps into earth. Cactus wren and sagebrush vole skitter for insect and seed in the mesquite and paloverde. Raptor birds soar in updrafts above, stayed at the ready, to plummet for rabbit or quail or snake. The old adobe house turns luminous as the star that colors it, molten gold in the light that remains.

The old man lifts his head from his reverie. He looks at his watch, takes it off his wrist, shakes it, puts it to an ear. He looks out toward the fallow ground to the west of the house, where the land swallows in what's left of the day. The old dog lifts her head, as if to ponder this turn of the world as well, and then her ears twitch and I hear it too — the rumble and growl of engine and piston in the distance — and now the stock-and-combo gooseneck rig comes rolling in, with a column of spiraling dirt trailing behind. The steel body rattles to a stop, sending mourning doves aflutter and hunter cats askitter, as a great wave of dust crests over the whole thing and volutes on ahead, until the dust will trough and settle before it's stirred up again. We fix our eyes toward the end of the porch as we wait for a form to appear, hearing a creak of hinge, a clap of steel, a crunching of boot steps over the gravelly path — and it's Ham shuffling up the porch steps, in that stiff-hipped swagger of his, the old dog up now and tagging back in a wheeze at his heels.

Pree' hot, Ham says.

No doubt as hot as any day has gotten, Rose's Daddy says.

Ham takes his hat off and palms the sweat away from his head. He stoops and scratches the old dog's head.

That crate should seat a man, Rose's Daddy says.

Ham pulls the wood crate over beside us, crouches down, and perches himself upon a paper label colored over with tangerines and leaves. He holds his hat between the bow of his open knees and fusses with the shape of the rim. Then he just stares at it.

Then speak, Rose's Daddy says.

Pearl is gone.

Rose's Daddy stops the swing of the porch swing.

Gone to where?

She went and left to be with him.

She went and left to be with whom?

The thoroughbred. She took off after the thoroughbred. She said she missed her ole Holy Roller. So she says. But what she really meant was she and Daughter Pearl couldn't take it here no more. Couldn't take this hellish place no more. Said it was no way for a woman to live. For anyone to live. Said I was either coming with them or I wasn't.

So?

So, said I wasn't. Told her if she had to go, go. Told her this harder spell of weather surely could not go on forever. Told her anyway somebody had to stay and keep the place up, as a man can't just run away when things get a bit hard on us, now can he?

So be it, the Indians would say.

Yessirree-bob, Ham says.

Listen to me, Ham, Rose's Daddy says, your Pearl will likely be home soon. She has been gone hither and thither before, for one reason if not for another or a dozen more. Surely you need not trouble yourself. When the woman is ready, she will come down from her mountain. She will come back as she always has. You have still got her right here in this world.

Yes, I do, Ham says. That I do indeed.

Is that bolo Navajo? Rose's Daddy says.

Ham gives the silver tips a tug and looks up. You know you got her too, he says. You got Pearl and you got me and we all been close as kin from the beginning, don't you know it without me having to tell you it? And you got lots of people you've knowed around here for near a lifetime. So don't you think it's time you picked yourself up and stopped actin' weepy like? You got to buck up, man. Act like a man again, old man. 'Tisn't right to go on feeling sorry for yourself this way forever. It's no good to be giving in. It don't look good. Nor is it good. You're making every-one feel bad, asides yourself.

Rose's Daddy clears his throat and turns his head and looks out toward the lemon grove. I saw another bolo close to that I almost bought for myself once, he says. But it was Zuni, I believe.

Anyways, Ham says. I come out to see how you're getting on with them roping cows. They working all right? No muleys in the bunch, is they?

No muleys.

You putting your time in?

Not so much as I ought to be. Yet I have been teaching some. Been showing Girl here how to work the heels. And I would say she is picking the skill of it up in good time. Is that not right? he says, looking my way.

I'm picking it up okay, I say. I push off to put a little swing back into our porch seat.

We shall be doing fine come rodeo time, Rose's Daddy says.

You'll have them barrels beat, Ham says, looking at me. You would have had 'em beat even if Daughter Pearl was still here to enter the show. She hadn't been rehearsing as she should on that horse a hers as it was. She was too busy gallivanting about town doing who knows what she was and wasn't. But I try to keep out of women's business, as is my policy.

Ham turns a cheek to where the sun is plowing shadow into the field.

And I know in that pause that Ham knows about Daughter Pearl and Son. Just as the old man knows. Just as everyone in town knows what Son does and who he does it with, in particular lately, the one.

What time you getting your water in, compadre? Ham says.

You got to check with that kid of mine, Rose's Daddy says. I am these days leaving him to corporal things a bit more. He has got to come to understand the working of the place sooner than later and so to do it on his own for a change. Besides, I am lately wearied.

You want I ought to go and check on him? Ham says.

Perchance you might, Rose's Daddy says.

Ham rises and gives a nod of the head and sets his hat back atop it. All righty, then. I'll adiós you for now, he says.

By dawn of the next day the land around us is shrouded in still, metal-colored water, all the furrows topped full and so ribbing the fields as to make it seem there's a colossal grating of some giant cattle guard fixed upon the land. The water had come in the depths of the night, as it sometimes does, and much to Son's chagrin, as it will ruin his plans for sleep, or whatever other pleasures and proclivities — as the old man calls them — that Son aims to keep to. Now Son stands out in knee-high rubber boots — wellies, he will say, that never work welly enough — shoveling a gopher hole closed and likely cursing at the spillage and wastage of water and, as well, of his time and vitality. And he will come back to the house to fill his canteen in a mood too cross for words to soothe over. And he will lave handfuls of water over his head at the sink. And he will doctor his blistered lips with ointment. And he will look at me with that wearied look, burdened by the work before him, burdened by this spell of heat, burdened by this land and all the oughts and duties that surely go with it. As he is burdened by me and all that I too expect of him.

IT WAS A tiny metal box that had been blessed by a holy man and given to me as a baby. The box was a book, the side of it etched with pages, the spine of it ribbed with words all worn by now and which I can't remember from back when I wasn't reading yet. The book was engraved with the face of a saint, the forehead and the nose and the stole around the shoulders carved high in relief and worn to a shine. It was brass, is all the box was, might have been just tin, but it opened like a book with tiny hinges worked into it and it closed with a thin latch. It smelled metallic and oldtime and mysterious. It was small enough to fit into a palm, meant as it was for but a child's hand, and inside the metal box were tiny garnet beads strung on a fine gold chain, the only piece of jewelry of any importance to me, even more so than the ring I've now got on my finger.

I ask Son about the tiny metal box and the string of beads the day I notice them missing. He just shrugs, as he does, and turns away. I can't keep a watch on your things, he says. I got stuff to do. Then he walks out of the room.

I find the old man sitting in the parlor in the afternoon ticking of the clock. Girl, he says. A chain, I say. Of garnets. He gets up from his chair and goes over to the sideboard and takes a swipe of a hand over the wood of it, as if to conjure what has been lost, leaving his fingertip tracings written in the dust. Go ask Rose, he says.

It's not until several days later that I find what belongs to me. It's when I'm in Saringo's Tack and Feed, where I see Pearl Hart's daughter, Pearl, standing at the counter. She's wearing the tiny garnet beads around her tiny white neck.

How can I help today? the man behind the counter says.

I came in to buy a quirt, I say.

How are you? Pearl's daughter says.

Have you also got the box for keeping the beads? I say.

She turns away and tells the man she'll have a look at a hackamore — a bosal, please, not a side pull. A pale blue vein in her temple throbs her heartbeat out. The fan overhead beats in slow pleading. I swat a fly away from my face and she flinches.

I want it back, I say. The metal box too.

She covers her throat over and holds her hand there. The pulse in her temple quickens. The man behind the counter looks at us and clears his windpipe with a rough cough.

It was given to me, she says.

A thing can't be given that doesn't belong to the giver, I say.

The hackamore, she says to the man.

I hold the quirt up, standing ready to do I don't know what, and this gets her to look at me and now she can see it in my eyes. She can see that I mean it.

For heaven's sake, the man behind the counter says.

Why cry? I say.

Then she undoes the chain.

I REACH OUT to the empty side of the bed, the space not yet heated by body or dampened with sweat, and I slide over onto it, feeling the reprieve of cooler sheet beneath me. I lift the hair off the back of my neck and pile it up high on the pillow. The fan whirs overhead, like the sound of a small airplane on a runway in start-up for takeoff. I roll this way, then again that, sleepless in the bit of breeze that wheels off the ceiling, restless in the pitch and drone outside in the night. I think about the day gone by, my visit to the Padre's office, telling him the story of finding Pearl's daughter wearing my garnet beads, running through the way things went again, hearing the sudden trouble I had in speaking to him. My hello came out without composure, the *l*'s so dulled by my nervous tongue, and other words caught and turned backward on my trembling lips, shifting the meaning of things, upsetting what I had intended, as the sentences went off ajumble and without me. Did I say too much? Or not enough? Did I look too weepy, or did I smile too quickly, talk too loudly, or sound too girlish and silly?

What is it that makes me so fluttery around the Padre? Is it because of who he is and what he knows? His nearness to a god, a god or a kind of knowing I can't say I know or ever did know or would see a need to know? Or is it something else? His manner of speaking? His voice is what it could be—the way he carries words to me, the way he says my name. Katherine, he says, in a deliberate and caressing way, taking care of all my syllables. And the way he shakes my hand and holds it some before letting go. And how his eyes will settle upon mine, making me so uneasy as to have to look away. What else could it be? I picture him and see his stance. Is that what draws me to him? Or is it maybe his height and his shape? Or the color and cut of his hair? Or the style of his shirt? Maybe just that, just the shirt, the white of it, or the wrist in it as it is poised in the cuff, or the weave and the hang of the fabric, or just a button undone.

What is it that catches the eye and the heart at the same time?

I flinch at the ping of the egg that breaks through the sac as it does every month. I turn onto my other side to face the wall. A gecko skips across the adobe. My heart jumps a beat and leaps ahead. I roll this way and that, listening to the night aquiver, so awake I am in the gathered rub of hind legs, in the thin-pitched screeching of insects, so alive in all that's alive. Gila monsters belly their way through the grass and the weeds, as limes swell and burst in the trees. My bones feel ready to rupture from out of my skin. I throw the covers off and move back over to the empty half of the bed, flipping the pillow to its cooler side, rolling over again to yet the other way. I use a corner of sheet to rub the wet off my flesh. I listen to the stir and hum of the whirling blades above. I listen to the blood, the way it pulses as it does through my pillow.

How could I make it happen to have him?

No, not here. Not in this place. I would have to go to him. But what? Go back to his office? But not his office, not the church. And not his home, not with his wife. All right, a ride. I could suggest a ride. We'll find a cool place near water, find a place to settle in shade. As if such a place existed anywhere nearby. But if it did. There could be a somewhere I haven't found here yet. There might be a smooth bank of shady trees alongside a cool piece of the river. We would tie the horses, let them pasture in what might be left of the wild grass. We would sit watching the river flow, water that would be ever so clear and embracing, watching and amazed at the way it pools and riffles, the way it courses through the boulders and molds itself over the stones. There would be only the sound of the water, the sound of our breathing, the silent roar of the day. I can see us from above, as if I were the eyes of some up-there-in-the-air being, my gaze affixed on us to stay us in place. We're side by side, our arms brushing one against the other, our wanting the same. And now he will turn my way and our touch is no longer manner or accident. We fall back, that's how it is, simple as that. Our bodies together, just that way. Our mouths, our mouths, our mouths. Our arms, our legs, our tangling together as one. And then, then everything. Then the happiness of having.

And I'm shaken back to where I am by the sink of the mattress and the whine of the springs.

Girl, he says, as he climbs into the half-empty bed.

I can't say why I behave toward him the way I do. Can't say why I don't plead with him to leave. Why instead I roll over to him and put my arms around him and let him rest his head against my chest. Why I just hold Rose's Daddy like this in the night, hug him and rock him for a long time. Until he lets go

and gets up and walks down the hallway, going back to his bedroom, where he will rest the rest of the night in his own half-
empty bed.

*And what does a man do when the darkness falls upon him?
How might he so relieve the pain that tears at his heart night and
day? What can rend the blade from the chest? Who might take the
suffering away?*

*Why must this grief come, after I have lived a life of willfulness
and uprightness? When in spirit and deed I have aimed my arrow
for the honorable mark? Where is the safety that should be from
ordinary decency and dutiful living? Where is it now? I have cared
for my land and my family with steadfastness and probity, in goodness and in tenderness. I have tended to my friends and my neighbors, been charitable to the elderly and the needy, am ever gentle
with children and animals, birds, trees, the land, all living things.
All things believed worth doing I have done. I have turned the
other cheek. I have dealt no harm, nor have I dealt falsely or with
cowardice. Yet right living has not kept me from misery.*

*What foolishness I speak, to believe in any kind of otherwise.
Yet what might I be guilty of but wanting only happiness back? Of
wanting a life of having back? Or have all my expectations been out
of place from the beginning? Perhaps as are every man's?*

*Could it be I have lived too much for the flesh, expecting gain in
this? Could I have labored too much for vanity? Have I been too
carefree as to the good of the land? Might I not have been mindful
or attentive enough?*

*Yet who is there to say? As who can there be to comfort me? The
son who grieves me so very bitterly? Who can know what has become
of him in his great regard for but himself? It seems he believes that*

living by principle brings no reward in the end. It seems he sees that all of us must lose, no matter the way in which we go about our days. So with this thinking does he justify his taking? Yet meanly and hungrily he takes, with little care for the rest. And still he is loved, however unjustly. With his young heart near withered beneath the breastbone. With his young mind weakened by sloth. And as to his soul, I say, how could it have become so lame? Why? Who is it that has failed him? Was it I, I who failed him? Now who is to catch him in his falling? And how am I to help him when I cannot rise from my own descent? How can I lead when the way is lost to me? When the blinding haze keeps me from seeing the steps out ahead? When the heat parches my tongue, my throat, my lungs, my being? When the burn has seared my fingertips so as to prevent me from feeling? When the clotted air shuts the music of others from my ears? The music of living is no longer—it is dried and blown away as the dust. And where be the water that may again quench the thirst? Where be the food that might nourish? Where be the hands that would soothe?

Lo, I tell you, the loneliness I feel even among the others. When all that seemed beauty is now beyond reach. No, no longer. I am past remedy. I am too sluggish to pull myself up, too loath to right myself, too lame to walk through my days or sleep through my nights again. I can no more waken myself to anything near industry. Not with this body worn, the muscles slackened, the bones laced with age. I am but a bended tree, blighted and galled, unable to recover itself in the wind. I am wearied, I tell you. Let come what shall come.

SON GOES OUT for the early morning feed amid the *who-coos* and *no-hopes* of the inca and the mourning doves. He opens the top halves of the Dutch doors, and the desert air and dawn light flood inside each stall. The horses one at a time come to him and whicker and snuffle and toss their heads. He goes inside the stalls and fills the troughs with water, and some of the troughs he fills with grain, and he splits pallets of green hay into sheaves and shakes them out for the horses to chomp on at their leisure throughout the day. He slaps at their flanks. He murmurs words. Then he wheelbarrows a load of fodder out to the corral, where the roping cows are huddled, and there fills a common trough with a mix of filler straw and but a bit of green hay for them, and he opens the spigot over the mouth of another trough until the water brims to the top. The cows shoulder their way over to the troughs and stand leaning one against another among a snarl of insects, with that look of not-a-thing in their eyes, their jaws rotating sleepily, the skin on their hides flinching, and their tails swishing at the spurs and the bites of the flies.

As Son moves through these dawn rituals, the morning star tacks to the sun in its fade toward day, brightening again in its will toward vespers. Whiptails gather a breakfast of insects and spiders, regal horns squirt blood from their eyes at their foes, iguanas bask upon rocks at first light. Collared peccaries cleave broken tracks in the sand. Angel's-trumpets yawn open their corollas at the cockcrow. We stand and look upward and outward, seeing time the way it so rolls away.

When the morning water run is over and the engine of the watertruck has cooled enough, I climb into the cabfront of it, using the door as a handhold to lift myself up and inside. I slide onto the cracked and sun-bleached leather seating, its yellowed stuffing sponging through in places, and reaching beneath I press the lever and scoot the whole bench forward, and the coils and the rods and the springs groan because the workings are old and bent and stiff. I adjust the sideview mirror and catch a glimpse of myself, seeing myself differently—a grown woman now. It seems a sudden and shocking thing, and yet I'm still the same as I've always been, in the what is gone and the places lived, in the here where we are and the what we are in—that same girl and different, I am.

IT WAS IN the middle of another long afternoon, within the monotony of the heat and the dust, the flat and the straight, the chafing and the blistering. It was a shot so loud and stinging that it would forever ring inside our ears, if it should not be immediately and mercifully blown from memory. The blast shook the whole adobe house, inside and out. It shook screens and hanging things, webs and bottles and leaves, the animals, the help, setting flesh atremble, hides aquiver, wings aflutter. It pounded the ribcage and spurred the heart. It emptied the breath right out of the lungs, leaving a sizzling in the blood. It blew from his bedroom and ran throughout all the rooms of the house. It bled down the hallway to fill the cool dark parlor before bursting out into the kitchen. It rattled kettles and teacups, potlids and silver, bowls and traps and bins. It flew out the open windows, clattering panes and blinds and shutters of those that were closed. It rose into and up the chimney, gusted up into the cupboards, eddied beneath all the doors. It got rocketed as far back as the melon shed, where it was swept over cement. It got sucked in through the toolhouse and ricocheted out and away in a *whooosk*. The blast drummed the doors of the watertruck, pricked the ears up on the shaky old dog, sent the hired man running, left the Mexicans stunned. It howled down the dusty road, stirred the dust up in the dirt-bare fields, and then went tornado'ing off into the wind, sounding a hideous moaning. It moved as far off as far could be, into the vastness beyond, settling into the wobble and spin of moons and planets and stars.

The bedroom wall would be left all pocked and scoured with buckshot. It would be me and Son left to haul buckets of water in and scrub up what Rose's Daddy left us. We sponged and rinsed the walls in the slash and the warp of the light of the blinds. We got down on our knees, choking, gagging, keeping ourselves from weeping in the reek. We climbed onto ladders, reaching tipped and upward to the ceiling. We rinsed our hands of the stench, again and again, though the odor of the water would forever remind us of our ghostly task. After the cleaning was done, we piled up and hauled away and we patched and we spackled and painted. And still we could see it, the wound, the way it was imprinted in the walls and the ceiling, all as it was and would be. As the wound had been imprinted in us.

What is there to do otherwise, but abide by what has been given?

Son and I will take all of what the old man had to leave us. We will live in it and sleep in it, drive it and feed it. We will care for what's left here just as the old man had taught us, the way he had cared for it all himself. We will will ourselves to do the work that needs doing, carrying on with the days coming on in sameness and routine, with every day a seeming repeat of the empty day past, all within the victorious dust and still unmerciful heat. And the birds will rise up and cry out in warning. And the sun will peal in its glory and might.

LET US BOW our heads and pray.

Good people, we are living amid a most unsettling and strife-filled time. We are thrown into a calamity that has uprooted many of late and thinned our congregation. Most have lost livestock and farmland and business, many of you loved ones and homes. I see the anguish of the days in your faces. I see the weight of the losses and the burdens in your eyes. I see doubts in the loll of your shoulders, questions in the slump of your heads. How can we have been so betrayed? you may say. It is an old query, raised time and again: How cruel might a God be to have put us into existence only to then abandon us? And you are silent in your suffering as you wait for a voice to speak.

But you find only silence.

God speaks not, nor does He show you His wisdom. And if He did, you could likely not understand the subtlety of the words or the magnitude of the thought. For God's wisdom is double to that which exists, and His utterance the nuance and grandeur of all that is.

No, you do not find the Eternal One by searching. For in searching you have positioned yourself as already lost. And your lot will be to wander in this world without end.

All you need do is believe.

It is this easy: believe the spirit to be within you, and you are of the spirit. For each and every one of you is of the spirit, each is of the divine unity, the Eternal One, you are of God. I tell you, you are God.

Then behave as God, I say. Straighten your backs and lift your heads and gird up your loins. For when was this world ever without suffering? And who would not believe that our world is necessarily a world of opposites? For one half of a thing cannot exist without the other half. Pain exists only in relation to pleasure, just as happiness is but the other half of sorrow. There is no sound without the silence, no up without a down, no order without chaos, no subject without object. There is no man without woman, no birth without death, no entity without the void. No light exists apart from the darkness, for surely the day is forever one with the night.

> *He maketh sore, and He bindeth up.*
> *He woundeth, and His hands make whole.*

And so you will see misery pass away, just as the waters pass away. Just as the wind blows through the grasslands so the seeds may be set adrift. You will forget your pain, I promise, and be again as the morning.

Now, good souls, I tell you, stop the search. Only want and look outward. Put yourselves into attitudes of reception, and then you will see. Be in perfect knowledge of the goodness and spirit of the earth, the universal beauty to which every particle is related, those persons near and dear to you, those persons, as well, far off or despised. See these trying times, not as a curse, but rather as a test of your abiding faith and delicate intelligence, and at destruction and famine you cannot but laugh. You need not wait for your God to speak out of the whirlwind. Hold the infant in your arms and see how perpetual is the Messiah. Every day a Christ is born. Be assured that the divine kingdom is yet here upon the earth, and that you who so make the effort will without effort enter into this kingdom.

The Padre drinks from a glass of water. He begins again.

I tell you: prophecy is innate in you. Be a prophet. Be a help-mate and a teacher. To him who has lost a suit, give him one of your two. To him who has lost the warmth of child or the breath of wife, listen to tears and regrets and reach to place a hand to a hand. All sincere conversation is worship, every loving touch a benediction, your hands a light, your eyes, grace. Yet do not expect to know the greatness of your gesture, as it is of no mind. Simply give and you will receive. Life depends not upon your having more than others. For what profit can there be in the material life? When all your accumulations shall go to others, and even your name will be worn from the stone and forgotten. Soul circumscribes everything, abolishing time, abolishing space. So I say, give now while you are able. It is the only way, your only salvation.

For the word good is to God, as the word evil is to devil.

We walk in the valley of the shadow. Our days upon earth are but shadow. Yet we who live in the shadow of death are able to see the very light of life.

> *From the unreal, lead me to the real.*
> *From darkness, lead me to the light.*
> *From death, lead me to immortality.*

And now let me bless you and keep you.
Amen.

WE MOVED THROUGH days gauzed with worthless dirt, numbed and dazed within layers of but more dust, with everything about us in a stage of drying up and decay. We kept our faces muffled over with bandannas, our sleeves, our hats, with whatever we might use to breathe into for relief. We rode perched high up over the road in the watertruck, aiming toward some sparkling cradle of water ahead, every time arriving to find our visions gone to vapor, the water before us but shimmering blacktop and crawling sand.

We sought to providence a resting spot. We turned off the

road and drove along the canalbank, with the old dog powdering a trail alongside us. When we got to the zanja madre, we stopped and got out of the watertruck, stepping out into paled clumps of scorpionweed and buffalo bur and making our way to the jetty. Son found a place to put the container down, and he opened it and reached in for a handful of ashes. He released his grip to toss a handful out over the water, and as he did, the wind kicked up and ash flew right back and into our faces.

As if the old man had one last thing to say at the end, after all.

It seemed then the only message passed on to us. For Rose's Daddy had otherwise left without a single word. There were no last words at all, no farewell he had to bid, no thoughts for us to keep and carry on with. We added betray to betray. We searched and we searched. We searched for hours, days. We reached into the pockets of shirts and pants and jackets for his whys of leaving. We looked for his ink left on paper, a poem maybe pinned to a pillow or weighted beneath a vase, a saying that might have been clipped into place or dropped to the floor. We needed to find his script writ out on a mirror, or a note of his left tacked to a door, maybe a letter somewhere cubbied into adobe. We walked through all the cool dark rooms of the house, needing a way of knowing. We went out and sought for what we hoped for in the corral, moving about the stalls, peering into the grooves of the walls and the corners of the floor of the tackroom. We picked over shelves of bolts and nails and studs but found no plans or wishes that might be intended for us. We rummaged throughout the toolhouse, eyeballing every post and beam for what words there might be posted. We stood at the edge of the cement gully, staring down into the musty trough of it. We stood out in the middle of the melon shed, surveying the concrete floor for something scrawled. We ran our palms across the dashboard of the watertruck, finding nothing but grime and the forever cover of dust. We looked into the clouds of the old dog's old eyes. Finally we quit seeking, finding nothing anywhere otherwise.

On an afternoon soon after, Ham drove out to the old adobe house to show me something that had come to him in the mail. The envelope bore Ham's name, but the letter inside was addressed to no one, though it was clearly written in Rose's Daddy's hand. Nor was the letter signed, making it seem as if the old man hadn't finished all of what he had to say, as if he might have been waiting for answers to his questions so that more words could come from him. We would never know why the old man hadn't put his name on the paper. We knew only to keep the message from Son.

EVENING COMES AND the sun anoints the old adobe house in a splendor of golden color again. Remnants of the day spill inside, settling in rods of light that fall upon walls and floor and table-tops. Toward the east, looking out the kitchen window, the sky begins to deepen and cool. I watch as another little eternity rolls by, one day blown in and away, and after, the same, and so time gathers again, and we begin another beginning.

There's a scent that holds the memory of the start of things, an old-spiccy smell of cologne that ignites a wanting. The scent drifts into the kitchen to find me, and as if there were hands to it, it reaches and touches, coming in from as far off as the other side of the house. It fills the room, covering over the smells of domesticity—the sizzle of meat in the pan, the lemon suds brimming in the sink, the bitter coffee dregs left in the bottom of the pot. I untie the cloth that's wrapped around my waist, letting the sweet old-spiceyness spark a where and a what there once was, reminding me of a time ago. But there's something that's off—the scent of change, what it carries is wrong, a seeming not for the better that tightens the knot in my gut.

We meet up at the front door, Son gussied and reeking.

What? he says. Did I go and blow a stirrup again?

You could at least look at me, I say.

He doesn't.

Dinner is just about done.

Who asked you to cook any dinner?

How come you're all duded up?

I'm tired of mopin' around the place.

Me too.

You ought to get out some, then.

If you go out—Son—no! If you do.

Do what you got to do for yourself.

Don't go.

Don't tell me what to do and don't.

He goes out the door and shuts it hard behind him, setting the windows to shuttering in the panes, putting the old dog's tail to dangling between her haunches.

It's like someone coming up out of me when I cry out, like a hot ball of something bursting inside and rising out from a place deeper than any place I knew there was. It's a scream that burns at my throat and widens my eyes to a sting, a cry that makes my skin curn-up and my scalp feel aflame. It takes the breath away. Sparks shoot out and spiral about, as from something afire in me, now out and out of control and surging ever higher. Then there's no more breath, no sound at all, no answer to my call, only a terrible silence, an emptiness too absolute. A kind of tingling feeling around my mouth. My legs wobbly. Walking as if the house were in a lean, or the planet were gone off its axis. I put a hand to a wall and try to right myself. I will myself not to tumble and fall. There's a slow, rising volume of the cricket shrill. Then that suck of air comes that shuts the ear closed and makes the queer ringing louder again, makes the shallow pant of my breath harder and coarser, as if breathing from a tube underwater. The panting turns to gasping, as if there were not air enough in the room to breathe, not air enough in the whole house to breathe. As if there were not air enough anywhere in the world left to breathe. And I'm running in a sudden to the bathroom, fumbling with the toilet lid, plunging forward, giving over, vomiting into the bowl. The retching done. I lift my head, towel my mouth, wipe my eyes, hold the towel to my nose, smelling his cologne for a moment. No. Don't. Don't. Then spit what's left in my mouth into the towel and go out. I move about the house, room to room, like a dumbstruck animal. I stand in the cool dark parlor, in the lost time of the old clock, checking the hands the way they are set on the face and so to check myself, noting the time in order to put some order back, to know where I am, to steady the teeter and sway all about me. The smell of the cologne becomes the smell of vomiting, the sour sweetness everywhere and sickening. I rush back to the bathroom, wait for another wave to carry the stuff up and away. All of it out, all of him out, until again the heaving stops. I splash the water over my face, then see the face in the mirror, a face hot and red, the alien look in the eyes, not mine, afraid, and I turn from what I've seen and don't recognize. I hardly feel my legs taking me back into the kitchen, standing me up in front of the window. I leave out the light, allowing the ending of the day to dim all the things about—the pots, the dishes, my hand on the teacloth, the diamond ring on my finger, letting the dusk swallow all of everything up.

I make my way back to the parlor and on down the hallway, passing the closed door of the master bedroom, master and mistress forever gone to us.

There is no one to call.

There is the Padre to call.

But I don't call. I just look at the telephone, affixed and silent on the wall, and I go and get the stepladder and take it into the bedroom. I climb up and reach for the brass handle and pull the cupboard door open and blow the dust and brush the cobwebs away before dragging Rose's old suitcase out, the one Son and I had used during our honeymoon. There's an ache in that vague somewhere inside, just having to see the thing and the time and the places attached to it, being snagged for a moment by the happiness that had once been.

Hold it while ye may.

I sweep the rest of the dust off the empty suitcase with a sleeve. Take clothes from drawers and put them into the suitcase. Reach for the satchel and put things in it too.

I heft the suitcase onto the benchseat of the watertruck, toss in the satchel, climb in and start up, clutch and shift, and let the clutch out. I holler out the window for the old dog to go on back. She fades out the side mirror along with the old adobe house, fades away with the lemon trees, the surrounding fields, the pasture, the stalls, the melon shed, with all of everything lessening as it gets taken up by the evening.

The empty drum of the tank rattles like a wanting. That's all I remember of the drive. I'm here in what seems but an instant, turning into the church lot, the wheels of the watertruck climbing over the curb, making the entire bulk of it tremble and lilt. Through the settle of dust is the building lit up before me, the tan stucco, the low-pitched roof, the broad facade, the arched windows adding some ornament. A young Mexican man, holding a long pole with a duster head at the end of it, stands in a swath of electric light. He looks my way, then goes back to dry-mopping the film from the glass.

The church has been dimly lit for evening. The altar is covered over with a ruby-colored runner, and large candles on brass stands are aflame at each end. There ahead, where I first saw the Padre, is the pulpit rising upward by but a single wooden step. Across from it, a chancel for the choir. There's a scorchy smell in the air, like hot paper maybe, or more like ironing, the smell of the heat of the day as it's settled about the place. I make my way down the aisle, the lights from the pillars halo'ing the floating layer upon layer of dust above. I walk slowly past the rows of empty pews, the dutiful hymnals propped upright in their slots, my bootheels tapping out a metered wooden beat much slower than my fluttering heart would be. I walk the way alone today, as I walked the aisle as the bride I was. What a short time ago, that matrimonial occasion, and yet how far back in the past it seems. Time and its oddities. Look how I have traveled.

The Mexican man comes in through a side door near the chancel.

Señorita? he says. He holds his duster upright like a shepherd's stick.

I came to talk to the Padre.

Sí, sí, this way.

He takes me out the back way of the church, and I follow him along a pebbly, lit-up walkway to the entrance of the add-on part of the church house. He takes me inside and shows me to a door where a light creeps out from beneath. I knock on the wood, my heart knocking about inside my chest. Then the light comes pouring out all over and around me.

The Padre doesn't say anything, but his smile does.

It's an awkward kind of talking in its intimacy and formality, with the Padre sitting at his desk and with me seated across from him on the other side. I spend most of my effort holding back what would surely be an angry wailing, choking on the words Rose, Rose's Daddy, crying about Son, crying for myself. After a short while we fall into a spell of silence that I'm helpless to break. The Padre says nothing, just sits and is quiet too. I shift about in my seat. He asks if I have had supper and I nod my head yes, though it wouldn't be true. He offers me a stick of chewing gum. I take it, not wanting it, just holding it in my hand, soft and misshaped in the heat, turning and kneading it, pressing it straight. He says I might want to get a good night's sleep and then we can talk about what we need to talk about at the fresh start of the next day.

I follow the Padre out of his office and down a hallway, past a meeting room and past a classroom and past a kitchen and past a supply closet, all of the rooms lit-up as if there should be people in them, and we go on into a narrow room with walls lined with books on both sides and what was a time ago a modern sofa that he says yet pulls out to make a bed. There's a shuttered-over window that I wouldn't think to open, though who knows why. It smells like church inside here, with its kind of musty and bookish odor, and mixed with the air of what you know you should and shouldn't do, somehow anyway, but really don't know, as such rules could only be somebody else's rules. I settle my satchel on the single chair and go out the door and down the hallway to the bathroom, feeling myself wandering and lost. The hallway smells of cleaning and rigor. The bathroom door sticks with fresh paint. The walls and woodwork and ceiling gleam white, and an outside light from the porch colanders in through the ironwork latticed over the window. I pass a glance at myself in the mirror and see again that startled look in my eyes, see a face changed in a single day, and this time I don't flinch but instead have a long, good look before turning away.

The foldout sofa is already pulled out and a blanket and a pillow and fresh sheets are left for me. I make the bed up, tucking the corners of the bottom sheet under and in, the way Rose showed me how to do it. I crease the top covers back into a neat geometry and I case the pillow and set it at an angle and turn the bed into an inviting place. I put the lamp on and turn the overhead off to home the light, take the book out of my satchel, and place it next to the lamp. Now I've made my place.

I take my dusty daytime clothes off and fold them in a pile and put them on a shelf, thinking to climb into the bed naked, as is my habit, but feel it something like a sin here, and so I take my shirt and shake the dust from it and put it back on before I climb under the sheet. I blink, my eyelids swollen, a bitter taste lingering on the back of my tongue.

What of the laws that gate our promises?

I scan the comfort of books on the shelves and will to read them all. There's time. I take comfort in this and close my eyes to the night. I try to sleep. I turn on the light to read for a while.

In the morning there's a kind knock on the door.

The Padre comes in and sits at the edge of the bed. He smells like mint chewing gum, even this early in the day. I wonder about my own breath. He asks me about my night's sleep. I sit up with the sheet tucked against me and I comb my hair back with my fingers.

No sleep really, I say.

My heartbeat beats so hard I know it shows in my throat and

through my shirt. It beats so loud as to call regard to itself —*don't go, don't go, don't go* — if it be heard.

Why be embarrassed? he says. You look perfect. You are perfect. Don't you know this?

I scoot up in the bed and wipe the night from my eyes.

He picks the book up from the bedside table. *Popular Cosmology.* Popular cosmology? he says.

I brought it with me, I say.

Don't forget the Bible, he says. That's too a good read.

Someday.

That's all right. When you get to the other side, God won't cast you out because you weren't interested. He doesn't work in those ways.

How could anyone ever know such a thing?

It's beyond language, he says. Therefore, impossible to explain.

I'm just fine without an answer to the question why, I say.

He smiles and touches my hand.

I have no place to go.

Tell me.

There's a tap on the wood. The door opens just enough for the Mexican man to put his head into the room to speak. Padre, he says.

Come back to make the room up later, Jesús. Gracias, Jesús.

The door closes and the Padre turns back to me. I'm here to help you work through what you must, he says. That's what I'm here for. I'm here as your teacher. I'm here as your guide.

IT WAS ALREADY midday before I got back to Old Border Road. I arrived into a different commotion of sorts, with Son and the hired man and a new cadre of Mexicans moving busily about the south field. The hired man had run the disc around the perimeter of the bermuda to make a firebreak and was now tractoring back to the canalbank. The Mexican men stood lined along the bar ditch with drip torches and fire swatters and waterjugs in hand. Son conducted this business astrut in the midst of them — pivoting on a bootheel and pointing directions out, taking his cap off and scratching his head and putting the cap back on again, shoo'ing the old dog aside time after time. The watertruck clacked and bucked over the corrugated drive, and I slowed it down but kept going, not looking Son's way. I took the lane through the whitewashed old trees, the fruit hanging leathered and shriveled in the heat, driving on and then braking to a stop in front of the house. The watertruck shuddered to a quit. It hadn't even begun to tick to a cool by the time Son had caught up to it and had the door open and was grabbing me by the fistfuls, dragging me out to where there's a flare of my heart in a moment of hope. I thought he was about to take me into his arms and I'm ready to cling to him and breathe him in as he tells me he'll never again let me go. But instead he hauled me out of the cabfront and flung me aside, reached in, and threw the suitcase and satchel out too, cursing that I'd held him up by disappearing in the first place and by taking my time about getting the watertruck back. He didn't even look me in the eye. He just climbed up into where I had been, and clutched and grinded and shifted and took off in a huff, leaving a powdery cloud of earth behind in the wake.

I waved the dirt away and turned toward the house and went inside. This all-over feeling of being new here came over me, that sense of not belonging, of being placeless. Even in the bedroom we shared, I could lay no claim. You could see how the bed had been slept in in the night without me, the way the sheets were bunched and tossed. You could see the press of Son's head left as it was on the pillow. A nearly full cola bottle sat like some guest on the table next to the bed. I went into the kitchen, where there was a pot of coffee left to go cold on the stove, a mug with half the drink still in it, stains ringing the countertop, spills of something flyspecked and sticky, a plate with remains of beans and yolk and tortilla. A dirty pan was set into the sink among a bunch of crunched eggshells and splatters of red sauce and grease. So he can manage to eat without me, in any case.

The old adobe house creaked and groaned, as if it were digesting a meal. My stomach felt hollow and wringing. I gazed out the kitchen window, past the dead but still-clinging stalk of the climbing rose, past the withered heads of the old lemon trees and out toward bursts of dust moving along the empty road. The world was weighted differently now, as maybe it is when you believe you're suddenly and truly alone. I had known this cloister of solitude before, known it as a kind of truth, you might say, making every piece of sky you see more prized, and any music you hear turned more serious to the ear, every look in every eye necessarily meaning everything.

I opened the screendoor and went out the back way and looked about. Son was over by the melon shed standing among the hired men, likely discussing how they would manage the blaze while figuring in the wind. I've been in on a few of these burns on burn days, back when I stayed side by side with Son most of the time. I had listened to the caution and the reasoning, seen the ways of managing. I had seen the flanks of fields ignite and arise, seen great chains of fire run aleap like feral animals in a chase, watched the angry kindle until it begins to dim, until the smoke rises higher, until it blackens and drifts, seen the way everything gets turned so quickly to nothing.

I went back into the house to collect some things, passing by our wedding picture and turning it facedown on the table. I could smell the smell of fire by the time I had put a few more shirts into the suitcase and was choosing another book to put into the satchel. I went out to the porch and could see the flare of a backfire downwind of the burn site. The head of the site combusted in warning-colored light, and soon the entire field burst into flame—the whole thing turning wild and trembling, the air shaking feverishly, all of everything looking aswim and awave, the fire burning in raging shapes that boiled and hurled outward and upward into the ether. A mass of towering smoke-cloud gathered and spiraled above. Then it was done—like that—the fire gone out, the charred and simmering field turned an absolute black, a few serpents of smoke coiling up here and there. There was a glimmer of metal that sparked along the road, and through the carbon and smoke the watertruck appeared.

Son pulled up to the front of the house. He got out and came toward the porch and saw me sitting there on the steps with the suitcase and satchel. His clothes and skin were black with ash and soot, as if he had been up inside a chimney or come out of a coal mine or been in some story where he would be the bad guy. He took his cap off. His putty-colored forehead and sandy-colored hair were oddly pale next to the black rest of his clothes and his skin. He had a disagreeable, if not a riled, look in his eyes. Now I could see other things about him that were unappealing—the centipede-like scar on his forehead, the blisters on his lip, his set-too-close-together eyes—and I was glad for every bit of distance it put in between us. I was glad for whatever it is that makes it easier to leave.

He looked at the suitcase. Now what? he said.

I had more of my stuff to get, I said.

Well, you can't take the watertruck with you again.

Then I'll take the pickup.

You can't take the pickup.

What else have I got to take?

That's your problem, I guess, ain't it?

I was gratefully put off by his stance and way of speaking. He walked past me and went into the house and let the screendoor slap behind him. I got up and went to find the hired man.

Sure, Missus, he said. Fire's douted now. I be happy to give you a lift into town.

SIX

HARTRY

The hired man squints into the noon sun, his face raccooned with ash and soot from the burn, and then he becks his head at the Ambassador, curbed in the dirt and baking in the day's heat, happy, he says, to do the acquainting. The idling thing is an oversize, sand-eaten, and bister-colored old four-door, sun-bleached and patchworked and seeming foreign inside, with a reek of old cigar smoke and diesel grease and a kind of oiliness or spiciness not easy to identify. A deity of some alien notoriety dangles from a string affixed to the rearview, a yawning opening holes the panel where the radio should go, and spongy filling creeps through the rents of the leather bench seating. The sill of the back dash is bedecked with an array of billed caps labeled with various feed names and fertilizer brands. But for back and front windshield, the glass in the windows of the vehicle no longer exists, and hot dust boisters in on us, setting the caps aflutter as soon as we're moving. The engine rumbles along between hitches of sputters and coughs and pings, and black smoke billows out the tailpipe like crepe-paper Halloween frills. I fan the calamity away from my face and tell the hired man that I believe your rings need cleaning, and he looks at me and lifts the cap off his head and then dons it again and tells me, You can say that again, Missus. He grins, showing a gummy orifice where there ought to be teeth.

What's happened to your radio? I say.

Allow me, he says.

He reaches across my lap and pops the glovebox open and brings a transistor out, which he hangs by the wrist loop onto the rearview along with the swaying deity. Then he thumbs a switch on it that lets go a scratchy mariachi song. He puts a foot to the gas, getting more backfire than heave, and he taps a beat out on the steering wheel, moving us along like this to the music.

After a time we're come into town. We're riding down Main and I'm all the while looking out from the passenger side, wondering what people are wondering who are looking in at me.

You can drop me off at the coffee shop.

Much obliged, Missus.

He swivels the wheel with the flat of a hand and swings us into the lot. I gather my belongings and muscle the stiff door open, the hinges and the joints of the Ambassador groaning like an old man, the dust bleeding out of its gutters and seams. I thank the hired man again through the glassless frame, calling him Hartry, as is his name, and he responds with that gappy smile and a touch to the bill of his cap.

Just as it would happen, there's someone I know sitting in the window of the coffee shop. It's Ham, holding a mug to his lips and looking out my way. He twists about in the booth and signals me over as soon as I've come through the door. I go over and put the suitcase under the table and slide into the seat across from him.

What are you doing riding about with the hired man for? he says.

Son said he wouldn't drive me into town.

Why not drive yourself into town, then?

He said no to the pickup and no to the watertruck, either one.

What happened to the sedan?

He sold it.

What you lugging that suitcase around for?

My clothes are in it.

Your clothes.

I nod my head.

Oh, he says.

The swamp coolers cool it nice in here, I say.

You want something to eat or drink?

Iced tea is fine.

A fly lights on the table and Ham whacks it flat with the back of his menu. People at tables around us jerk to attention. Some of them turn their heads, look at Ham, look at me, see the suitcase, think what they think. The waitress comes over and Ham hands her the menu, showing her the red splat. She puckers her mouth and gives him a look. Then she leans over him and swabs the fly blood off the table with a dishtowel.

It's one way to get your attention, Ham says.

What's it today? she says.

Grilled cheese, extra cheese. And bring the little girl here an iced tea.

Ham watches the waitress walk away. She's sweet on me, he says.

She's been here forever, I say.

Just about, he says. He arranges his knife and his fork in their proper places.

What you plan on doing? he says.

There's a place I used to rent that might still be vacant, I say.

You can come and settle out at our outpost, he says.

The waitress comes back and sets a full plate before him and a glass of tea in front of me. She gives Ham another one of her looks. He gives her a look back. She turns and walks away.

You can be my guest, Ham says, at least till the gals be home-come again. And till you and Son are able to settle whatever of yourn needs to be settled, he says.

He offers me part of his grilled cheese and a few said-before words about being married. He says things about the workings of matrimony not being as easy as people would have us believe, more so after the gambol and the frolic of the honeymoon are over. He tells me times are especially trying for the newly married, as couples haven't yet the know-how or the skill-of for what it takes as to the workings of the setup.

Often as not, he says, young kids such as yerselves succumb to the husband-and-wife routine with nothing but simple mimicry as any kind of guide, meaning that of which has been commonly done by common others come before. They brand each other with their wedding rings and too soon get caught in a loblolly of the unforeseen, he says. They get penned in and choused about and confused by all of what's expected of 'em.

Ham's face is lined with ruts and gullies, his slate-colored eyes set deep. His voice is caged and pitched from the depths of his chest, and his words are passed up and raked through the gravel and scrape of his throat. He goes on to say something about Son and how as a husband he ought to be treating me more delicately, regardless of unsettling things that have gotten in our way. He says something about Son being lost—poor kid! poor the both a yous!—says how it takes time aplenty to get over a tragedy such as the one we've been hit with. As he speaks, the very sentences break and fade into air, the way the ice in my glass disappears into tea. We sit across from each other in the booth, Ham yet talking and me listening from a distance. We sit in the dissolve of afternoon light flooding in on us through the windows, light exactly such as I have seen it before in here, making the place ever more known for the time spent in it. The light runs awash over the backless stools and over the row of red vinyl'd bench seats posted at each windowed booth. It pours across the wide aisle of checkered linoleum in between. I see myself up and moving about the place, slowly, as if moving through water or part of a dream, filling orders and coffee cups, as I used to do, speaking into the steamy hole of the kitchen as I clip my ticket to the chrome wheel. I am not so long ago a girl in school and working here evening shift, yet the span of those days seems hardly as if it could be. How can it all be the same and yet nothing is? How does time get away and then show itself back, right where it was and it is again? I'm reciting the day's litany of baked pies and fresh cakes, remembering every name. I'm standing beneath the overhead globes, bringing forth and carrying away, smiling casually, while all the while keeping an eye out for that someone or other who should walk in the door and spark my eye. I never knew who it was I was looking for. I only believed that one day the whoever it was it was supposed to be would walk in and find me and put a stop to the longing. And he would say to me, Sorry to have kept you such a long time waiting.

It is but one of the myths people tend to be rowcled around by for the better part of their lives, Ham says.

I look into the old stone eyes. What is? I say.

Marriage, he says. You're not listening, is you?

The waitress comes toward us, and as she does, Ham lifts his coffee mug at her. I turn to look through the window's powdered-over glass as she makes small-town chatter and pours the refill. Outside, ropes of dust pay out across a rain-shadowed and fevered land. The sun burns hot atop the macadam, turning it from a licoricy solid to a hellish liquid. Paint jobs fade from every car and truck parallel'd and slotted in the lot. Buckled crusts of shaled earth splinter and fin in the bake. Tumbleweeds skitter past in the dearth.

Ham lifts the coffee mug to his lips and blows the steam and the hot off it. He takes a cautious sip. He says, I want to do my best to help you two arbuckles out. I want you to know that I am able to help Son get more work if need be. The desalting plant is about to get a thumbs-up, and as I know the señors running the outfit I might be able to bespeak Son a job. And until the meantime, the boy could help me out at my spread, as there's a lot of work needs doing before bronc'n and bull'n time. Asides, it might just be that a life of sodbusting has come to be too much of a struggle, and maybe it ain't worth it to him anymore with the old man gone. It would still be possible to sell the entire place, and likely yet profit-able given the water rights that come with it. You kids might be better off. Hell, I might even buy the place myself, if Pearl gives her say-so. She's a better mind about these sorts of deals than me.

He tilts his head back and empties the mug. Then he reaches into his hip pocket and tugs his wallet out and drops a couple of bills next to the ticket. He offers to carry the suitcase for me and I grab the satchel and follow. He picks his hat from the stand as we're leaving and flags a good-bye to the waitress, moving toward the exit in that stiff-hipped swagger of his. He opens the door, the dust drifting in like fog, and we walk outside to the blast of heat that awaits us.

Ham's rig is parked in the choppy shade of a date palm across the lot. He opens the passenger door of the crewcab of it, and I climb up and slide inside to a woolly heat and onto the burn and stick of naugahyde seating, arranging my legs around the suitcase Ham has put at my feet. He comes around to the driver's side and gets in and starts the engine and soon we are slithered onto Main Street snakewise, the empty horse trailer abuck and arattle behind us. It's the hot and quiet part of the day, known commonly as siesta time, as most anyone would know without my saying so. The few vehicles we pass on the road are filled with drivers who drive sleepily, as if the hot air were too thick to move through, their driving become a mix of the afternoon hour and an old-timer style. I roll my window up to keep the dust out, then roll it down to let the wind come back in. Soon I have almost got a system.

I sit back and take the views of town in as we move through. We pass by the only hotel, its sign boasting of a swimming pool and a banquet hall and a honeymoon room. We pass the jewelry shop, and a sinking feeling comes over me when I see the blown-up wedding photograph of me and Son that Mr. Gomez has postered up in the window to help him sell his diamond rings. We pass the grocery store, its windows butcher-papered over with prices and sales for the week, and I scan them out of habit, then realize with a catch in my gut there's no reason now to take heed. We drive by the five-and-dime, drive by the laundromat, the tortilla factory, and the tack and feed, by the liquor and hardware and paint. We get to the end of town and come to a span of concrete and steel, the water below the bridge now diminished to creeping eels. Aside the river is spread the historic prison, its legend vast and its name famous. Now the wooden frame of it is propped up and stove in, and its stone edifice is rubbled over and patched together by whatever it takes to mend it. Its guards of iron palings tine shadows in silica and gypsum and scrub. Its sallyport casts an archway of shade over ghosts that are said to come and go about the place. We drive over the bridge and our silence is drowned by a steady *whooooooh* sound, like somebody blowing across the mouth of an empty bottle. Then we're to the other side of the bridge and we hit blacktop and are abruptly brought back to the world of audibly solid boundaries.

We keep each to our thoughts and ride on in the quiet.

Soon enough we've come into a reprieve of privately heavenly shelter, a corridor of desert olives and fan palms and dappled light running along a wide driveway. The wrought-iron gates are left open today, and no man appears in the gatehouse to greet us. Ham pulls the rig up to the front of the pink mission and he helps me out with my suitcase and takes my hand to help me down out of the cabfront. We enter the house through the arched portal, passing through the long dark entryway cooled as it is by tiled floors and stucco'd walls, then out of the zaguan and across the stony path of the courtyard to Daughter Pearl's room, and why, Ham says, shouldn't I use it?

It's plenty enough to keep you out of the williwaws, he says.

He goes over to the window and throws the drapes aside, and the light bursts upon swarming motes of dust. He gathers loose garments that are tossed atop the bed and piled onto the floor, and he opens the closet door and tosses the wad inside. I go over to the window and look out at a grove of date palms, the shaggy trees all clustered with drupe.

As you can see by all the foofaraw, he says, that girl a mine ain't been wanting for much of anything. She's been spoiled from the get-go, he says. And yet not a single gracias out of her, no matter the advantages of generous parentage and proper schooling and decent society.

Son's fond of her, I say, speaking into the glass. Awfully.

They's growed used to each other since they was itty kids.

Anyways, he says, I want you to make yourself to home about the place. Mi casa es su casa, as they say. You'll be doing me some good by giving me a bit of company. It's too quiet around here with the gals away. So please don't thank me.

Thank you.

Ham puts a little finger inside an ear and shoggles it about and makes a sound somewhere between a snort and a grunt. Inner-ear itch, he says. Only thing that fixes it.

YOU TALK LIKE you got a bad case of romantic in you, Son had said. You talk like you're lost, he said.

He got up from the table and walked over to the kitchen sink and poured the rest of his coffee into it. You ought to quit reading so much of the time, he said. That and your daydreaming. All you're doing is sounding like somebody else you're not. All you're sounding is loco.

WHAT ARE YOU doing, Girl, just staring off into space? Rose's Daddy would say if he walked in and found me in Daughter Pearl's room, sitting as I am at the edge of the bed. He would turn and have a look about, nodding his head at what might be causing my unease, though how could he know the feeling of being fostered out? He would try to comfort me with what he might see as reasons that could be reasoned away. He would probably comment on the hard shade of the lavender walls, or maybe say the canopied bed was a bit claustery, the curtains and pillows and throws all too many and frilly, enough to make one feel smothered in in her sleep. No wonder, he would say, wondering aloud—though keeping his voice low so as not to insult Ham in any way—saying, how could Daughter Pearl's choosing so differ from her mother's refined taste in things? He might say, Our children are really less of our doing than a parent believes, knowing Ham would anyway agree with him in this opinion. Take for example that son of mine, Rose's Daddy would say, nodding at the picture of Daughter Pearl and Son, framed and placed on the bureau top, each of them holding a purple ribbon up for their given livestock winnings. Just a couple of kids they were then, with no more than a couple of years between them, he would say. And in those yesteryears yet somewhat innocent. Or maybe not. Who can say, when we try to hold to our long agos, and with our memory confounding so our hope for things? Yet together those two have grown equally and are much the same, meaning—and I say but the truth—with so little generosity of spirit, with so little integrity, neither one of them believing in a single important thing.

Rose's Daddy would take his hat off and run a hand over his forehead to the back of his neck—that hand, patchy and withered as the skin on a river toad is.

We turn in the silence that comes over us, regarding the room more completely. We study the clutter of childhood strewn about: the stuffed creatures that are bunched on the bed, as though stayed to watch over those who would be lost in their sleeping; the ribboned winnings at animal husbandry pinned along the sashes and the rods and the beams; the adult-bodied dolls stiffly posed among the shelves in miniature mode-of-the-day clothes. We pause at the loud posters of pop song characters that rob the lavender walls, sweaty-torso'd and feral-hair'd, their mouths opened to shout. Stacks of cakes of makeup and tubes of lipstick, disks of gloss and bottles of enamel, halfmoons of headbands and spirals of ribbons, barrettes and hairpins and rollers and combs, files and tweezers, and whatever the rest of the stuff that covers the top of the bureau over might be—all this Rose's Daddy will eyeball with great curiosity. Are these but girlish paints and polish to play in? he might say. He brings his nose close to the eyes and the teeth of the glamour stars and models taped to the glass. He lifts a sheet of her astrology calendar, noting with curiosity the red X's that mark the girl's moons. He opens a bottle and daggles himself with a splash of scent—lilac or violet or lily of the valley?

That could only be the mother's doing, Rose's Daddy will say, pointing his hat at the gilt-framed painting of the thoroughbred hung beside the bed.

I look around and wonder, what does Son see in this girl, Pearl? Or see in any of the rest of them? What does he see in all his other-than-me's? I don't have to speak the thoughts aloud, as Rose's Daddy knows me well enough to know. And always he tries his best to soothe. He will say how it is too easy to get caught in trying to make some comparison of worth with respect to yourself and Daughter Pearl, or whatever other female company there be for Son's keeping. When there is no likening to be made, he will say. When the fact is, it does not take much to turn a man's head. There will always be some woman or another who will catch the eye and make a lively man lean a different way. There will forever be the temptation to reach out for the other. It is but an urge built into us, is it not? And most remarkable yet, is that our desire to act does not spur us out and onward more often, that whatever rules we are harnessed to keep us from going astray. Unless some kind of agreement can be made otherwise, which I did so attempt, in Rose's and my case. Or until one day a man just tires and gives out. Then what more would there be left to him? In any case.

A man does know his time, he will say. He cannot be blamed.

But this I will tell you, he too will say—what Son does, you ought not to believe it is anything to do with you.

The old man's words bring little comfort. Am I not enough to sway and keep him engaged? I reach for the picture and bring it closer to my face. The two are rangy and pale eyed, with the same wheat-colored hair and sun-dotted skin.

They could be brother and sister.

And Rose's Daddy will look at me in a way that I see such a notion would not be an impossibility.

I look at him to say, If it's so, why wouldn't they know better?

He will fiddle with the edge of his hat brim, curled one-sidedly where his doffing hand has gripped it so often.

Nothing anyone could prove, he will say, or even wanted to. And it is long past what anyone could do about it.

I will nod.

I will shake my head.

I worry about what you might think of me for leaving, I say. Leaving Son, leaving the house, leaving all the things that need caring for behind. I still think a lot about what you and Rose would think of me.

Yes and indeedy, Rose's Daddy will say. For were we not family? And do not the dead surely lay their claim? Perhaps more so than do the living. Whereby the laws of the fathers have been set into place, this we know. A bell and a pomegranate, a bell and a pomegranate. Do as commanded or elsewise live in fear. Girl, I tell you this—death is but one less day to be afraid.

And he will square the hat back atop his head.

THE OLD MAN had told me a story, a story about a woman who had lost an only daughter, a woman who had come to motherhood in the late afternoon of her life, so to speak, a daughter not yet to reach the dawning of a birthday of twenty. The daughter had left a handwritten will, odd as it was for one of such a tender age, anybody would say, and filled with but vitality and youthful exuberance. Lo, the girl was mature beyond her years, he had said, and as they come, somewhat precocious.

Now in this will the daughter lay out her requests in detail and in relative depth, he said. She asked that the mother, if it so be that she be alive at the time of the daughter's death, should dispose of the said ashes according to the girl's wishes. And the wishes were exactly these, that the mother should seek three places within all the seven great landmasses that cover the earth, and that the ashes be scattered in those three sites that the mother would deem holy.

And it came to pass that the daughter gave up the ghost.

And the handwritten note was found during the midst of the mother's grieving, placed in a drawer of the daughter's bureau among a gather of keepsakes and fewtrils, with other remembrances and forgotten things.

There was no father. There was no family besides.

And the mother did so mourn.

Scattering the ashes required toil and yield and will, means and reserve and fortitude, all of which were the greater burden in the mother's grief and in her already graying days. Henceforth, it took the mother years to carry out the daughter's last wishes. Yet she held her countenance and completed the task before she was herself sent to the grave.

Why should the mother do it? I said. If, after all, the girl is dead?

A question worth pondering, indeed, he said.

Inconsiderate, I said, to inflict a burden that would be obeyed through guilt.

Maybe obeyed through necessity, he said. Or obeyed through virtue. Or obeyed through the desire to perform an act, an act of beauty, an act that might be called, in and of itself, sublimity.

And for this the mother went to all the trouble?

Who can say? he said. Yet would not the planning and the tending become consolation? Would not these efforts thereby be turned a blessing?

Did the mother get over her grief?

Is grief something that ought to be gotten over?

Well, what I mean is, how did she seem?

I know no one who knows, he said. No one, so I am told, spoke to her upon her return. She came home after the last scattering, it is said. Neighbors saw her unloading her bags and her duffels from the vehicle, but she soon after disappeared. Friends say they gathered one day to make a visit, hoping to bestow an offering of baked goods and a bouquet, as her home seemed open and welcoming from a distance. They knocked on the screendoor, receiving no answer. They put their noses to the mesh and peered in. They called out, yet only to quiet. They went inside and walked room to room, repeating the mother's name. They found the house in perfect keeping, the beds made up with ironed linens and the dishes stacked in the drainer, with sunflowers freshly cut in a vase, with handkerchiefs and underthings drying in the sun on the line, the water-sprinkler yet on on the lawn.

HE OPENS THE door and I want to move into his embrace. He knows this. I can see it. I can see me in his eyes. He comes forward and puts his arms out and pulls me against him. There's a hard pounding of heart between us—mine or his? Or both?

Please, the Padre says.

He gives me a pat on the back and puts a halt to us.

Please, come in, he says. Come in and talk to me. He says he is happy I have called on him. He says, Do you mind removing your shoes? A house rule, he says. Not mine but my wife's. To keep the dust out, is what she says. Though who would hope for any such miracle here? he says, bursting into the pleasant laugh I've heard him laugh before. He touches my shoulder and leads me into a room.

I hope I'm not disturbing you and your wife tonight, I say, knowing the wife has gone away for a few days.

My wife's gone to the coast to partake of a music festival.

I stand in the warm homey glow of the place and look about the room, hoping the dishonesty of my words doesn't show on my face. So much to read, I say, and I nod at all the books stacked in the cases that line the walls. Atop the cases are rows of gleaming copper pots in pregnant shapes. There's an urn centered on the mantel that makes me think of family ashes, and there are figurines seeming to belong to some long-ago arranged along a sideboard. All about are growing things for tending—delicate ferns dangling on hangers, wandering jews pedestaled on stands, creeping greenery coiling along the rods and the sills. Everything is placed just right according to a given eye, to say a certain thing to any other's, and this, you can see, has cast some fraud upon it. There's a notion spelled out in the assembly of things that I take to be the wife's doing, not the Padre's—ideas of hers as to how to live in the proper way, a way of being, even in this newly built abode of faux adobe we're in. I decide I don't like the wife. I don't like her dried flowers posied in vases, or her faded embroidery mounted in oval'd frames, or those overly posed family photographs she has nestled on a chest. I don't like anything.

Come, he says. Sit down.

I follow him and take a seat on a loveseat and fold my hands into my lap — I see me folding my hands into my lap, I hear me saying things that I don't know what I'm saying, I see me listening to him say things. What is he saying? Practical things about the practical world — things about housekeeping, about collecting things, about life, about his wife. I decide he doesn't like his wife either.

The Padre gets up and lights a stick of incense. Then he goes over to a cabinet and takes a disc from a sleeve and opens a record-player case. Smoke begins to swirl about the room. The sharp trill of flute smothers the quiet and winds about us as the smoke does. He opens the door of the cabinet and takes a couple of tiny glasses and a decanter out.

Home remedy, he says.

I take the glass he hands to me and sip. Strong as tequila, whatever it is.

He watches me drink. Eau-de-vie, he says. Water of life.

He keeps looking at me, his eyes welcoming as open doors.

A ceiling fan sets the buds and the stems and the leaves of the plants around us atremble. I look down at my hands and see them shaking too. I take another sip of the drink, feeling the burn of it down my throat and the hot thread of it moving into my chest. I drink the rest of the glassful, wipe the drips off my chin and my lips — water of life, beads of sweat, what would be the difference?

If it were red wine, would we be drinking the blood of Christ? I say.

Given a different intention, yes, he says.

He reaches for the decanter and fills my glass to the brim.

The second is smoother going down the throat. It loosens the words to make them come up and out easier when I speak, but still what I say isn't what I mean. I empty the drink again and this time reach the glass toward the Padre. Smoke and melody snake about the room. I sit back and hold the glass with both hands, wanting to steady the swimminess in my head, and then I'm speaking, the words pouring out strangely easily.

I think it would be wiser to believe in gods, I say, or god, I say, with a small *g*, as I see it, all things being equal, that is, as a person would be happier probably, in any case, seems to me anyway, but then that would be believing in believing, is what the problem is, now that I'm thinking about it.

We are born believing, he says. Some of us just stop paying attention.

I'm paying attention, I say.

The Padre takes a drink of his drink and looks at me with his open-door eyes.

Anyway, as best I can, I say. Though maybe I haven't been. Or maybe I wasn't, is what I'm saying. I don't know. Because how could I have been looking, with everything the way it just went and slipped out from under, when we must not have been looking, or something, me and Son, I mean, because we should have been able to see what was happened to Rose's Daddy, the way he was going, and maybe could we have stopped him from going that way? With him doing what he did. If we'd been looking. If we'd done something differently. God, everyone must say the same thing about the same things. I could be a recording.

What would you have done differently? the Padre says.

I shake my head. What was Rose's Daddy's rush? I say. I've

read over what he left written, trying to understand. I try to imagine what he would have to say about it, about doing such a thing, and I hear him at times, really—and no, I'm not talking make-believe, about believing in spirits, I'm not talking ghosts or anything like that, but just what we remember, is what I'm saying, or trying to say, the way the sound of a voice lives on in you so you can hear the voice, hear it when you want to and hear it even when you don't want to—anyway, you know what I mean, I'm sure you do, without the person even being there, they're there.

Voices speak through me at times, he says.

Why did he go? I say.

There are those who find it too sad to live without gods.

That sounds preachy.

Forgive me.

I'm sorry.

You're sad.

I'm not sad.

Not sad?

Angry, maybe.

Understandable.

I have an unfaithful husband.

Adulterous, you mean.

Right. As in roaming around with other women, I say. One of them in particular.

Sex between two people should be approached as a divine act.

Is that another one of your truths again? I say.

You pick things up when you read, he says.

I read, I say.

But not the Bible.

No, not the Bible. Though Rose had one, an old one, and I would look at it sitting there always in the same place and gathering dust. Seeing it always bothered me. I felt it like a parent looking back at me, is what I think it was. But the stuff in it, it's popular enough to know without having to read it. I mean, who doesn't know the story of Adam and Eve? With the snake and that. The forbidden fruit and all. The tree of knowledge and such.

Making love ought to be approached as prayer, he says.

A lot of angry stuff in those old Bible stories. I think that that tree-of-knowledge thing, that was meant to be a lesson of the meanest kind. What's that tree supposed to be about but what it is we're cursed by, that we're punished forever by the knowing of our dying? Isn't that what you'd call our fall from grace?

We have never fallen from grace, he says. You are better off not believing such stories. Just believe what you feel. Take what you know from what there is inside you to be true.

What I feel? Okay, what is that? Too much? Not enough? I should pick one. Where do I start? I'm sorry, is what, sorry about the old man, sorry about Rose, sorry when it comes to Son. Maybe sorry for myself, mostly.

Here, he says. He takes his handkerchief from his pocket.

I put it to my nose and smell mint chewing gum.

Start from the start, he says.

Well, then, I think I've come to the end.

Nothing ends without something beginning.

What's that but going in circles? I blow.

In the spiritual life you may know joy in life.

I lean my head onto the back of the loveseat.

My head is spinning, I say. It must be that incense stuff.

Love is the true redeemer of souls, the Padre says.

He puts his glass down on a table and takes a cross-legged seat on the floor in front of me. He reaches out and takes hold of one of my feet.

Please, he says. Why pull away? Why should you be afraid?

Who says I'm afraid? No, I just need to blow my nose again. I need to wash my face. Where can I go wash my face at?

Then ashamed, maybe? Don't be, he says. Don't turn your head away. Here, give me your foot. Give me both. There. Feet are very humbling. Mary Magdalene washed Jesus's feet.

The Padre's fingers sink like clamps into the flesh of my foot. He rubs a thumb along the spine of the sole. Here is your liver, he says. Here is your kidney. And here, this is your heart.

It hurts there when you push.

It won't after a while.

WE RIDE OUT to the potrero to check on Ham's livestock, to cut what he calls the colicky beeves from the rest of the herd so the vet can do the day's doctoring. I ride a gentle appaloosa that Ham's daughter used to prize—until she just growed tired of him for his gentle and knowable ways, he says. Ham rides a palomino that was his wife's everyday favorite, wanting to keep the horse from going barn-sour before she comes back home and wants to get back on him again. Ham tells me he's heard from Pearl, that she writes to say she has had luck breeding the thoroughbred and to say too that she and Daughter Pearl will stay to see the foaling. Meanwhile, they will enjoy the northern climate, though the mountain refuge has not been as cool as it was known to be before. The spell has been cast wide, Ham says.

But it is anyways lucky we have the means for the gals' retreat. If I thought you'd be in any kind of good keeping, I'd send you up north to join 'em. But I'm betting you and Son are not beyond a reckoning between the two of yous, sooner than not.

A handful of vaqueros trot ahead of us on grulla ponies, Mexican men hired as needed, some of the best punchers being keepers. They round up the stock to move them a bunch at a time into the pens, where they will filter them on in through the chutes and from there into the arena. The vet's border collie skirts the herd along with the men, the working dog all the while clipping and snapping at heels to gather and steer the livestock onward. The drove moves about like a cloud, changing shape but without pouching or breaking, their cloven prints blown loose and risen into the air as soon as they're set into the earth. The tracks vanish into the blind of dust and sun above, where new batches of worlds are forever taking shape. Up there, where heavenly bodies are colliding, where stars are burning out while all the while we spin in the blue, in the realm of the very small here below.

There's an explosion of dust—a shudder and thud, a crying out, a man pitching from his horse. He lunges at a calf and bulldogs it down to the ground, setting off a commotion of yipping and hawing and whooping among the others. The downed animal looks stunned, as it just lies there on its side with its legs splayed out. The vaquero picks himself and his hat up off the ground and hazes the cow's head with the hat, and the cow rises up on unsteady fours and looks about stupidly before it turns and trots back into the herd.

You gotcher one fine bulldogger there, the vet says.

He's my top waddy, Ham says.

He really took that dogie down by the horns.

Ever one of these men gets worked up about rodeo time, Ham says. Half a time they got contests of their own going on among themselves.

You got you a training ground here for good wrestlers, the vet says.

I wish't they'd cut the horsin' out and get on with the doing of what work we got here to be doing.

Yet it ain't right to hobble the spirit out of the men now.

You could say so, Ham says, if you was wanting to be fair about it.

You got to sabe what's fair or not for yourself, the vet says.

Fact is it's a helluva time to be sporting and funning about in this godamighty heat, Ham says. Take a lot out of man and animal, as you know better than everbody. What I know is these buckaroos ought to be preserving ever bit of their fortitude for what work we need 'em doing. And not wearing our animals down none neither.

Especially as my doctoring fees are by the hour and you've got a lot of vacas needs eyeballing and treating, the vet says.

You needn't be reminding me, Ham says. He swats at a horse-fly buzzing too near his head.

What you been feeding? the vet says.

I feed 'em all good, Ham says. Specially the ponies. They get a mix of corn and barley, cottonseed hulls and alfalfa hay, molasses and a bit of silage, and some cornflakes and cheerios to boot if they's some left of it in the kitchen. I got a pearburner so we can add the prickly to the fodder. Beeves get this elixir too, but with a lot more plain hay in it for filler. And they've got a girt of grazingland I keep irrigated alongside the river for 'em to feed off of as well. They even get a bit of shade there to keep their hides nearly cooled off.

I believe the colic's likely been brought on by sand what's got mixed in with the grain, the vet says. It happens now and again. I been seeing it with an awful lot more stock these days. Sand's pert near in everything and in every place.

Or maybe too it's the stress, Ham says.

Could be in addition, the vet says. Heat is tough on any animal. You got to watch 'em for the coughing pneumonia and the emphysema they get from the dust. You got to watch 'em so they ain't drying up and dropping over with their tongues all swolled up and hung out.

Nosirree-bob, Ham says. Won't let that happen.

Nope, the vet says.

You know what we want, Ham says. We want that certificate of approval from you, is what we want. We want these animals in top form come rodeo day, and I'm counting on you to get us in shape, even if it cost me some extra dollars. As I'm counting too on us getting closer to a break in the weather, he says. I'd give the Good Lord the pay dirt necessary for that prayer to be answered. This curse a heat can't go on forever now.

The vet takes his hat off and scratches his head.

You wouldn't think, Ham says.

No, you wouldn't, the vet says.

Let's get us a header and a heeler.

You're the hacendado.

They nod one to the other.

Speckled outbursts of starling birds lift from the withered branches of an old pecan tree as I lead the appaloosa toward its pool of shade. I stand the horse and watch as some of the men drive another part of the herd into the pen. A couple of the vaqueros wait inside the arena and prance after the stock once they've come in through the chutes. A nimbus of dust rises up and takes shape, like some celestial body yet chained to the earth in its drift. One of the men trots through the mass to the clear, working the stiff from a rope and building a loop of it. Another man trots at the heels of a weakling and waits for the header, now looping overhead until the lasso should take the proper shape and weight on. When the header nods ready, he comes about and tosses the rope and catches both horns and pulls back. The heeler rowels his horse and moves around again from behind and throws the lariat and catches both hind legs as was his aim. The calf stumbles, but the riders don't topple the animal, and their horses know to keep the ropes taut enough and to wait for the cue. At this, the vet rides over and eases his horse up to the cow, and he plants a foot on the cow's head and leans over and stabs a needle through the hide and into the flesh, injecting the medicine. He quick marks a line along the animal's forehead with a greasepaint stick, and saws his horse to back it up and waits as the men untie and recoil.

Let's vamoose and go on after the next of 'em, he says.

The appaloosa stands patiently beneath me, borne up as we are on a vast desertland, shaped by splintered plates and buckled crusts in a constant state of stretch and crack, causing the earth to solidify and rift, if I'm remembering my geology correctly. We're moved in our repose through currents, caught within the eddies of westerlies, the great mountains in the far away snagging every cloud and withholding any vapor or bit of mist or drop of rain. The sun is distorted by its own fevered glare above, and little sandspouts whirl about in the dirt and skitter out across the vega before us. I sit under our modest yet glorious cover of shade, the horse swishing her tail at the flies that bite, watching as the men run through the herd and do what they do again and then over again, all the while taken in by the might and the spectacle of all of it.

THE HOT-STAR sparkle of diamond catches my eye, a glint of light seen in the adamantine luster, in the fire crystaled inside, in the faceting as was intended for matrimony, in the merging of elements complete. Inside too I see the lies bedded and the promises cleaved that disturb what remains of any brightness there might once have been. I close my eyes to any regret. I let the startle of flesh and the stroke of breath carry me to another place, where each thought becomes no thought at all.

It's like a door slammed and I'm startled awake. That fast are we fallen and come to our senses again. Or come out of our senses, if you might say it that way, and come into our minds again, come into the ordinary, as if we're suddenly no longer touched by whatever wand had so touched us. For what happened between us isn't any of what I'd imagined it to be. Not after the words, the mouths, the caressing, the groping, the fumbling at loving. Not after the clothes are off. Not because what I had seen was not what I had thought it would be, as far as the shape of the head not being cut and molded the way Son's is, and the other different things about another body that might take you by surprise and so frighten and arouse. But it was once the Padre had come into me, once he was inside, it was that quickly finished. In a minute—no, less, not even, less than a minute, in an instant—it was done. He was finished.

He lifted his gaze upward, his breath caught hard and quick, as if he were hearing something from above that had in a sudden come to him.

It's not so much that it was over for the Padre—over in just the obvious way, in that all that was stored up was suddenly gone to spill in me. But more that he behaved as if helpless or ignorant as to what he could do now. Do with me, I mean. Anything, do anything, do something—my body could not have been more pleading at the time—but please, don't just roll over and turn away and lie still. Don't abandon me. Don't say, Forgive me. Not just, Forgive me. As if doing nothing but speaking a few words of apology was all that would be needed. As if he believed he were some kind of saintly being or other and needn't do a thing but simply ask for forgiveness and expect that he should get it.

THEY SET AN eight-second clock for the bronc riding and other roughstock events, Ham says, because eight seconds is the best you can get out of any bucking animal. Experience proves you cain't expect any much better, as after eight seconds the horse or bull will tire enough to change the game. Every cowboy goes into a show wants a good bucker so as he can make it to the short-go. Or she. Cowboy or cowgirl, he says. Though most ladies will stick to their barrels, as you know. Not all, but most. As maybe they've got the better sense as far as the sexes is concerned, he says.

Ham gives his bolo a tug and stares at me as if he either remembered or had forgotten something.

You want good buckers, I say.

As I was saying, he says.

You were saying, I say.

Now, for the bulls you got to train with the dummy to get what you want out of 'em—that's that itty box there with the antennae on top a it, he says, pointing to the contraption in the corner of the tackroom. You take your young brahmas, who are naturally aggressive and got the drang to buck, and you get them used to a thing on their back that they don't like from the get-go, and you will have 'em to leap and to kick and to whip about each and ever time in no time. We use the dummy pert near a year afore we put a rider atop the bull at all.

You mean until the live dummies get on, I say.

They ain't so dumb, he says. Them boys know what they's doin' and what they's dealing with. They trust the stock to be tough and the stockmen to deliver. You want toughest of the tough. You want rank. Good riders expect that. And you don't go relying on finding good buckers from what's come from somebody else's remuda, or relying on luck, he says. You got to breed for what you want. Then you encourage the animals to do what comes naturally—to toss every cowboy gets astride of 'em right off and onto their pockets, is what.

Ham reaches to his hip and digs into his canvas pants and pulls a watch and a chain out. He flips the silver cover open, and when he does, the sun hits the metal and strikes at the eye like lightning.

Where goes the time? he says.

He puts a hand to the middle of my back and leads me out of the tackroom and toward the arena. He keeps talking, with me all the while reined alongside him by what he knows and cares to tell me about.

Now later on today, he says, what we got to do is introduce a few of the animals to the rodeo chutes. The aim is to keep the bulls and the horses bucking and yet at the same time get 'em used to being in the pens and being around people. Atop of all that of which we must check that ever one of 'em is properly branded and weighed and named. You can help me out with that part, if you've a mind to.

He tugs a raggedy old bandanna from out of his pocket and swabs his forehead and the back of his neck with it, the flesh on him darkened and withered nearly to jerky.

You'd think there'd be yumidity here with the way the sweat's coming off me today, he says. He puts the bandanna to his nose and gives a hard blow. He looks into the rag. Yet they's nothing but dust coming out, he says.

Isn't it crazy, I say, to think that in this plague of heat people would still keep the sport of rodeo going.

Crazy to think we would not, he says.

It reminds me of those poor countries you hear about where they're in the middle of some war, one against another, both inside and out, but these same people are able and civil enough to compete in games of ball kicking or bat swinging, I say.

I won't make to any comments on the morals of mankind, Ham says. He slides the post back and swings the wooden gate open. He nods at me to go ahead on in, and we walk across the arena, the dirt powdering up at our heels, the sun hammering down on us from above. We head toward the shade of a stand of cottonwood and eucalyptus that lies on the other side of the fence, all of everything trembling in the heat.

Far as I'm concerned, Ham says, is once a man starts talking about honor and morality, you'd best get to counting up your forks and your spoons.

We climb to the low rung of the fence and look over to where a brahma bull is grazing in the pasture.

Brahmas are the reason rodeos got to using barrel men and bullfighting clowns, he says, as bulls a this type are likely to attack a downed rider. That there is one rank bull you see before you now — downright nothing but mighty. The very reason we named him Bodacious.

He looks anything but near his name, I say.

He's upward of two thousand pounds, Ham says.

The bull doesn't move but to rotate his head to look back at us. He regards us with glossy eyes. He has large, pendulous ears and upcurving horns and a hide that is velvety smooth and hangs in excess in the dewlap and underbelly. The bull gives a twitch of the skin and tosses off a skitter of insects and then turns his head back to look out at some distant yonder, caring less about our presence than we do about his.

These animals know what heat is, Ham says. They can take it aplenty. Nowadays we got better breeds, like these ones. And we got nighttime rodeo to ease man and animal's burden and suffering both in the sporting and the gaming. We got electric lights and a good reason for using 'em too. Asides, it's more complicated than you might want to think, he says, these reasons men have for competing. Goes back as far as the start of any of the oldest stories, whether wrote about or just plain spoke enough of.

Dear Katherine,

You need to come home. You need to take my apollogy. You need to know how I am sorry for doing things I should be sorry for. You need to know that sometimes all of us does things that are not right for each other but that we cant help it even though we try. Since we are just humans. Right!? I promise we can work on things. I promise you will see and you wont ever want to goe and leave another time. Because I need you and you need me too, admit it. Just come home now and we can try it from brand new again.

Love, Son

P.S. Please pick up some groceries on your way home.

A COUPLE OF days went by after the letter and before the telephone call. I was out in Ham's tackroom going through pages of the names and the weights of the top stock when Ham came in to holler my name. You got a caller, he said. There was a hard stomp inside my chest, thinking it might be the Padre. What to say? What not to say? Never complain, Rose's Daddy would say. And never explain. And the old man would be right. It's a bad sign of anything to prosper between the Padre and me if I were to have to explain to him what happened between us, or didn't happen, I should say, and in doing so be complaining. If he cannot divine it, he could not truly understand what I'd have to say. And he, after all, being a doctor of divinity.

But no, it wasn't the Padre calling me. It was Son, and his voice sounded fitful in a way it had never been and it sounded truly grim. He said he was calling to ask me to come back to him, like his letter said, and didn't I get it or what, he said, as he expected by now to hear from me. It was hard to know correctly how to take his manner of speaking, whether for better or for worse, given the words attached to the tone. Finally he gave up trying to spur me to a defense and he shot for simple bargain and appeal.

Why not we give it another go-round? he said. Don't you know we've got a rodeo to be working toward? We've got to be a ropin' team, me and you. His pleas were filled with reminders, filled with we got this and we got that. And we got a lot more too we could work on together, he said. We were good at a lot of things, us two, and you ought not to forget it and just the hell go and let go of it all.

C'mon, Son said. Just come home, he said.

SEVEN

DAUGHTER PEARL

There would not have been time enough away for the place to have this much changed, only time enough away for me to have changed and so to see it this way. It's like going back to somewhere from when you were a kid, where you are grown in size now and are surprised to find what you return to turned as small as it is. It might be just the eye that betrays. Or maybe the hazed light is what blanches and dwindles what's seen, draining what color and deforming what form there once was from everything. The way it happens in the fading of a photograph, or in the lessening of memory.

Ham drives on and we face each out our own side window, looking at fields that lay pummeled or let go to fallow, at land scoured by windblow and sunbake, at the many acres man-burnt and mantled in black so black that they gleam like aluminum sheeting in the heat. Ropy-necked wintering birds, come strangely early, scatter about like a toss of debris to pick at what might be left to forage for in the stubble and ash and soot. Farther off, a cultivator still hitched to the disc sits outcast, as if someone just gave the task up and left the piece for attraction or pondering, the machine to be meanwhile taken in in time by ephedra or snakeweed, as what was once fertile earth turns to scrub. We pass through the old lemon grove, the whitewash on the trunks of the trees all but washed out by the sun, the burnt leaves dropped from the stems to clutter the saucers of dirt that top the roots beneath. You can see the old adobe house as we approach it, with the grove disrobed of its emerald cloak, the way the house looks sunk into the hummock from here, as though the thirst of topsoil were sponging up the adobe and wood and clay, and the mud within the thick walls become no more than decayed straw or dusty clots or maybe just empty space. You can see how if a wind lashed through, the tiled roof might be shucked off the house in a minute, the beams and joists then to buckle up and give way from the frame and all the hollow walls surely to topple.

Ham pulls up to the front of the house and sits the truck in idle. Right away, Son comes out the door, letting the screen slap loudly behind him. I get this kind of fizziness in the blood when I see him, and a sinking feeling that comes after. He stands there in the glare, in the lunatic'd trilling of cicada, looking out at us. I spot the old man and the old man's wife on the porch behind him, standing as if they had been waiting for me the whole time I was away from the place. Son raises a hand and whisks the vision away, and in a blink of an eye they're but a picture of what was.

Ham flags a hand back.

I'll be gettin' on then, he says. You two be all right.

All right, I say.

How you move is who you are. If this is true, then what is Son but someone without enterprise or aim? What then would he be made of? I watch him walking toward me and see only what he is not. He is not a seeker. He is not in pursuit of. What future is there held in him that could move him eagerly forward? He moves with a demeanor of carrying too heavy a load. His long arms dangle with but a lackadaisical sway, and his long-muscled legs advance him sluggishly, indifferently. His face is wearied, the look remote, his eyes diverted by hardly a thing. He is still tall as to any average, but fallen into himself, making him appear to have lost some inches. He is desert tinged, as he has always been, his hair sandy toned and bitter-brush stiff, his skin coarsened and ruddied a reddish tan. He is colored as one of the desert animals—the pumas, the song dogs, the bighorns, those creatures antlered and hoofed, or rodent and reptilian, where any of them will blend into the textures and hues of their environs and then just up and disappear on you.

Son puts his hands on my shoulders and leans to kiss me. His lips are dry as seedpods, the skin on his cheeks like burlap. His chin is prickly. He pulls me close to him, his body, the body I know more than any other other than mine, having once known the feeling of feeling it as my own, now feeling it entirely as what I do not know. The arms that cling to me are stony, without moisture and give, the smell of his skin, bitter, sandy, peppery, not the same, and still every bit him.

WE HAVE GOT to get a get-go, Son said.

And this snapped me into seeing him differently, hearing a something in him that yet drove him on, something to be aspired to, something to be hoped for. How could it be otherwise? When there's yet the spirit in him for the sport and the win of the rodeo—a striving enough to lift him, to lift me, to lift us both from the stall of things.

And so we would put our time in, despite the heat, riding around the hot part of the days. Son and I took the horses out of the shade of their stalls and harnessed and saddled them, though they didn't want to leave their water and their shelter at all. We paced them slowly, and still they lathered and baked in the heat, champing and foaming at the bit and whorling their heads when we loped them, as we all the while tried keeping ahead of the brown cloud folding over us. We rode along the furlong, rode paled in dust, rode dirt-caked through nothing but desert waste. We rode with bodies of dirt rolling up about us, like roving animals they were, come from out of the ether, shapes that shifted and disappeared into fits of wind. We kerchiefed the grit from out of our eyes, moved on through sagebrush and bunchgrass, arroyo and brecha, into mile after mile of no place of shade. We passed burnt animals spread out and pecked at by prey birds. Zebratails peeked out of the creosote, sidewinders coiled up in the dirt of the sun, cats baked in the stingy shade. The old dog wandered off in the dust, and we tracked after her and led her back to water and home.

We rode out along the canalbank and deeper into the day. Son dismounted to open the metal traps of the water gates, letting the water sluice through and funnel in, the garbled voices of holy men heard in the spew and the gush of it. The horses stood at the edge of the cement ditch, and they dropped their heads, blowing between drinks, snuffling their dripping muzzles up at the finish. They stomped their hooves and leaned again to drink.

What thirst there can be. Thirst as great as any yearning.

I was slid out of the saddle like that. I tossed the hat off my head and was right down inside the cradle of the ditch, and I lay back in the buckling onrush of water, letting it riffle my hair and slap at my face, letting it bloat up my clothing, blur over my eyes, brim into my ears, as I waited for the water to all but fill me up inside.

WHY DID YOU let the bird die?

Forget about the bird died.

Why is our wedding picture up here on the mantel?

Put it there for you, Darlin'. Put it there for us. For our happy memories. So we can remember what we're supposed to look like.

I see the photograph and how my eyelashes in it are matted together with mascara from the weeping. See the satin of the bodice of the dress, the way it's spattered with the dark that poured forth from my eyes. I know the stain beneath the tulle on the lap of the dress, though I carry the bouquet low enough to hide it from the notice of others. But what am I hiding with that smile but girlish foolishness? Or maybe fright?

What did we know? I say.

Who ever does? he says. Asides, it's done.

Where are the pictures and all the rest of the doodads up here your mother had?

Here, Son says. In the burn pile here. To light up first cool evening comes through. He reaches into the pit of the fireplace and peels a blanket away from a great mound of things — Navajo bowls and crystal vases, brass candlesticks, tiny figurines carved out of desert stones, a hand-painted box, conch shells collected from the coast, Rose's old Bible, a family album of letters and

honors and clippings, a lot of photos in frames, one with the eyes of a child looking out.

That stuff won't burn, I say.

What doesn't gets hauled away. I'm tired of looking all the time at what was.

What do you call us?

Is, he says. I call us what is. He comes over and puts a hand up inside my shirt. Let's go make us some kids, he says.

Don't be kidding around.

Let's go and practice at it anyway.

Let me settle in.

I'll get you settled in.

He puts a hand around my shoulder and leads me out of the kitchen and scoots us on through the parlor. When we near the open door of Rose's Daddy and Rose's bedroom, I stop to look in. Son tugs at me, but I persist. Bars of white light drape the bed, the bed still made up the way it was when I left, with Rose's lacy-edged pillowcases and her best set of linen sheets all ironed crisp and everything tucked in just the way she would have liked it. The bed she withered away in. I see her there, reaching out to me with her spidery fingers, see me rolling her and molding pillows about her to prop her into a change of placement. I see the long braid, come loose from its coil and draped like a rope along the delicate pedicles of her thinning spine. I hear her bones cracking in the shifting of her position. I smell yet the camphor of balms, the ointment of zinc, the iron and salts and metals that rivered through her body, as with every body, smell too the last breaths and the mottled flesh, the fester and rot of what's gone — smell all of this, even through the spackling and primer and fresh coats of paint covering the ceiling and walls. I stand and wonder, seeing a room that was

once put to ruin, with now the whole smoothed over and seemingly righted. I look inside, thinking of how our yesterdays will all the while deform us. Just as through memory we deform every yesterday.

Look. This is a room where the dead have lived. This is a room where the dead have gone and done their dying.

Where is the dried rose I put to stay on the pillow? I say.

In the fireplace with the rest of that pile of junk, Son says.

He closes the door.

The dead are just dead, he says.

I stand looking at the woodgrain of the door at my face.

How can it be so strange to comprehend? I say.

Comprehend what? he says. What's it you can't comprehend? Their lives are just done. So's having to live the way they had in mind for me to live, that's done too. Living with all their tales and their make-believe. Living for something now because I'm worried about when I'm dead, is not what I call living.

The clock stopped, I say.

What did the old man want anymore anyways? he says. He was selling his water to outsiders far away as the coast. Fussing about watering the roads when everything else around here is drying up on us. He told a lot of stories but never told one about the long run. Well, as he liked to say, in the long run we're all of us dead anyways.

I open the glass and insert the key, and it grates in the slot at the wind.

Now the old man's gone and he's nothing, Son says. And she's gone and nothing too. And this place is nothing.

The clock begins to tick again.

What've you got in mind that might be something? I say.

How about getting on with the living of my life? he says. For the first time in my life. I've got me some ideas. But let me tell 'em to you later. Come here, he says. Let's do it the way we used to do it.

He pulls me by a beltloop and leads me into our bedroom.

What about fixing the hands to set the time right? I say.

The time's right, he says.

AND WE WOULD go dancing again. Son would get duded up in his newest pair of denims and pearl-buttoned shirt and his walking-heel boots. He would saddlesoap the boots and splash his face with aftershave. I would get out my after-the-wedding dress, which I had not worn since our night of matrimonial celebration. I would wash and set my hair, run a razor over my legs, put a frosty pink to shine on my lips.

There was a place in town where a band yet played on Saturday nights. We went inside and stood like a couple of moles, waiting for our eyes to adjust to the dark. A bar loomed up amid the lights, as did the bottles behind and the customers among the stools that rimmed the wood. A man tending appeared on the other side of the counter, sliding back and forth it longwise, like fingers running over frets on a guitar. There was a stage ready to be lit, with instruments and equipment set up and a bunch of tangled lines and paid-out cables looped about. There was a dance floor fenced in by tables and chairs and only half-filled yet with people talking and drinking in the dim. There was a door-to-door perfume smell in the air, and a smell of spilled and soured beer, and too a musky scent, all of it mingling in the stale fold of tobacco smoke.

We took seats in the back and waited for the woman in the short skirt to come to us and for the live music to begin. There were songs being piped in from overhead, songs about getting drunk and aching hearts and being sorry. Son was already eager to dance, even to recorded warm-up music, but I said I needed something to drink first. A woman came with her corkboard tray and put little napkins out on the table in front of us. She readied her pen and wrote our orders on the pad on the tray. Son watched her the whole time, his eyes moving from her pushed-up and glittered bosom to her colorful drawn-on eyes and back again. She finished writing and looked up and smiled at him. Back with the seven-sevens in a minute, she said. She left to retrieve our drinks.

It's not polite to stare, I said.

C'mon, he said.

There would by now be a couple of couples out on the dance floor. Son is as good a dancer as he is a rider, and it has always been easy to catch on to his feel and his time and to follow. We would take breaks after several dances at a stretch and go back to our table and drink our drinks, and we would order again and go back out to the dance floor once more. We two-stepped. We west-coast'd and disco'd. We slow-danced and line-danced. Son rotated his hips and frapped his feet and winged his elbows and knees. He had his arms outspread, moving them about up and over his head as if aiming to throw a rope. He screwed his mouth up in drunken concentration, and his brow broke out in a sweat. In his feverish dance I could not help but think he hoped every woman in the place he took notice of would be taking even more notice of him.

We went back to our table and our drinks. There were two women seated at the table next to us who had come in during our dancing. One of the women said to the other, first you do it this way, then you flip around and do it that.

Son turned his head and asked her what she was drinking.

WE GIVE THE hotshot to the hired man and get him to work the chutes and the gates. Son heads and Ham comes to work the heels, and they each one teach me to heel too. Then one of the two of them coaches me on the paint on a couple of runs through the cloverleaf. We cool the horses and water them between runs. We get water for ourselves from our waterjugs and canteens. We cough and we spit and we curse the dust.

Son says, *Whoooo-ee!* calling out in the voice of the old man.

Ham tells us we're toughened as brahma bulls in this heat.

Some nights, we trailer the horses over to Ham's place, where he will put the arena lights on and play host to what he calls his authentico ranchero rodeo. Most of his vaqueros and a few of the outside hands and old punchers will gather for the contest. Some people come for but pure spectacle. Others show up just for the sake of showing up.

One night it's nothing but bronc riding. Ham picks his roughest stock, some of the animals meant to be broken and ridden for working or pleasure use, others chosen specifically for the sport of rodeo'ing. He saddles every horse with stock saddles meant for everyday riding. Rules at Ham's are that riders may ride with their free hand down, instead of held up and in position for any judge to see. They may hang on to whatever keeps them in the saddle—horn or horse, reins or mane, prayers or curse words, whatever it be—in a ride-as-ride-can kind of style. Folks from town string themselves along the perimeter of the arena, propped on rungs of fence, or wooden benches, or bales of hay. They fan themselves with their hats and hoot for each rider gotten atop a stock pony or a brush bronc, cheering every one to stay on for the clock.

Eight seconds can be a godamighty long time, says one old puncher. He stands beside me at the fence, and I nod and smile and avert my eyes from the man's nose, most of it gouged out, I suppose, by some hack surgeon's knife to rid it of the cancer. Or maybe the vet's knife, could be.

Lookee here, he says, I have the crooked limbs to attest to them seconds.

The old puncher reaches an arm toward me to take note of, and I'm made to look. He just as quick takes the arm away and uses it to shake a fist as a rider in a big-brimmed felt jumps out of the pen gate. The puncher hollers out to the rider, Hold hard to the apple, man! But the rider too soon hits the ground in a blowup of dust. The pickup men ride in fast and nab the riderless animal, the horse still folding and kicking, until one of the pickups catches the strap at the horse's flank to release it, the other man fogging the bronc back into the pen. The fallen rider rises slowly, uses his big-brimmed felt to brush the dust from his chaps, and he hobbles off, every bit of gesture done high-cowboy style.

Gives me the mulligrubs anymore just looking at them guys limping back to the gates, the old puncher says. Here we go for the next go, he says, elbowing me, and we watch as the horse is readied in the box, and the chutegate opens, and the bucking and the leaping and the yips and the shouts start up all over again.

THE SUN IS already in a rage overhead by the time the day's first water-run is done. I put dried beans in a pot to soak and fill the waterbowl up to full for the dog, stopping to check that the stove-burners are off before heading out into the pouring morning scorch. I walk along the walkway, the flowerbeds that border it now littered with the bones of picked-over gophers, and the feathers of oily old crowbirds, and the dried and coiled skins of lizards and snakes. One of the hunter cats scratches at a creeping thing yet crawling in the weeds. I scoot the cat away, and it scrambles off the porch and takes off out across the burnt grass of the hummock. I'm thinking it's some kind of semiprecious stone or globular mineral I've come upon, but when I stoop down I find the heart of a tiny critter left in the dirt, the muscle of it turned dark and hard as an agate. I pick it up and feel the leathered feel of it. I drop it into my pocket and go on. I think to give the tiny heart to the Padre, to make up for the things that haven't been said properly between us.

A couple of the other hunter cats lie panting in the shade out in the melon shed. The old dog's dusty old tail protrudes from beneath the watertruck. She scoots out from under when I get in and start the engine. I let it idle a minute, the old dog standing beside, her tongue aloll and panting in rhythm to piston and cylinder. I sit and take the familiar smell of the cabfront in, the solidly good thing about the watertruck that it emits. Was it my grandfather's lap I sat in? Or was that my father? Was it a truck, or a jeep kind of vehicle? I'm in a spell of talking to the Padre about what I feel right now. I'm wondering at the long ago, trying to explain to him the way days past will follow us place to place, even into the unlikely. I'm saying, how much of it can even be called validity, our so-called memories? Things and feelings I can't be sure of or remember well enough to tell, but I tell them anyway because they are known deeply and have shaped me, and so must truly be. And the Padre will take my hand and squeeze it, understanding me, agreeing.

Go on now, I say, clutching into reverse.

The old dog stops her panting with a clap of the jaw and she trudges off.

I head down the rutted road with dwarves of dust trailing behind the watertruck. By midday these forms will grow giant and spiraling, until they are watered over again come evening. I throttle down and head straight up onto the mesa, the watertruck chugging steadily up the steep. The road at the top follows a meander scar, filled these days with but slickrock and sediment, the flood of sideriver long disappeared from it. The road veers away from the old channel and comes to a lake-size hollow in the ground, a pan layered in mineral and what they call loess and varve. All about is nothing but dun-colored, wide-open country, a cloudless and contourless land, ravaged by sun, and with little shelter from the savage rays but for those few patches and folds of shadow, the occasional safety of dwelling and shade, and then certainly the cover and refuge of dark to come that follows day's end. Where is the romance and glory that you can find in your ordinary western story? It's more dry-pan and cinderplain here, more brimstone, more empty, more punishing—more everything and nothing here.

I turn off onto gravel section line and from here drive through what were once miles and miles of lush groves, now all of it gone to acre after acre of dying trees—lemons and oranges mostly, some exotics such as tangelos and mineolas and tangerines. The stands are long bared, changed from evergreen to failing, the leaves dropped from stalks and twigs, the once ever-emerald blades gone from glossy to dirt colored and brittle as crickets fallen to skirt the roots, bare spurs and branches reaching upward like outspread hands begging for rain. Some of the fruit on the dead trees are persistent, shrunken, leathern, and yet attached. There were old families here that owned these groves. Not so long ago, when people had money. When people had water. When people had important names.

The watertruck rumbles along. The gravel section line ends at the escarpment and winds in a dirt road down the steep incline back to the valley. The river lies thin and shimmery below, a silvery necklace chain. I clutch and gear down and roll the window up to keep the dust at bay, and at the bottom of the hill I turn onto the main road, putting me now at the opposite end of town, having arrived to it the roundabout way. A man, doused hat to boots with dust, stands wearied at the roadside with a thumb out, but I keep on. I glimpse him in the rearview mirror, see him taking the hat off and turning to look back at me, making me take a look at myself. And I wonder, as might not he, what it is about us that makes us look at all, or not look, makes us stop, or go on.

In little more time I'm come to the church. I pull into the lot and find a crosshatch of shade under an old mesquite, where a flock of top-knotted little quail are sent ascatter into the apache plume. The sun peals overhead. The rays burn through my clothes. Heat rises through my boot soles. I walk across the lot in the best hurry the hot allows and enter the reprieve of the sanctuary. There's an unoccupied coolness inside, an easy stir of fans above. A powdery light pours in through the windows. I take the smell of leather and varnish in, the mustiness of old wool coming from who knows where or why there might be wool around here, an odor of dying flowers, although there be none upon the altar today. I walk down the aisle again, toward the tall wooden cross on the wall behind the altar, past the rows of wooden pews and the padded knee benches, past Bibles and songbooks bracketed on the pew-backs. A song from the wedding day plays inside my head. The wrong song. I will admit to it again.

To be betrothed.

To be be-truthed.

I put my hand into my pocket, finger the hard tiny heart, and walk on, going out the sidedoor of the church and across the church lot to the church house. I knock on the door, hear the voice say to come in. I open the door as the Padre rises from the chair behind his desk. He's dressed in a long white garment, not of the Indian kind this time, but something other. The room smells of coffee and books and ladies' perfume. In the visitor's chair in front of the Padre's desk sits Pearl's daughter, Pearl, source of perfume. The Padre stands looking at me, with both hands on the desk. Daughter Pearl cranes her neck back and looks my way too. Her hair is pulled back with a wide red headband. She grips the arms of her chair with her elbows winged back to prop herself into position, and I'm seeing one of those ropy-necked sandhill cranes out in the fields, with their plumage outstretched during their courting and mating games. Who knows what shows on my face, thinking this. She gives me a tight half smile back that says she knows something that I've not been privileged to. Or she would like me to believe.

Had I known you were coming, the Padre says.

I shouldn't have come, I say.

Wait, he says.

Daughter Pearl keeps with her bird pose and the smile closed tight.

Really, no, I ought not to have . . .

Jesús appears behind me at the door.

Lo siento, Padre, he says.

No problema, Jesús.

During the clumsiness and exchange I can turn and slide by Jesús and go hurrying down the hallway, my heart galloping ahead, passing room after empty room — a playroom filled with children's things, a meeting room of folding chairs, a kitchen of sorts where elderly women are usually seen shuffling about in the steam. I go out the door of the church house and cross over the pebbly walkway, stepping head-on into a cluster of buckeyes that flutter about the nopal. I fan them away from my face in a panic and hurry into the church. Take a seat in a pew at the back. Gather myself. Try to breathe evenly. What am I to say? Find the words and harness them. Try. I sit in the vaulted shadow of arches and beams, see the Padre leaving Daughter Pearl in her seat, his needing to go after me to find me. Wait. Try to think of what I came to tell him. Will I be able to say it the way I had thought to? Then let him speak. Give him a chance to tell me our story. I sit with an aching growing between my shoulder blades, just holding myself upright suddenly turning to work. Why does he take his time? Just wait. Maybe apologizing to her for the interruption. He won't be long, he tells her. He will be here in a minute to put everything right again. We will try. He was nervous, he will tell me, confused. You are young, he will say, and didn't know what to say, didn't know how to guide me. He will explain what it was that happened to us that night, tell me what's happening now. He will explain it all. For wasn't there friendship between us? And most of all, love, love between us, wasn't there love? he will say. Who else but you, who other than me, is there really to talk to? I sit in the pew, my body sinking into itself with a heaviness of not belonging, a loneliness more deep than I could ever know the where or the why of. Yes, how those yesterdays can deform.

Light flickers in the doorway. But it's Jesús who comes in and starts down the aisle. When he sees me sitting here he nods and turns back to go out the way he came in. All right, Jesús will tell the Padre where he can find me. Give him time to get the message, give him time to come out. I sit in the silence. I sit in the falsity, sit in the wrong. I wait. I wait a long time. The light beaming in through the windows fades and dims. Birds shriek outside in the trees. I get up and walk down the aisle, open the door, go out. A lone cloud hangs in the sky.

A cloud.

I take it as a sign of some kind.

SHE HAD COME back down from the North with a new quarter horse. The animal she brought with her was intelligent and built to run, and Daughter Pearl had the whole time away been working him as she should. Now she watches her father back the heavy-rumped animal out of the horse trailer. He bridles the horse and leads him to the post and tethers him. Son fetches the saddle, made special and light for winning and with a rounder skirt to allow the horse more go, and he swings it up and sits it squarely atop the racing pad set between withers and loin, tightening the girthstrap after. He stands to admire the saddle for a time, the wide pommel meant to accommodate a woman's thighs, the horn thin to better fit a woman's grip. He rubs his hands over the new leather. He studies the ornately carved silver that decorates the breastplate. He tugs at the tie-downs to check the fit. He hollers into the tackroom to fetch the bell-boots, and Daughter Pearl comes out with them, and together they put the rubber protectors on.

The hired man saddles up and readies the paint. There you be, Missus, he says to me.

Ham flips the breaker switch in the cooling light of dusk, flooding the arena with spectacle light. Ride those animals about and warm them up before we start, he says. And take yer time of it, he says, as we got plenty of it. The evening's still giving yet.

The paint's warmed up, I say.

Daughter Pearl mounts the quarter horse and trots him out, her long braids flapping up and down on her back in a steady rhythm, the horse not breaking time when it lifts its tail to drop a load that leaves a trail of steaming lumps in the dust. Son tosses his rope to a fencepost and sends a row of grackles, their cries like whining bedsprings, rising outward in a spray over the arena, where the hired man works to roll the barrels into place. By the time the barrels are set, Daughter Pearl has ridden back with the quarter horse beginning to ribbon with sweat.

Let's see who be the first to go, Ham says.

He flips the coin and she let's me call it.

All right, querida, he says, you're on.

Daughter Pearl sidles the horse to the ready mark. She pats the crest and leans forward and mutters some words to steady the animal. She looks over to her father. Be on yer mark, he says. Git set. And he whips the flag down as Son thumbs the timer to a start.

The horse comes out in a flash and she runs him at all-out speed, entering the first pocket and setting the horse up to make the turn, her legs hugged about the ribcage, her hand on the pommel, horse and rider both tipped on edge and rounding the barrel easily. She sets up for the next barrel and runs it tight, going the opposite way this time, looking into the turn, then aiming ahead and onward for the third barrel, taking it with not a wobble or a touch, and at this she lets the head go, running the horse like all get-out for home.

She reins the horse to a stop and it rears in a great explosion of dust.

Fifteen seconds! Son says. He gives a whistle of approval.

That's what you got to beat, he says, looking at me.

I turn my head to spit the bile taste out of my mouth that has worked its way up from my stomach into the back of my throat. I look at the paint's withers and check to see if the quivering is in him or in me.

On your ready, Ham says. I stand the line, the paint champing at the bit and tossing his head. I nod at Ham and he gives the count and cuts the air in a whip of the flag. The paint leaps out and off into a run, and I lean forward over the shoulders and let the head go. I suck my gut in and round my back and lift up out of my body to make myself light so the horse is free to glide through the course and do what he was made to do, all the while feeling the great fury of machine beneath me—hooves pounding and mounting heat, the lungs blowing loud and coarse as storm wind, nostrils flaring, girth heaving—my bootheels awhump against the hide, my arms stretched in a reach out toward the top of the animal's head, fence and posts and trees blurred and streaming by, my heart pounding hard and fast as hooves in the same race. I rein out but not too wide, and we turn the money barrel tight and I let the head go again for the distance of the second, rounding that barrel easily too, and now on to the last, but no, the head goes high and the horse is too soon thinking about the out and not seeing the barrel we've come to—too close, felt it, my boot hitting metal, but keep going, keep on round the third, don't look back, stay the course, a straight line now, just run full out, and my heart pounding out the meter to go on run run go on run.

I rein back hard at the cross of the line. The paint blows and snorts and tosses his head, and I let him circle and prance for the cool-down.

I felt it wobble.

You done toppled it, Son says. He shakes his head, turns away.

Ham looks at the watch and adds the seconds on. But otherwise you run it in good time, he says. Next time.

Son stays quiet.

Daughter Pearl sits her quarter horse and smiles her smile.

THERE WAS A showdown come sundown. It started when Son told me that Ham told him there was a soon-to-start date for the building of the desalting plant. Son told me he aimed to apply for a job. Before it's too late, he said, and all the work is took up by others hungry for it. He told me about plans to lay fifty-something miles of bypass drain intended to carry the reject water away. It'll be a good long project and employment to count on for a spell of time, he said. I know I could run a backhoe easy as making pancakes. I said to him, You've never made a pancake in your life. He stood and looked at me. I looked back at him, trying to see what I used to see.

Things are about to change, he said. Ham has offered to buy the place to help us out, old adobe house and all, and I'm ready as hell to sell the entire getup, he said. I'm happy to have it go to Ham. He's family.

Family, I said.

I've got us in mind to go and buy a nice double-wide with the profit we can make, he said. We'll set up along the riverside in the middle of a good stand of cottonwood. Get us some rich pasture for the horses. Put some time into riding. I've a yearning to go into rodeo'ing professionally, he says. Start out as a sideline until I'm into the bigtime. I know I'd be good.

The wind whined down the chimney flue.

C'mon, we could have us a real nice place that isn't the work to care for it is here. I'll even put you in a garden if you should want me to do it.

A garden.

Once the rain comes. It always comes. It don't stay like this forever. Anyways, you got to think ahead. And my plan is to take life easy for a change, as it oughten to be taken. I'll get me days of nine-to-five and ride nights, honing my skills at the ranch rodeos, keeping myself in the ready for the big shows. Darlin', I'm hearing coins jingling in my pockets. I'm seeing bills to be padding my wallet fat again.

I said something about time enough off for the keeping of his important evening hours in town, and the ways he might find there to spend the money he sees coming in. He said something meant to hotshot me back. And then there were words — words stored up and ready to fire for the longest time, words spit out like bitter seeds, words flung out recklessly and said too many times by too many people in too many fights, words that I will not go on about here for the shame of the sameness of them.

Our voices hit higher decibels. One of us walked off to another room and then the other one did. Doors were slammed. The old dog put her tail between her legs and slinked out of the way, looking for out. I thought for the dog's sake and stopped holler-ing. Son went to the front door and opened the screen, and she scooted past and off into a trot. I sat and stared at the wall, as if there were something to be read in the wallpaper of it. My way of putting a halt to the quarrel was to quit talking at all. Son's way was to tell me he had best get on to the tending of his business in town.

I peeked in through the crack of the open door of the bathroom. Son stood in front of the bathroom mirror with a comb in his hand, trying to get his hair to go just right. He combed the hair all over to one side, as if to tame it, then went and combed it all back the other way. He took his time making the part, making the line of it precise. He raked all the hair forward and made the line again. He combed the fullest section of it over, and the little bit of it down and to the side. He kept trying to work the wave along his forehead out. He wet the teeth of the comb with water and ran the comb through the wave. He pressed the wave flat with his hand. He cursed and threw the comb into the sink. He cursed once more, picked the comb up, and started combing his hair this way and that all over again. I waited for him to come out. I waited for him to see me standing here and quiet, and for him to say he's changed his mind. When he came out, his hair was wet and pressed into place, his mouth contrary, and he didn't look at me at all. He went over to the rack and reached for his hat, and after all the fuss with his hair, he put the hat atop his head. Saying nothing and not glancing back, he opened the door and left.

WHO KNOWS WHY they did it? Ham says. I'm ashamed to be telling you about it. Yet it be your husband and therefore you got to be told. Asides, word gets around town soon enough, even with what few folks is left of it.

Why who did what?

I'm not sure whose idea of the two of them it was, or if they just up and done what they done on impulse or for entertainment's sake. Alls I can say is they's mighty lucky to be let off. If it were not for the decency of Mr. Gomez, those two would be locked up. But he didn't press any hard charges, Gomez didn't, not formally, anyways. Though both kids has been slapped with six months of public service. Some agreement made between Gomez and the sheriff, sheriff says.

What charges for what?

We was just looking, Ham says, doing a shrill, mocking voice of his daughter. We was just playing around, she says. Ham lowers his register and says, But while Son has got Gomez cornered and is going on about this and that and the other thing to make small talk, Daughter Pearl is meantime reaching over into the glass cabinet to pick herself out a fine diamond ring. You know that cabinet way in the back, back where there's that old-timer at—what's his name?—the Israelite that sits in the glass box with them oddball glasses atop his head, fixing watches and other itty-bitty jewelry items. The old-timer would not've seen much anyways, even if he'd a picked his head up with them jeweler goggles on. Daughter Pearl must've figured she was clear to help herself, as she reached in and took out the ring real quietly and nonchalantly like, as Gomez says she did. He says she comes over and gets to chitchatting with him and Son, who I guess were chewing some pretty good fat by now. After a bit, she and Son say their adióses and head out the door and get into the pickup truck, and the two of them damned bandits just drive right off.

With a diamond ring she's wearing? I say.

It didn't take Gomez too long to see the thing missing and to curse hisself for having had his back turned. He right away puts a call into the sheriff and the sheriff takes off looking for Son's pickup. It got spotted parked out at the levee. Finds the two of them there and, well…

Better don't tell me, I say.

Finds them parked, let's just say that, and the sheriff hauls them in. They says they was planning to take the ring back to Gomez anyways. They says they was just borrowering it for a day or two as so to get the feel of the fineness of it. They says they had ever intention of taking the thing back. Says it was a joke. A prank, they says. To show how easy it is in this town to go and take such a thing. Hell, I don't know what to say, he says.

You're saying what you need to say, I say. You're saying what I need to know.

Alls I know is the sheriff hauls their asses back to the shop. Gomez is by then in the window, untacking that poster of you and Son on your wedding day he had up to advertise with, in which you look mighty nice in that picture, by the way. Daughter Pearl takes the diamond ring off her finger and is weepy and apologetic like all get-out, sheriff says. Just wanted to wear it about town for a while is all, is what she says, and they would've brought it back soon enough. Gomez takes the rolled-up poster and hands it to Son and tells them to get on out, that he doesn't want to have to look at the neither one of them again. Sheriff says Gomez was so upset his mustache was twitching, like he was about to have some epilectric attack or something.

Gomez is a decent man, I say.

And them kids is awful dumb. Or something.

I look down and study the cover of dust on my boots.

The sheriff says he took each aside and said if ever one little thing goes wrong with either of them again, they will be busted without question. He must've thought one way to scare Daughter Pearl with the threat of this was to make her take a good hard look at what being locked up is like from the inside. So he's got her working days at the jail, in the kitchen, helping with the cooking and the cleaning up. She's been put on probation for a good three months.

What about Son?

He'll be picking trash up along the highway starting Monday, they say.

Now don't get all weepy, Ham says. Could have been worse. The sheriff is been more than fair. It could have easily gone to the courts.

I nod my head.

Didn't the sheriff have to haul you back home once? he says.

He did once.

He had eyes for yer mother, didn't he?

Probably.

This world.

This world, indeed.

EIGHT

THE QUECHAN

We meet in our coming and going out on the porch in the too-early morning, me telling Son there's a bowl of boiled eggs on the table and still-hot coffee in the pot, and Son telling me about not being away all day if my aim is to take the watertruck. He lets the screendoor go in a hard slap behind him, clipping my answer at the close. I turn into the settle of what's left of what's said, and head out and into the dim. The engine is still ticking when I climb up into the cabfront. The tires whine over the soaked and darkened road.

Hold it while ye may.

What a wholehearted wish it once was.

I head into the day's direction, turning off county roadway and onto highway, with the sun breaching over the blades of the peaks. The route cuts through a terrain pregnant with little desert animals that lie hidden underground, and all about the dormant seeds of plant species scatter and root and wait the drought out in secrecy. The landscape is whiskered with desertbroom and beargrass, panicgrass and rabbitbush, and other shrubs and scrubby thicket that might feed off the parched and mineraled earth. Gravelly washes wrinkle out from the shadows of the rocky bajada, aproning open onto sandy flats. Desertspoon and soaptree hatch the landscape to cast a laggardly shade. Nubbins of colored sunrise ebb into the pale above.

Yet happy pair.

Together we had washed the words away. Then even the tracings of etchings left were scoured to nothing by dust and by sun.

The watertruck rattles and coughs and pings in its work up to speed. After a time comes a rougher stretch of highway, and soon enough a sign posted alongside. I clutch and shift and ease the watertruck to a stop and open the door for a closer reading, seeing on the road below a foot-size, sausage-shaped, gaudy-colored lizard of rarity where I'm just about to put a foot. It looks up and flicks its tongue, and I close the door and touch the pedal when suddenly the tires are blipping over something other that feels living. I hit the brake and look into the side mirror to see a little desert hare splayed on the blacktop behind, and already the monster lizard is crawling over to feed off the thing.

My mouth waters up with that bile taste.

Not to be taken as any kind of sign. Just accident. No more than circumstance, chance, nothing as onerous as foretold. I give my eyes a squeeze shut and wonder at my will in the matter. I open the door again and this time I vomit.

YOU WERE SO big I couldn't breathe, my mother said. She said, I had to sit up in bed at night to sleep. I was breathless. Sleepless near the end. Could not get a wink with you. Ahh! she sighed, in the colossal way she always did. She sat on the bed and was rested back onto pillows bolstered against the headboard.

You were waxing gibbous, I said.

Don't get smart with me, she said.

Anyway, it was lunacy.

What lunacy?

You would have to be crazy to have a baby at your age.

I was young.

You were my age.

I had no idea about the pain.

How could you have until you have it?

You just wait.

I plan to.

She clucked her tongue. She sighed again.

My mother's closet was packed tightly as batting, the dresses and blouses and slacks crushed together airlessly. I put the flat of my hand into the body of the whole and spread to make an opening. I fingered about the neck of a wire and peeled a filmy pastel out and held the dress up. This one might do, I said.

Before you, I had your waist, she said.

I turned to the mirror and raised the dress to my chin and smoothed the below of it out, pivoting one side to the next, smelling the smell of her perfume as I regarded her colors held next to my skin. I saw her there in the mirror with me too, my mother, leaned against the hardwood of the headboard with a hard look on her face.

Who you going to this wedding with?

I'm going alone.

So go.

What do I do about shoes?

Just don't mess the dress up.

I turned to face her.

She turned to look out the window.

I plan on getting back into that one, one day, she said. She picked her tea up from the bedside table and took a drink. The ice tinkled in the glass. The glass left a ring.

THE PAINT STOOD tethered to the post, eyes more closed than open, as I worked the curry brush over the shoulders and withers, my hand made small as a child's on the animal's great muscled neck. He huffed out a coarse horsey breath that waffled the dusty air about us. The earth trembled beneath. I turned toward a commotion in the distance and saw Ham's rig coming our way. It twisted and bucked over the washboard road and slowed for a clutch of baby quail pacing behind a skittery mother bird. A hawk sighted in the fevery light above.

The rig rumbled past the paddock, hauling a great burst of dirt behind. It came to a halt in front of the stables, and the towed sandwhirl voluted up and ahead, gobbling the rig up entirely. You couldn't see a door opening but knew by the stiff creak of the hinge and the crunching of boot steps that someone was coming. Ham appeared out of the heap of mounting cloud that surrounded him.

I called his name out, as if the dust had deafened us.

Ham came over. He cleared his throat.

I pulled the bandanna up over my nose.

News, he said.

Some good would be good.

Wouldn't it, he said.

We stood in the midst of swirls and drifts until the kickup

subsided and all settled about us again. Ham went quiet as the dust did. I waited for what he had come to say. Then I got impatient.

I tugged the bandanna down off my face. What? I said.

He reset the hat on his head. Daughter Pearl, he said.

What about Daughter Pearl?

Going away, he said.

And to miss the competition? Hard to believe, this far in.

She's with child, he said.

I shoo'd a fly away.

Ham mopped his neck with a handkerchief.

She's going north to be with her mother, he said.

Gives me a real chance at the barrels now.

You had it anyway.

I made some comment about hoping the paint had not soured too much in the layoff and went on to brushing a hindquarter.

I noticed it you been laying off some, he said.

I've not been feeling myself lately. I'll be over it soon.

Ham put a hand to the bridge of the paint's nose and the horse tossed his head.

You might have to fight him a bit in the beginning, he said.

I looked out past burnt pasture and off into empty space, but no words would come to me. The paint lifted a leg and stamped it down. I went back to brushing him.

Am I smelling envy? he said.

I kept brushing, still trying for what to say.

You don't want to be wishing such a thing as a baby upon your-self, do you, now? Ham said. You at your age? Because from what there is to go by, I might speak a mind altogether different. You got ever bit of the world to go yet. Why add more cargo to it?

Ham's voice got softer. You savvy me, don't you?

I shrugged. I'm going in for a mane comb, I say.

He followed me into the tackroom. It was musty and on the dark side inside, as it's always been, but for the mullioned light that broke in through the little window. Everything was kept in the disorderly order the old man had left it in—the rows of saddles all atop their perches, the headstalls and breastcollars mounted on the walls, the reins and bits and cinches and spurs draped on hooks and on pegs. Tins of horse ointment and tobacco were left in their place on a shelf. The old man's old pipe sat cold in the dish atop the old metal desk. All of everything as it was, and all of everything so changed.

There was a great weight to the place.

There was the empty of missing filling the room up.

Ham startled me by coming over and putting his arms around me. I turned and put my head on his shoulder, feeling a pang of something inside where a life was beginning. I stood leaning into him, letting him embrace me, waiting for the ache of what was, and what wouldn't be, to go away.

Now, he said. Now, now, he said.

He patted me on the back. He felt as light and dusty as a raggedy-man made of hay and dressed to scare the field birds away. As if the air here had dried clear through to his marrow and lymph. There was the light boniness of his fingers on my back, the kindly patting becoming a stroking, and now the brittle hand traveling down my spine in a more deliberate and caressing way. I started to move away, but he held me against him, and I arched my back to look at his eyes, to see if I could find something there to know him by, but he brought his face close to mine, and I turned from him and felt his raw lips scrape the flesh of my cheek. I pulled out of his arms and was sorry for him and at the same time feeling guilty for whatever I might have done to tempt him.

Right then, Son should walk into the tackroom. He looked at us with an oddball smile, as if he knew something about the way the world works that I never did or would.

SPIKES OF LIGHT bolt up from the earth out in the distance. I turn toward the sight, heading off onto narrow dirt road and into the brush, the watertruck screeching at the bites and the scratches inflicted to the tank of it by the catclaw and mesquite. Soon enough in the clearing ahead the aluminum dwelling comes into view, ablaze in the sun's rays. A giant saguaro towers out of the roof of the add-on added on to the side of it. I pull the watertruck up and a dog slips out from beneath the place and barks meanly in greeting. A woman appears at the sidedoor and she hollers at the dog, and it stops the noise and trots off with an air of injury or insult, either one.

The woman stands in the glare of the sun holding the door open. She is big, despite her lack of height, dressed in a calico skirt and a man's undershirt that she has girted about the waist with a concha that parts her bellypads in a bottom-heavy way. She wears a ballcap with a logo on it, a necklace of fetishes, and hoops of silver bracelets that slide up and down both forearms and make dainty chimey sounds when she reaches out to me. She takes my hand, her fingers ringed and thick as dumplings, and I think of the gila monster, likely still feeding off the meat and bones of the little hare back on the road.

The woman is Quechan. You can see this in her broad face, rounded with weight, but still the high bones that abut the sockets remain prominent, her eyes dark and deep set. She nods me inside.

The place smells of bark, or what could be a kernel or a pod, or some kind of root. My eyes adjust to the dimmer light, and forms come forward, becoming knowable things. There's a card table and folding chairs in a kitchen area. A daybed appears in what would be a livingroom, with a large chair of the reclining type, and a television set set out in front of it. There's a paint-by-numbers painting of a smiling clown hung on the wall, another one to the side of it—the same clown but frowning. The Quechan woman looks at me, without a sign of much of anything showing on her face. She raises her arm slightly and cues me through a short hallway and into the next room. There's a long wooden table set up in the middle of it, a plastic bucket under the table, a rag in the plastic bucket. There's a single metal chair, a little wooden stand, a shelf with some bottles and jars above a sink. A naked bulb drops from a cord above.

Put the purse on the floor there, she says.

Now here, she says, and she opens a door.

Go in, she says. You make water first.

The bathroom is little bigger than a telephone booth. I lift the lid and sit on the toilet seat. My bladder is full, but nothing comes out. I rest my arms on the half sink in front of me and lay my head on my arms. The whole trailer quakes as the woman moves about it. I have a sudden urge to call out for my mother. My throat aches in thinking this. *Stop it. Don't go feeling sorry for yourself.* And I raise my head, having heard the words.

The urine starts. First a trickle, then an outpour.

The Quechan opens the door. Come, she says.

She leads me back into the room where the table is. She takes a muslin bundle from the pocket of her skirt and ties it around my neck. Her breath smells like smoked meat. She says to get up onto the table and I do, and she goes over to the window and opens the shade and lets the light pour in. She brings the single metal chair over and sits looking at me for a minute. I smile, who knows why. Nothing yet shows on her face. She asks me questions about flow, about weight, questions about the days, what I know and don't. She asks about family. She tells me what she has to do.

There's a hook on the wall for my clothes and a robe that looks taken from a hospital, but the name on it has faded. She has me put the robe on and says to get back up onto the table and to lie down on my back. She takes my shoes and places them just so under the little wooden table. The shoes look helpless and left alone, open mouthed and calling out.

The Quechan has her back to me. Her arms wing up and down and up and down in some task. She turns around and comes over and swabs my eyes with a cotton swatch that has something cool and soothing on it. She puts an unguent onto her fingers, rubbing it in circles on my forehead. There's an odor of food about it. She rubs more of the oily stuff on the top of my head too, in the place that was once a soft spot, rubbing in circles there until there's heat. It's warm in the room, but I'm beginning to tremble. When did I last shake this way? Some time ago up north it must have been, in the cold. I close my eyes and think of places away from here. I think of my father's house, the darkness of the walls of hewed logs and chinking, the coolness of the rooms, the smell of woodsmoke, the quiet of the woods outside, the quiet inside.

The woman puts her fingers into my ears and rotates them. A shivering of another kind runs throughout my body. She mutters words in another tongue — or is it the twisting of her fingers making the sounds? My mouth fills up with saliva. I swallow and swallow again and then cannot stop swallowing and have to keep swallowing. The veins in under my eyelids flash on and off like warnings. The padding of the woman's soles going out makes a worried sound.

She's gone from the room a long time. I lie on my back on the table staring at the wall, listening for movement through it. I wait. I think about getting up and going out to find her. I think about leaving. I stay where I am. Finally she comes back. She carries a tray of things that she puts on the little wooden stand. She opens a bundle of dishcloth, and inside there's a hot water bottle and rubber tubing and kitchen gloves, a bottle filled with clear liquid, square cuts of clean rags, scissors, twine—why twine?—a folded towel beneath the whole of everything. I close my eyes again and listen to her in her arranging, hearing the right placement of things, hearing she has done this before, hearing many times before. She murmurs words to herself, reminders maybe, or rules of some kind, or maybe she could be praying. Birds scratch and chatter in a skirmish atop the roof.

Put your knees up, she says. Now you hold still.

A fly lights on my forehead.

It's cold, what goes inside. Then it's like a blade.

Don't move.

I'm sorry.

Doing good.

Stop.

Not much more.

How much more?

Hold on.

Please.

We're just about over.

Okay.

Cramps?

Bad ones.

Good.

It hurts.

Keep your legs up.

Oh, God.

There. She pats my foot.

Can I get up now?

Lay here and keep still for a time.

How long?

I'll be back.

She goes out of the room and comes back with a musty old pillow that she puts under my head. She has a mole as big as a nipple on her neck. She asks if I need something to drink. She gives me a glass of water, and I take a sip of it and lean back. She tells me everything will be all right. She stands beside me for a while, gazing out the window but not seeming to be seeing anything, her eyes oily and dark within their coal hollows. She tells me the rain will soon be coming and reaches for the glass in my hand. The rain always comes, she says. We need not worry it along. She speaks now in a voice that is different from her tending-to-me voice. She speaks in a friendly, mercantile way. She says she sells cleaning products of top quality that you can only buy straight from the dealer. She says the name of the company, says she has been a distributor for them for a long time. Yes, I say, nodding my head, I've heard the name of the company before. I feel a twinge of pain from where the life would be. She smiles. She tells me in her selling-to-me voice that once I'm mended I will want to come back out for a visit and take a look at the stock in the pantry that she's got. We have soaps and detergents that will clean anything, she says. Dishes, tires, dogs, clothes, tools, plants, shoes, whatever you have or can think of, these soaps will clean. All of what we sell is one hundred percent guaranteed, she says. Or you get your money back. She gives me a wink to mean it.

Okay now, she says, speaking again to me in her tending-to-me voice. She pats my hand and turns and goes out.

My tailbone is sore from the hardness of the table. I worry about how long I can keep still as she has said to do. I start to feel a leaking going into the napkin she has put between my legs, but the leaking doesn't feel thick enough to be blood. I don't know. I wonder if I should hold in what's coming out. I want to call for her, but I won't. I close my eyes and wait, listening for her behind the closed door the whole while. She's a clatter of dishes, a humming, a smell of cooking beginning, something cabbagey and oniony, or a kind of root food, it might be.

My heart beats the meter of a clock out in me.

Let time be what it is.

Who was it said this? I wonder what it means? I think it must mean nothing. Or could be it means everything.

It's dark outside when I wake. Crickets call out in their high-pitched shrill, while night bloomers unwhorl their sepals and petals. I raise myself up and turn toward the window, see the haze of moon caught in faint halo, ringed as it is in sunbeam, held in the however long of earth pull we are fixed in.

PEARL HART KNEW a lot about breeding. She had a way of holding an ear when she got to talking about it, and it seemed to be a subject she talked about a lot. When she was giving breeding advice her eyes took on a look. She would wave her arms about in the air and up her decibel level. She would slap at the table and stomp at the ground. Her hair would go loose from its knot at the nape and unravel in a wild mane down her back. She would leave it that way, not bothering to knot it up again, not missing a beat of her testimony either.

Mares, she said. Trouble with mares is they stay with you and need a watchful eye and all-the-time care. And when you've got your mares, well, then you've got your foals, and soon enough your colts and your fillies too, she said. I once had a friend in mares who would park his car in the barn and sleep out there in the backseat, just to be at the ready for the foaling. Now that's a claim on your time, not to mention your spine and your backside, she said. And aside from the comfort of the sleep hours you don't get to keep, there are the sky-high vet bills that can drain your outfit bigtime. Mares are a huge claim on the pocketbook. That's why my part, you see, is in the siring.

Most definitely, she said.

Pearl Hart knew a lot about water as well. There was a day we would ride out to a part of her property so she could show me a giant groundwater irrigation pump. There's something that ought to impress, she said. We sat our horses and she spoke about drive shafts and vertically stacked centrifugal impellers as we watched a stories-high giraffelike metal apparatus bore deep into the aquifer below. Or was the thing drawing the water upward in through its throat casings? I don't know. I didn't ask, or rather, I couldn't. The groaning sound of the pumping machine's workings sent an unsettling vibration through the bones. The earth beneath seemed it was being shogged loose from us. Waves of nausea rippled through me. I felt a sweat breaking. I felt a sinking.

Rights, she said.

About what?

Rights, as in water rights.

Water rights? I swabbed my forehead with a shirt cuff.

That's right, she said. Surface water. Groundwater. Rights.

Only know the water stories Rose's Daddy told, I said.

Pearl took a little cigar out of the silver case she had in her pocket. She lit the little cigar and talked the smoke out of her mouth. Yes, he was quite the storyteller, she said. And wouldn't I know, she said. Wouldn't I, indeed. But he tended to leave a lot of parts of the stories out. I bet he didn't tell you much about selling his water to outsiders, did he? He probably didn't mention that many of us around here look upon this so-called way of doing business as being treasonous. Unless those of us at the district level, whose concern is for all of us—the greater good for the greater number, meaning in all fairness—unless we as a district should determine the price and the amount of water to be sold, otherwise that water ought to stay here, for the overall betterments of this place. Undermining our already failing local economy is a betrayal. I bet the old man didn't have too much to say about that, or the tension between us it created.

I don't know, I said, as far as the economy goes.

And that husband of yours follows suit, by not knowing any better. He doesn't seem to care enough about the land given to him for his keeping, or the water that goes along with it. He cares for little but the one thing. Well, that and rodeo'ing, so that makes two things, I guess.

The machine grunted and churned.

My cheek muscles puckered and watered my mouth.

Now don't go getting quieter on me. It's not as if I'm telling you something you don't already know. I mean to help, she said. Really, she said. I do.

Her smoke rolled out in ropes and coils in the air about us.

I should have done a better job of keeping that boy shoo'd away from that Pearl of mine, is all I can say. She fanned at the air to clear the smoke away and she looked at me. You've got to do something for yourself, she said.

Do what? I swallowed the bitter taste down.

Some advice. For starters, I've got a water lawyer for you to talk to. You can't sell the place when it's time to sell without the water rights to go with the house and the land property.

Son's been talking about it, I said. He wants out.

Then it's time you got your name put on things.

The giant pumping machine jabbed away and ruckled on. I breathed with my mouth open, trying to calm my stomach down.

C'mon, she said. You need to brisk up a bit.

Pearl knee'd her horse and led us out to the shade of a big cottonwood. We got out of our saddles and benched on a tumbled-up bale of hay. She carried a canteen of water and reached it my way.

I'm not feeling just right lately, I said. My head was dropped toward my knees.

Pearl put a hand on my back. You'll feel better in a few minutes.

Her hand felt good there. I held still, not wanting her to pull it away, but after a minute I lifted my head and took a long drink of the sulfury-tasting water.

Lean back, Sweetie, she said.

I rested my head against a pillow of hay.

How about I tell you my buffalo story, she said. Or have I told it to you already? she said.

I would've remembered a buffalo story.

She lit another cigarillo. I looked at the dry bale we sat on, thinking how quickly everything could go up in flame. She waved the little cigar about and talked on as I listened and kept an eye on the smoldering glow.

So we were out on roundup for a couple of weeks up near Wickenburg way, sometime back. One of the ranchers up there had a mind to expand his enterprise, so he added a small herd of bison to his capital of cattle. We rode out to the rincon he had parceled the bison on, and where these great animals could roam, you know, as buffaloes are known to do, and made our camp among them. The rancher that invited us had a handsome outfit. There was a chuckwagon and a chef assigned to it that had cooked for one of our past American presidents—he was good, I tell you, that chef was. And there were a lot of good men riding good horses on that particular outing, men you could talk to and drink with and sport with, if you know what I mean. Pearl gave me a wink and a nudge of an elbow. That was one dandy roundup, she said. She sighed and smiled and took a puff on the cigar.

Where was Ham?

He was along, of course. He wouldn't miss a good time.

He didn't mind?

Mind what? My style? My men friends? You are young, she said. She laughed and shook her head.

I'm feeling better now, I said.

She looked at me a minute, seeming to be judging my condition for herself, then she went on.

This one night, she said, I had to get out of my tent to relieve myself. So I crawled out and put my boots on—I was buck naked otherwise and did not want to linger any out in the cold, cold as desert nights can be, you know—and I went out under the most magnificent cover of stars there ever was to be seen, and found a good-size boulder nearby to squat behind for a bit of privacy and to admire the sky by—and my! what stars there be there. So I hunker down and get comfortable and let the sight above fill me with delight and wonder, and I begin to let the pee go when suddenly the boulder seems to be moving. And now the entire boulder is absolutely moving, and it's grunting with indignity as well. Lord, did I ever buck up and trot off quick-like. She laughed and slapped at her thigh.

Feels good to laugh, she said. You ought to try it more often.

I gave her the smile she asked for. I lay back listening and she would go on.

There would not be much time for visits with her, this most remarkable woman, this Pearl Hart. She was too soon gone back north, and with her daughter with child to follow. And she would never come to say good-bye. I don't know why. Though maybe, in all honesty, I might have the tendency to do the same. But in the time we did have, there were more good stories, and she had things to say that she would leave me with. She spoke as though she knew what was. She spoke as though she knew who she was—seemed to me she must have, in the very act of naming herself, in the very deciding from the beginning who she would be.

What do you want? she asked me once.

This was early on in my married time with Son, and hardly knowing her. No one had asked such a forthright question of me before, unless I was knocking on a door or reaching for something. I stood there before her, a bit stupefied and likely flushed.

After that I thought about Pearl's question a lot. I'd be standing at the kitchen sink, tearing at onions, or mixing a bowl of kibble for the old man's old dog, or riding alongside Son, watering the roads with the watertruck. Whatever I was doing, I would all the time be wondering about the very thing I might be wanting.

When I saw Pearl next, I told her I had an answer. She smiled her smile. What perfect teeth she had. I wanted such perfect teeth. Maybe that's what I should have said. It would have been a simpler wish altogether.

But I told her about what I'd been thinking. I told her what it was I wanted.

What's holding you back then, Sweetie?

I hitched a shoulder. It would scare me to death, I said.

I bet it would scare you to life, she said.

SON TAKES THE frozen dinners out of the freezer and puts them into the oven and sets the timer. When the bell goes off I get up from the sofa and go into the kitchen and see him putting forks and plates and glasses of milk out on the table. He has set us up in the breakfast nook in the kitchen, and we sit there in the quiet, gazing out to the lemon grove as the sun begins to gild it into olden ruins. The steam from the food rises in little bodies before our faces. I feel again that big clot of something that spilled out of me, slippery as a fish coming out it was. It splashed into the water and sank into the neck of the bowl. And then more blood poured out. I sat waiting for the bleeding to slow, my legs trembling uncontrollably, up and down and up and down — more spasmy, really. I put my hands on my knees to stay them. Then I put the pad between my legs and went to lie on the sofa in the parlor until Son called me into the kitchen.

You're back to not eating all the food on your plate, Son says.

I feel kind of achy today. Crampy, I say.

Seems like every day it's that time of the month, he says.

I need to lie down.

You just got up.

I leave my full plate at the table and go into the bedroom and turn the ceiling fan to high speed. Loose papers skitter off the chest of drawers. A few clothes take on lives of their own. Everything about looks thickly edged, as if another cast were added to the three-dimensional. Things are become oddly textured and are too spongey or too dense, either one. The spring of the mattress has turned hard as wood, harder, like concrete. I toss the sheets off, brittle as paper wrapping, and lie with the fan blowing over me, feeling the rigid and the soft of things at the same time. Thinking of the milk soup my mother fixed when I was a child and sick. There was a crust of sugar on the top of it. I feel the spoon going into the soup now, but the liquid has turned gravelly and it scratches the metal that's going in. My mouth is so awfully dry. What age am I? There is a taste of the wood of the headboard where I left the baby-teeth marks. There is the relief of the ache, the need of the hardness then. My grandmother shaking her head. Go to sleep, she said. I'm falling off the horse again and there's no end to the falling — how lovely it is, the soft floating along of falling along. I'm going, I'm gone. I hit the ground. I spit dirt spit. Come on, spit it out. Gum comes out. A wad of chewed gum falls from my mouth and goes into my mother's hand. I back the truck and turn the wheel before going forward, but the turn is too sharp and the hill too steep and I have to back up and struggle with the wheel again and inch forward, but still it's no good, and just look at all the people out of their cars and waiting for me ahead, and the cars behind so close I can't back up enough, and you need to turn the wheel as far as you can, but I'm trapped on a hillside too steep to climb.

A door slams.

Time moves away in a vapor. And time comes back in on itself. It carries the sound of nobody here.

There are voices of people from a faraway and long-ago place. Someone's calling my name out. A woman's voice, I know it, but who? I open my eyes and see a dark thing big as a small being hurtling at me. I put my arms out to cover my face. I lift myself up in the bed, panting. My heart is risen out of my chest and moved up to pound inside my head. I look to see the nothing there. There. See. Nothing. Nothing but the pain. Like something inside me on fire. Worse. I lie back and turn to my side and bring my knees to my chest. I turn the other way. I roll onto my stomach. The pain, it won't dull, it won't change, no matter how I shape myself. Make it stop. I go back to my back and keep still as I can, thinking not moving might make it go away, but no, the pain is everywhere inside. I call Son's name out, but he's already next to me. I don't know since when. I've got to get up, I say. Does he hear me? Help me get help. Are my words coming out? You need to carry me. He must hear me. He's picking me up, but the hot knives — no, no, put me down. Can't walk. Oh, please, somehow.

Somehow we're moving through the dark, silently, starlessly. Wheels turning. No use wondering. Only care about no more pain. I call out for my mother. The man behind the counter speaks.

Yes? he says.

Doesn't he remember? He closes the book and puts the guitar

down. He leads us through an empty corridor. Our Centro Médico. What's left of a hospital. No, it never was. The man takes us into a room and puts a light on.

What can I do? he says.

He speaks as if he doesn't know me. I could not be making sense. My voice keeps breaking. My words crack, falling away into nothing.

We need a doctor, Son says. Why does he speak this loud?

The man says there is no one but him and he will have to do. Lie down, he says. But I can't without pain. They help get me onto the cot, and the man is shushing me, shushing me. He has Son unfasten my pants and the man lifts my shirt up. He puts his hand on the flesh as if feeling for warmth. He pushes on my belly and quick releases, and I jump at the touch and cry out. He shakes his head. He takes my temperature. You're inflamed inside. I know, I say. I could have said. He says he can give me a shot. He says we need to drive to an actual hospital. Actual? That's two hours west, Son says. I won't go, I say. Whatever, the man says. It's your pelvic cavity, he says. He turns from me in judgment. He furrows his brow. He makes notes on the clipboard, the laborious press of his pen turning a roaring scolding.

I'm sorry, I say. The words settle onto the tongue like a tasteless wafer.

The man holds a vial up to the light and sticks a needle into the rubber stopper. He draws from a syringe, taps the bubbles out, pivots me to a side. This will hurt, he says. He thrusts the needle into my hip. Go home, he says. Take these. Take all of them until they're all gone. He hands the bottle of pills to Son. The two of them standing looking down at me, each to a side of the cot.

That scar should've healed better, the man says.

Son touches the place on his forehead.

I look at the cracks in the ceiling.

I wait for something more to be said.

YESSIRREE-BOB, Rose's Daddy had said.

He was leaned back in the old oak swivel with his boots atop his desk.

The tribes were tough minded in these parts, he said. Indeed, they were known for their warrior abilities and their know-how as far as how to live amid this dryland habitat. They were not hunter-gatherers, he said. In the stead of, as with most, they tended their home country as agrarians. And they surely had no thoughts of such talk as property or water rights. For the earth did not belong to the people who so dwelt upon it. Rather the people belonged to the earth. They thereby did believe.

Rose's Daddy knocked the burnt ash from the pipe bowl.

Thus, when Governor Kearny spoke atop his mount to the surrounding chiefs, they would not have understood the underlying meaning of his discourse. Kearny stuck close to the words most invaders have used since ancient times, as he told the tribes he had come as a liberator, not a conqueror. Yet the loftiness of these liberators would be bowed down soon enough, and their haughtiness made low.

Rose's Daddy blew a quick shot of air out the pipe stem.

All were humbled, he said. For a torrent of hot was soon thrust upon our borderlands, and hell did so enlarge itself then, and in this very place. The newcomers were the first to succumb. Many of them backtracked eastwardly. Some fled westward toward the coast, seeking refuge, hoping to escape the penal fire that had come down upon them. The going was rough, and there was no water to be found for days on end in what should have been a fortnight's journey. But wheels stuck in the deep sand of the dunes along the way. And people became desiccated and hungerbitten. Mules and oxen died. Horses, babies, men, so many of them died.

He paused to fill his pipe bowl with a wad of full aroma.

And those that stayed here, he said, well, very few survived. Mainly the Indians, they who had learned to manage in this wasteland long beforehand. These people did what they did. They branded figures into their skin and covered themselves over with pigment. They buried what melons there were left to them beneath the ground. They punched holes into the burnt soil with sticks, and they filled the holes with seeds as was their way. All this, despite the heat. They embraced the boulders for shelter and lived within the shaded clefts of the earth. And they waited the fiery deluge out. They had no place they knew or wanted to go. Stay and wait, it was said the Indians said. And so be it, they did.

The old man rustled about in his pocket for matches. He put the fire to the bowl and the stem to his mouth. He shook the flame out.

Of course, then one day the rain did come. And the waters fell upon the fields. And the rivers swelled again to flowing. And the seeds greened from up out of the earth. And the fruit of the earth did so become excellent again, and there were bees and goats and honey and butter, and the land was once more comely to dwell upon. There were those who would make it to see these days, and some were left to speak of the past, and so too, of what remained.

Rose's Daddy studied the swirl of smoke about his head.

And among them it was said, Whoso believes that man is greater than his maker?

Now what do you kids say?

I REACH FOR the glass of water at the bedside table and swallow the iron-tasting stuff down with one of the horse-size pills the man at the clinic gave me. The dry tablet scratches at my dry throat. The fever is past, but I take the pill as he said to do, and now to take one every day until all of them are taken.

How many days have I missed?

It's Friday already, Son says. He stands at the end of the bed. You need to get yourself set up so you can eat something. Get your clothes on and come out to the kitchen. There's a pot a coffee on the stove. You got some mail in a pile for going through. A postcard from your mother from some place or other. A letter from a school.

Maybe tea, I say.

I'll put you some water on, he says. He goes to the window and draws the curtains open. Light pours in and washes over everything, and in that moment all is turned pure and good again. I feel myself brought into being. I get out of the bed, moving as if I'm just learning how to do it, thinking there might again be pain with as much as a turn or a shift, but no, no pain anymore, just that careful way of walking left in me. Just an empty place inside where the fire burned. A pure empty place where all will grow new and good again.

I go into the bathroom and turn the faucet on and the water sputters its rusty color out into the sink. I cup it into my hands and splash it over my face. I look into the mirror, feeling today as the first day of any. I fill the water glass and drink the water down, gulping it, breathlessly, filling myself up. Now breathing. I brush my hair and put my clothes on and go into the kitchen.

Son has put cups and plates on the table in the breakfast nook. I slide in and sit waiting. He puts a sugar bowl out, and knives and spoons, and he puts a tea bag into my cup and pours hot water in with it. He brings a plate of buttered toast and asks me about jam, and I shake my head. He pours a cup of coffee for himself and sits down across from me.

This is you, I say. I push the envelope his way. Did you forget to pay your posse dues?

I paid my posse dues.

He takes the envelope and works it apart with a thumb. He takes the folded paper out and opens it. He moves his lips as he reads. To hell with them, he says. Bunch a old losers anyway. He wads the letter and tosses it across the kitchen to the wastebasket and misses. He picks his coffee cup up and looks out the window. I go back to the pile of mail, sort through the bills, the final notices. Then I come to the letter from the school. The letter I had waited for for a long time, until I had finally not cared anymore, or so I thought.

Aren't you going to open it? Son says.

Later, I say.

Later, he says. And he gets up from the table.

After he leaves I sit in the pale quiet of morning light. Arrange my cup of tea to the one side of me, put it just so. Move my plate of toast more to the left. Fold my paper napkin into a perfect square and tuck it under the lip of the plate. Everything now has its order and place and I must get it all right. My spoon here, and here my knife. When everything is arrayed out before me correctly, I sit and study it, feeling the pleasure in the placement of things. Now to keep everything this way, the world this way, and there won't be any need to worry. I take a sip of tea, tasting the iron in it past the pekoe. I add more sugar to the cup, stirring clockwise, then set the spoon in its proper spot again. I don't eat the toast, but know it for its place on the table and am pleased for that alone.

It is all a starting-over.

THE PADRE ANSWERS the call on the first ring.

It's me, I say.

You, he says.

I went to the Quechan woman. I'm calling to thank you.

Life is ever fruitful, you know.

I suppose, I say, hearing his words as no more than glossy talk now.

This dream, he says. I've been wanting to tell it to you. And look, you called me so I could. I knew you would call. How did I know you would? Because I made you. You got the message. It's this power I have, this ability to forecast things, to will things. Believe me. It's something one has to practice at, and for a while, I was lapsed. But I have it again. I have it back. You don't believe me, do you?

What kind of dream?

I see you in it now, ever so clearly, standing beneath an immense archway looking outward. You were beautiful, and ready to head into some beautiful unknown. I can still feel it, the dream. I can't get it out of me, this vision of you.

The pen goes in circles and swirls and curlicues over the paper, as though with an intent of its own. My hand follows along as the Padre speaks. I listen to the way his voice deepens on certain words and rises on others, the way he will pause before going on in order to add launch to the next thought, the way he will soften to add tenderness or delicacy. I hear how the measure and pitch of his voice would work on the ears of listeners sitting on Sunday benches, their chins at a tilt to look up at him. Are they told what they already know? Or do they wait for some new truth to be spoken?

Maybe the me you dreamed in the dream wasn't me.

You are more than you think you are.

Tap, tap, tap of the pen. I straighten my back. So much has changed lately, I say.

Katherine. It's you, you have changed, he says. You have changed remarkably in the short time of our knowing. I'm delighted for you. Truly.

I may go back to school and make something of myself.

You are without bound.

I could use the rigor of it. The ritual and routine of it. A bell in the morning. Long hours alone. Books at night to look forward to.

Do what will give you to yourself.

The labored sigh of my mother escapes me.

All you need do is go find your story. Tell it. Then live it.

The scribbles turn to deliberate shapes of things.

Just a place where there are stars to see at night would be a fine start, I say.

They're out there, he says. So go on. Go forward. Go find your place. Let the stars pour their spiritual rays out upon you. Lean your head back and drink them in. Enjoy the great spectacle that the universe bestows.

Yes, so you've said this.

The ink comes out on the paper in spirals.

I speak to you from the heart. As I do the entire congregation. I tell you, most importantly, keep with your God and you will hear your God. Listen for God's voice in the sweet melody of the birds, in the grand call of the morning, in the beating of your heart. Feel His divine love and His wisdom in the warmth and the light of the sun.

I click the pen closed.

See the soul as well in the treasures mankind leaves behind. Go to your Moses, or Plato, or Homer.

Yes, go. I should go.

Go to your Beethoven, your Bach, your Brahms.

Go to your... Katherine?

Hello?

THE INSIDES WENT up in an immense surge of light and rushing of air, as if some proclamation had come in a sudden from above. Jesús went running. People tried. But no one was God. And everything inside was dry as tinder.

Church cat, the sheriff said. He had a look of wanting to settle people down with a why for it.

People stood by, nodding their heads, their faces radiant in the light, arms hanging at their sides, watching the groaning timber glowing hot as coal and blackening as the frame went caving in.

Just imagine how it happened, someone said.

I did. I could hear the totter of a saucer, see a spill become spark, a spark changed to flame. I could see the flame the way it flittered about for a minute — just a little bird, a sprightly hop before it shot up in a hot burst, turning a fit of bright shifting bodies of light. I could see the whole of the thing laddering heavenward, pillars of heat rising in the air of the in-between, bending and stretching all forms in the sanctuary, distorting the very emptiness of space above. There would have been a whiffling, or buffeting, like sheeting being opened and shaken, or sails caught in the wind, or a sound of coarse breath, a muffled calling-out, a wimpering in the seaming and knotting. The fire crackled and darted up the night-darkened panes. The ruby-colored runner atop the altar trembled before the cloth swelled to combust. The blaze rose in the sacristy and nave, with beams and pews roaring in glorious ascension, with the cross going up in a great serpent of flame. Bindings and pages of Bibles and hymnals reddened and bloated. Prayers and songs filagree'd upwardly, turning a float of cinder and drift of charred motes in the smoldering, all the words ceased now to nothing but remembering.

Amen, someone said.

THE SHERIFF DRIVES his sheriff car out to the house to deliver the news himself.

Where's that husband a yours? he says.

It's not my day to babysit him.

No need to be a wise guy, he says. How come you're never very nice to me? You still upset about the time your mother called me up to go and get you and drag your heinie on home?

Yes.

You sure like carrying your grudges, don't you?

I don't like remembering being locked up inside the back of that car of yours. I turn away from the slab of shade the sheriff has parked in. As if I were a criminal or something, I say. Just looking at the car with that metal grating between the seats, like

I'd been put into a cage, makes me want to grate my teeth — and all I did was move out of my mother's house and get a place for myself and bothering no...

Ah, the Sam Hill anyway. That was a time ago. You were balled up and confused. You're a grown-up now.

What did you come out here for? I say.

Pass a message on to that husband you got. Tell him we're letting him off highway cleanup duty early, he says. We consider he's paid his dues by now.

The posse doesn't think so. They don't want him anymore.

How about you? he says. You want him anymore?

The sheriff takes his hat off, the sun highlighting the pockmarks in his face.

I hear you been through it a bit, he says. I hope you're fine by now. Really I do.

I look out to the emptiness of the landscape, the dusty earth about us aquiver with cicadas and their kin.

THE LIGHT IS something from a time before. It has in it the fullness of what already was, as well as all of what could possibly be hoped for ahead. It's a starchy light, or call it chalky colored, as I can't think of how better to describe it. What it is, is the same veiled light that had come pouring in through the window to where we lay in the bed that morning back in our beginning. Was it Son that got up and drew the curtains full open? Because I can't remember here what I had seen looking out the window, only that the glass was hazed by the drift of alkali, or of quartz, or some mix of these minerals that so softened the lens on us. But I do remember we were in a motel room, one of those places with the same dollar-something name to it. We were just finished making love another time, and the night we had been through was still in us, and the morning was all over us in the bed.

Then the light is changing with no more of the past to be captured, and Son is talking to me about here and the everyday, putting us back to where we are again and the people we are since made into.

We ought to think about getting us another dog, he says.

The old man's old dog stops panting and draws her tongue in.

We don't need another dog, I say. We have a dog.

The old dog goes back to panting.

It would do us some good. We need something new.

Not a dog, I say.

The dog gets up and shakes, follows me toward the front door.

Where you off to? Son says.

To the foothills.

The foothills?

To buy soap from a Quechan woman.

A Quechan woman?

A Quechan.

Soap? he says.

Soap, I say.

NINE

AT THE TOUCH OF A HAT

He did not come by to say good-bye. His leaving came from Pearl to Ham and Ham to Son and Son to me. Ham told Son that Pearl had worked it out for the Padre to take the chapel up north in the mountains, as the village minister there had more than a serviceful since the inflow of desert folk. It was told the Padre spoke to what was left here of his congregation in a makeshift meeting house put up in the plaza—a rented tent much like the one Son and I celebrated our matrimonial day in on the eve of the vows. People said the Padre talked about listening inwardly and advised letting the voice inside you be your guide. They said he closed his eyes and raised his arms, palms turned heavenward, his fingers quivering. Said he opened his eyes back up, stuffed his hands into his pockets, and jingled loose change a minute before he gave a nod of the head and said he was leaving. So Son said Ham said people said the Padre said.

Someone said, There's not much of a flock for him to care for in these parts anymore anyways. And there be not enough believers left to believe it worth rebuilding a burnt-down church for too few to come and sit and repent in it. Another said, I heard the church up north is of a different order of faith altogether from the one we had us here — full of a bunch a cricket stompers up there, I hear tell. To this it was added, The Padre always claimed he could preach in any mission or temple or mosque or house a God there be. Yes, so another agreed, the Padre did so profess to speak universally. And atop a that he has the sense to find an otherwheres to go, knowing well enough he has to keep his belly and his billfold full, said yet another.

The Padre will do just fine. He has a way with people. This, it was said, just about everybody said.

The Padre had his way with me. This I've said to no one.

Or was it me having my way with the Padre?

There are ways of telling the story. I would say it all started with his words — the most earnest words I'd heard spoken about love, though what had I ever listened to of such consequence but those lyrics figured and trilled in some overdone song played over the radio? The Padre's voice, and the melody of his homily, were tender as a caress, is what I would tell him. I sat there in the pew looking up at you and saw you looking right into me. I felt myself lifted upward — levitated, I was, afloat over every other breathing lonely soul in the parish. I was changed that day, I would tell him. I saw you and all the world and me in it differently. I saw you in me and me in me, and I was awake again because of what I was seeing.

Call it atonement, the Padre would say. At one-ment.

He would begin our story with the handshake. After the sermon he stood near the front doors, in the light of the archway, next to his wife. Like royalty they were, smiling and greeting the church people, those herded together in the cool of the sanctuary, then to be singlefiled and blessed one by one and sent outside into the rippling heat that awaited each, every figure dissolving into the haze of the dust. I saw you in line with the others and coming near me, the Padre said, and I thought surely the look on my face would give me away. And we touched and it was like a great bolt of electricity moving through my body, he said. He apologized for the cliché. I said, I don't know why you apologize, and he touched my arm and smiled at this, not seeming to mind how young I was and not nearly as worldly as he, with me being yet in my teen years and too soon married and in need of someone.

The Padre insisted on making a spectacle of the communion, as I had never been through the ceremony before. After the psalms and the canticles, the readings of the creed and the evensong, I walked down the aisle to receive the sacrament, to repeat an oath of holding in common, to take a vow of opening one to the other, to promise the promise of courage of heart. I walked down the aisle, just as I had done on my wedding day, past all those people I mostly ought to have known by now, sitting too upright in the pews, dabbing kerchiefs at their necks and brows, hats and fans beating like wings—this not too long before most would desert church and town for kinder ground, leaving but dusty imprints of themselves in the church seats. I wore a white dress for this second promenade of mine, though a short one as to the mode of the day, and I had my hair done up with strawflowers pinned into the twist of it. There were vases of buckthorn and blue dicks and scarlet sage placed upon the altar. A woman played the organ and soprano'd a melody that was ancient and mysterious and carried a sound that resounded throughout the body. Shafts of ivory light shone in through the windows, the unearthliness of it making my eyes watery and my chin quivery. Chiseled figures were as witnesses suspended above.

I didn't know, was not practiced in, the ways to properly conduct myself to receive the rite. I didn't believe, really, not in the fable of it, nor did I see the importance of the ritual, and so I acted that day as if I were playing a part in a play, behaving in a way I thought might be expected. I surely didn't believe I was being saved by some holy man holed up in the sky. It was instead the man standing ahead of me that had lifted me up out of myself and was carrying me away. There he stood before the altar, waiting, and I came to him trembling and willing to believe, willing to believe in him, in us, with all of everything welling up inside me.

This be His body.
This be His blood.

The Padre said the blessing, offering me the bread and the wine.

There were days and weeks after when I day and night pictured different scenes between us. There were hours of stealing time away to talk on the telephone, and times I went into town in the watertruck to visit him afternoons. I won't soon forget some of the looks the older church ladies gave me on my way in to see him, the way they would glance over with their heads lowered, slowly blinking their old and wrinkled eyelids, scaly reptilians they seemed. Many of them had been friends of Rose's, but I didn't give notice to them, didn't say hello, didn't see the need to give reasons as to the whys of my frequent sightings with the Padre. I was thinking only about how this man was something happening to me, bodily and otherwise.

But why my need to sit here and tell it?
You might think it made up, or worse, just another old story.
But you try trying to admit to your life.

A SHADOW PASSED by the open window. I went to the door to see Ham standing outside. He had come by to explain, he said. That incident in the tackroom. He said he was sorry, deeply sorry, deeply, deeply, he said. He lowered his head and started acting weepy. It would never happen again. Please, he said. He reached his hand out to me, but I didn't take it.

You're like a daughter, he said.

A daughter, I said. I looked into his old stone-colored eyes.

What I saw was that Ham was the only person left to me that came anywhere near to trustworthy. There was nothing to lose by giving him the favor of any doubt.

THERE WAS AND is nothing to do but keep on. So keep on we do, those of us left in the calamity of the heat and the dust. We carry on with our routines, bolsoned all the while within stubborn currents of air, caught in prevailing westerlies. We haven't the effort or the time to struggle with pity or beseeching, with sentiment or presentiment, with delicacy or the lack of it. We have only to go forward and not get trapped in the stall of looking back. We move ahead in necessity. Call it will. Call it fright. Call it any of these things.

WE LEAD THE horses out of the stalls and halter them to the post, saddling in the ocherous haze of day's end. The wind nerves the dust up about us in dervishes, stirring the odor of hay and dung and clay. We switch the power on as a hard dark falls, and walk the animals out of the paddock and into the arena, where little bats swoop about in the light of the floods. Cicadas quit their ruckus of tambourines and maracas. Crickets begin a scratchy calling song.

We're an edgy, jumpy bunch only a week away from rodeo day. What is it but the chance of big money and the little spot of glory that comes with the win that spurs us? A reason to keep moving, is what I will say. Braggin' rights, is what Ham will claim, and a lot more than pocket change to have at that. All I know is it'll be mucho dinero and onward ho from this, come the win, is the one thing Son will say, over and again.

Come Rodeo Sunday there will be cowboys and announcers and judges, all drawn to town for the spectacle. There will be pickup men and timers, veterinarians and entertainers, chute bosses, flank men, prodders, and hollerers. There will be tie-down roping and team roping, steer wrestling and barrel racing, saddlebronc riding, bareback, and bull. There will be a day of old ranch sport after the big events are paid, games of branding and penning and doctoring, a show of wild-cow milking and stunt riding and fancy roping to boot. There will be men calling the times and the names out, gold and silver buckles won big enough to shovel with, a rodeo queen to wave a white-gloved hand in the parade. There will be cameras perched on tripods, fenceposts, beefy shoulders. History will be posted for keeping. Win sheets and photos will be framed and displayed.

I look at Son in his reverie, wishing to see what he sees.

I reset my eyes and look again and see him through a choke of road dust, bent over, picking beer cans and candy wrappers out of the pricklypear and knapweed that litter the roadside, a scrim of foothills behind him and aquiver in the distance, a metal-colored sun above. See him in that bright orange jumpsuit they made him wear during his month of penance, the short pant legs come out of the tuck of his boot tops, dust spuming from his bootheels as he scuffs along. The sheriff driving slowly by in his sheriff's car to check on the guilty on occasion, the sun lighting up like a white cross on the hoodtop, the yellow light flashing slowly like a sorry warning. Son keeping his back turned away from the road all the while, away from the eyes of passersby, those who would put a foot to the brake and idle forward for the show throughout the day. I pulled the watertruck up behind but never called Son's name out, just watched him moving laggardly down the road in a scorch of coarse light, prodding at the road trash with a poke stick, his hat brim pulled low over his forehead, a filled litterbag dragging behind like a dead animal of some kind. It's a picture in me that would forever change him. If something by now hadn't already finished it.

I never claimed to be Christian. But, then, isn't it always more complicated than simply forgiving?

SON AND HAM will pay the entry fee as a team. They need not get off a horse to win at their category of roping, and for this some people call the sport an old man's sport, but those others who know shrug such comments off. For it takes skill, each on a horse and handling a rope for both, and too the aptitude for the marriage of the two. Son is good at the setup and gets his toss right nearly every one. Ham is precise with the lasso after all his years of mastery, and he still has the reflexes and excels as well in the timing. And there are rules to hold to, rules that define the craft, rules as to barrier and cross fire, rules as to advantage point, heeler breaks, and head catch.

There is nothing to do but get back to the practice.

They give me the job of the stopwatch. We give the hired man the job of hotshotting the cows down the pen chutes and undertaking the working of the gate. He undoes the latch at the touch of a hat and throws the barrier back and scrambles clear of the way. The calf bursts from the chute hard and fast, and Son gives it its seconds of yardage before gigging the sorrel and lunging out in pursuit, Ham's horse pounding out right behind. Son builds the loop open and swings it aloft. He rises to stand in the saddle for the toss, and the lariat falls right over the horns and catches the head — nice! — but there's a jolt at the dally and Son's horse brakes and reels and in a sudden he's catapulting forward, all arms and legs in the air over the horse. Son hits the ground with a thick grunting sound and with it comes a great concussion of earth. Then the sorrel topples and rolls, making its own violent cloud. The animal rises up out of the dust like a vision. It steadies itself and lopes away toward the gate, leaving an eeriness in the emptiness of the saddle, the stirrups kicking out without aim.

Ham drops his lasso and trots his horse over and I'm ahead in a run to where Son is, pitched facedown in the dirt. I roll him over onto his back and he's looking up at me, furred with dust and stunned, his mouth open, breathless, soundless. C'mon, I say. Breathe. He breathes. He coughs and spews curses. There, I say. Ham stays mounted beside us, his horse sidling and jerking its head up excitably. Ham looks down at Son and nods his head. Got the wind punched out of you pert bad, young waddy, he says. Son just lies there, looking up to nothing. I reach a hand out to him and he takes it, but his grip is weak and he's turned all dead weight. C'mon, I say. Get up, I say. All he says is, Can't.

Don't say can't, I say. The voice of the old man gives me a start when I say it.

Ham slides out of the saddle and the hired man comes running and we huddle about Son, bent down and heads together as if to discuss some ball game strategy. Tell us what hurts, Ham says. Nothing, Son says. Nothing hurts. The hired man takes his cap off and wipes the sweat on his forehead away with a shirtsleeve. We look at Son. We look up, one at every other. We'll have to get him on home, I say.

The hired man takes hold of Son's shoulders and I pick him up by the legs, and we trundle out awkwardly as Ham trots ahead to open the arena gate. We have to stop a couple of times because of the weight of him. Ham comes back and takes over for me at the heels, the hired man taking the head up again. I hobble alongside Son, teasing him for the work he's putting us through, and he moans and chokes and spits. We put him down in the dirt again, dragging him out by the legs the rest of the way.

Ham has gotten his rig turned around so the outside light of the tackroom will shine into the horse trailer. He opens the trailer door and gets inside, shouts to stand clear, and kicks out hard lumps of dung with sideswipes of his boots. He spreads canvas feedbags over the trailer floor, then gets out and lets the ramp down, and he and the hired man lift Son up and pull him in. The old man's old dog, by now gotten caught up in the commotion, prances about panting and nosing things. I get her by the collar and put her to wheezing to hold her out of the way while Ham and the hired man settle Son inside the trailer and cover him over with a horse blanket, as I wonder, in this heat, what for. They close and latch back the door. Ham and I get into the cabfront and drive around to the front of the old adobe house, a sweep of headlights to guide us, the hired man and the old man's old dog following behind on foot in the thick dark behind—no moon, no stars, no galaxies, no movement to speak of tonight.

Ham sides the rig up to the porch, and he and the hired man stretcher Son out of the trailer with the horse blanket and get him up the steps. They slide him across the cement, cutting a slithering wide path through the dust. I fan the moths away from the screen and open the door, and we get Son over the threshold and into the house, stopping to rest in the cool dark parlor. Ham and the hired man stand breathing hard in the quiet, waiting for me to light the place to see what's next to be done. Outside, the crickets frenzy on in a high-pitched chirr and trill. The old dog skirts about nervously. What I see is that now it's up to me to decide, that what I say will be done, and that I must believe I know what's right in order for anyone to believe me too. Let's get him to bed, I say. They pick Son up and head toward our bedroom, and I say, No, go the other way. We'll put him in the old man and Rose's room.

They get Son onto the bed, and I get the pillow fixed under his head. The old dog goes over to him and licks his hand, and Son balls a fist and knuckles her in the head hard enough to hear the hollow below the skullbone. I give Son a punch back in the shoulder.

What's the matter with you? I say.

The hired man gives me a look, and I tell him he better get back and unsaddle the horses and feed and bed them for the night and shut the arena lights down. He nods, obliges me with a sure-enough and a Missus, and turns and leaves, taking the smell of horse dung and diesel grease with him. Ham comes back in from the kitchen with a pitcher of rust-colored water. He puts it down on the bedside table and fills the glass up and holds it out to me. Here, I say to Son, take this, and I tip his head forward and put the rim to his lips. He sucks the water from the glass and swallows hard and too fast, getting him choking and spitting until he's suddenly now bawling like a baby would be.

Sakes alive, Ham says.

You're all right, I say. But Son won't look at me.

Let's get rid of these diggers, Ham says, and then I'll take care of the justins. We unstrap the spurs and Ham acts as a bootjack with each of Son's feet between his legs to lever the boots off. I unbuckle Son's belt and go on to opening rivets, and Ham and I each pull on a cuff until we get the dungarees shucked. Son's legs and thick folds of dust spill out of the casings.

Could you be of any help here? I say.

Son doesn't move and won't speak. I unsnap the shirt snaps and he tries to shrug me off, but I keep at him. Ham helps me roll him over to one side and then to the other to get his arms out of the sleeves. We get Son back on his back again and cover him over with a clean sheet and turn his pillow. There's not a mark on you, I say. Not a scratch or a bruise or a cut. Nothing I can see that's wrong. Ham's right, you're just shoggled-up, is all.

You were big-holed back there bad, Ham says. But you'll be up and to tomorrow. You'll be back horseback and in ace shape come rodeo day. You'll see. Then we'll hit us some pay dirt. Don't think us borasca'd none, he says.

We stand attending Son and looking down at him, but he keeps his eyes closed.

I'll adiós you, then, Ham says.

I gather the bundle of dusty clothes up and turn the light out. Put the light back on, Son says. Now you can both get out.

HAM HAD BID his good nights and said he would be checking by tomorrow and would see himself out the door. I turned and headed into the kitchen with the load of clothes. The old dog followed close beside, as if in unusual need of me, and as we passed her dish I paused and saw she had water enough. I went on into the backroom to the washing machine and opened the lid, going through Son's pockets before throwing the clothes in. I found a book of matches, printed with the name of a bar in town, and a crumpled half pack of cigarettes. The watch pocket of his dungarees held a silver timepiece engraved with the old man's name, this, aside from Rose's Daddy's old buck knife, Son's only keepsake. A deeper pocket held a dirty handkerchief, and there was a tin of chew in one of the backs, a wallet in the other back. I wadded the clothes into the tub and shook the soap grains in on top of the stuff and pushed the start button. In the hum of the fill I began to riffle through what there was inside the wallet — a fold of bills, mostly singles, a gasoline credit card, a receipt. The driver's license described Son's hair as blond and his eyes as blue and him as six-foot-two and 160 pounds. The sheriff's posse card he kept for some reason, and when I came to it, an image of Son came to mind. It was the day he was sworn in, and seeing him afterward, the way he walked up the porch steps looking taller than he even was, his boots saddlesoaped, his denims ironed and creased for him, a new yoked western shirt looking right out of the box and white as to the rules. The tin of the deputy badge stuck on the shirtfront shone like the sun. The old man would have me run get the camera that day to take a snapshot. The old man would take a snapshot of the two of us too — both of us smiling, looking to be trying, or maybe even yet happy.

I was shuffling through the rest of the find when a photo slipped out of the packet and drifted to the floor, and I wondered which it was of me he would keep. I saw it was one of the little black-and-white photos that had been clipped from those that come in fours in a strip you get from machines they have in bus stations and drugstores. Like the one back in the beach town north of Angels City, where we had pulled off the highway that afternoon, and there was a boardwalk at the seaside we walked along. The place was lively with people out for a day and men haggling over their wares, and it was motley with trinkets and hand food for sale. We bought souvenirs for ourselves and postcards to send home, and we bought peanuts to toss at the seabirds. The air smelled of fish-and-chips and finespun candy, and it smelled too of fruity booze drinks and coconutty suntan lotion and Son's spicey aftershave. Pop songs about love played out a loudspeaker, and I couldn't help but sing out loud myself, bold and gay as we both were that day. Palm trees laughed brisk in the wind, and gulls screamed and careened wildly about us. Light sparked off the sea as though currented with electricity, the glitter on the water sharp enough to dim the vision. The day was a day meant for the word — oh, where would there be such a word? Only to say there was a buoyancy and a radiance all about us, there was whirlpool and mollusk and flipper, and nests, corals, shells, wings, flukes, kelp — what else? There was sand and current and wind and reef, and there was tide and pulse and drift. There were clouds the shape of fishes aswim that day. We stood embraced, watching the waves, the way they were ever so slow at the gather, the way they would mount and light at the crest. There would come the start of the curl before each surge and break, before the great things came pounding down, bursting into themselves with such force you could feel the tremendous ending of every one drumming throughout your ribcage. Then again, another beginning with the start of the next swell. Everything in us swelling, as we walked along in song and clinging one to the other and always in step, like dancing, our timing was. We had all the world between the two of us, right where we were, and too out in the beyond and in the what we couldn't even know of yet, and at the same time we had the knowing of going home to look forward to, and we were eager for it.

We wandered into a curio shop and there I saw the photo machine and led us into the booth. We swiveled the seat down to fit our heads into the screen evenly, and Son sat and fitted me atop his lap, and we put our faces together and got our arms out of the way, and we smiled without even trying and held still, waiting to be captured in a rupture of light, wanting the moment burned into us.

I felt a rush of that heat in me now.

The old dog put her nose to the dropped photo and I hazed her away, bringing myself back to where I am, thinking how very close we always are to being somewhere not here. And then I felt that stall of the heart, in the instant of something gone wrong, as I peeled the photo off the floor and turned the face of it up, seeing it was not a picture of me, not even of us. It was Daughter Pearl that Son held so close.

The old dog nudged me as I tore the picture apart, ripping eyes and lips and teeth into teeny pieces, childishly, dropping the confetti it made into the wastebasket, flicking the rest clean from my fingers. The old dog nuzzled and winced. The machine rumbled and agitated. My stomach churned out a pang of something no doctor could explain.

THERE HAVE BEEN callings and pursuits I've imagined myself in, in whatever hard wind of future that lay ahead, though never did I picture myself doing the work of cowgirl or nurse. But here I am, scuffing along in slung-heeled boots, carrying a jar warm and musty smelling and heavy to the brim with Son's urine, and wondering all the while where the time will be to keep the paint warmed up and ready for the barrels come Sunday.

The routine is, after all, a change. Now Son and I are together every night and every day, just as it was during the month of our honeymoon. But he hasn't left the bed, hasn't wanted to sit up once, hasn't used his legs, complaining they're not working yet. Yessirree, the old man would say, chance did so rejig that boy's ways indeed. And I would say, We have to be careful as to the details of our wishes.

Ham says he has seen instances such as these with other falls of the kind, oncet or twicet, he says, remembering particularly. There was a bullrider friend a mine, to give a example, he says, that got caught in the getaway. He was looking good prior—got his legs fit about the bull just right in the pen, resined his glove snug, and had a good hold of the bull rope, was scooted up just so on the upper of the animal's back, and with his knees clenched tight and toes turned out rightly and body squared over the horns, as all like to see, and he was out the chute and riding a perfect buck and waving to the queen—rollercoasting, he was, and right on until the buzzer sounded and it was time to let go the strap, and he swung a leg over the back and hit the ground on his feet. You should've heard the crowd and seen the cheering and that jackaroo taking all the glory in, and just then the bull, rank as all get-out, it was, came from behind and rammed his rider with such force the man was thrust into the air and throwed against the fence like a old raggedy doll. Clowns and pickup men ran the bull clear and got to the poor fellow and toted him out, Ham says. He was knocked cold. Suffered a concussion, the doc said, and a wounded spine, and a family turned horribly worried. But he had a lot of sand in him, as they say, and in a bit over a week he was up and walking again, though he did limp after and walked about with a stave, a stave he had made from a branch of a quaking aspen, the leathery bark of which was carved with the names of ever bull he'd ever ridden. An' the story ain't no bluff, he says.

I suppose the ending could have been worse, I say.

There's another misgo I seen, Ham says. That time a clown — a bullfighter really, is what they is — was matching wits with a brahma when he got tossed up like a bouncy thing, and when he fell, the animal trampled him. That was a bad one. Wife took the ol' boy to see the best doctor to be had on the coast. After treatment X and Y and Z, and money they ended owing up the wazoo to the bank, well still that clown was left permanently catawampus and was not walking any more barrels or getting any more laughs. After all a this his wife up and left him, which pretty much wohaw'd the man for good, Ham says, shaking his head.

We stand staring at the same patch of ground, with a feverous sun above.

In either of the two ordeals, nature is above all the only decision maker, Ham says.

That could only be, I say.

Seems to me, it matters little whether we make the two-hour drive to take Son to a hospital or if we don't, Ham says, as the damage is or was done, or it isn't or wasn't.

Worries me to think we'll do more damage putting him through the long drive, I say.

And in this heat to boot, you sure can't bet on betterments.

We don't want to hurt him any more than he's hurt.

What do a bunch a fancy doctors know anyways, he says, except for fetching higher prices?

It's not as if medicine is even a real science.

It's more or less a case of wait and see, is the way to reckon it.

I want to agree, I say. Best to keep Son still and cared for.

Just keep him eyeballed for the time being.

That's what we'll do.

In any case, I haven't got a roping partner, Ham says. To say the least.

If you can head, then I can heel, I say.

There's nothing much to lose but an entry fee.

The next day, Ham would go into town and pay the sum for us. But there would be no need to team-up come the event day. For there would be no rodeo Sunday at all.

Talk about timing, is all I can say, Ham would say.

He would be talking about the rain.

IT BEGINS TO rain Saturday, late evening. Clouds slowly roll in and collect throughout the day, and this has people looking up hopefully and placing bets as to downfall. The clouds accumulate cumulonimbus, their underbellies fiercely dark and tumid come afternoon. By the time the hired man is doing the late-day feeding and watering, the overcast heap has turned ragged and scud. The horses circle fearfully in the stalls and they won't eat, won't drink, either one. The calves stir and groan in the holding pen. Tree clingers and perching birds harbor inside old saguaros. Hunter cats take cover under the house or in clefts of the melon shed. Cicadas and crickets are hushed for once.

I go out to call the old dog in and feel the gather of current in the thick and mixed-up air. The ominous swells are dark and fast-gathering above, like a troop of giants set upon us, appearing loaded with weaponry rather than the bounty we had been hoping for for so long. In the end the storm might be called a blessing, but it arrives as hard as a trigger pulled, with no time between flash and sound in the first strike of lightning. The weather turns violent as some lesson put on us from the Bible. The sky pulses and booms and strobes, the rain heavy and going on steadily after. Looking out, you would think the fountains of the great deep had opened, with the water pocking up atop the hard ground, making it seem the earth were percolating. In a place turned sere and nearly blown to claypan, the rain but walters over the armor of it, with no sod to retard the flood. The deluge surges on in a rage across blind creek and arroyo, dry gulch and draw. It overflows canals, ditches, coulees, gullies, dalles. It fills wallows and potholes in, courses over broken ground and reg. It runnels gumbo, rills pumice, disturbs erg.

It makes an eyot of the old adobe house.

I stand with the curtain parted and with an eye out, watching the water veiling over the portal like a falls does. Through the pour I see the flowerbeds along the walkway turned spillway, with dead gophers and field mice and creeping things drifting past in the downrush. Mud and silt trickle down the slope of the hummock, melting the tumulous hold of the old adobe house.

Water swells over the ribs and the welts of the burnt turf. It brims up from the furrows, pools the fields, washes out over the road. It pours across the porch, and the steps are lost to the eye in the sink. The pickup appears afloat in a pool of eddies and whirls, the watertruck stuck in a swamp of flotsam. The old lemon grove comes alive in bursts of lightning, like a scrawny army of whiskery old ghosts fallen charge on us.

My breath dims the vision. I put a sleeve to the glass and rub my traces off. I turn away from the rain and look about, seeing the old adobe house—its rooms, its space, what it contains— seeing everything about the place as nothing it has been. Startling in its difference, and yet also more familiar than ever, as though I were standing here regarding it all for the first time, feeling the anchorage as something belonging to me. Or is it me that belongs to it?

Nothing gives. Windows and doors warp and stick and are difficult at the open and close. Cupboards and drawers and cabinets need a hard push or a pull for a budge. Newsprint peels away heavy and wet from the countertop, leaving inkings of forecasts. I throw dripping wads of births and fatalities into the trash basket. I open the pantry and find dried beans and macaroni swelling on the shelves, cornhusks and tortillas wilting, the salt clumping, a pile of tea towels on their way to mold. The wet seeps in from everywhere. It crannies in through roof fissures and wall cracks and casing seams. It beads along the beams of the ceiling. Thresholds won't hold it. It fills and puddles the grooves and the niches of tile and board. It fogs mirror and glass and pane, brings iron and tin to the beginnings of rusting, soddens cardboard entirely. It dampens furniture, mattresses, drapery, rugs. I walk room to room, the clothes on me dank smelling and steaming, putting buckets and pots out for roof leaks, collecting batteries, flashlights, the old man's old buck knife, towels, rags, duct tape, and twine. The storm cuts the current off, and I burn Rose's old oil lamps to brighten parlor and kitchen. There are holiday candles stored in the sideboard, and those ugly stubby ones kept for power outs, and these I use to light the old man and Rose's bedroom, where Son lies restless in the bed, amutter in his sleep. He's circled in flame, appearing ready for sacrifice, or resurrection, or something else mystical and unexplainable.

The rain will make it dark as night for days.

I go in and hold the light up close. I see Son look at me and not see me. Hard shadows gutter the lines in his face and mudden the sockets. He speaks in broken sentences. He speaks of a dream he's been dreaming, a stampede, he says. Run, he says. Leave. He might yet be dreaming. He mumbles. He trembles. The house rumbles in the thundering above. A moth flutters in the lamp globe, its wings to singe in the flame. I put my hand to Son's chest and feel the parch of the flesh of him. I listen to the water dropping into the bucket, steady as a pulse will pulse.

I blow the flame of the wick out.

The old dog stays close at the heel, and I use the flashlight to guide us, leaving Son in a gibber of broken sleep. I peel my clothes off and leave them in a soggy pile on the floor, lift the damp sheet, climb into the empty bed. The old dog lies down alongside on the floor on the Navajo and is soon aswim in her dreams. Her haunches jerk and her limbs twitch, and growls roll out from low in her belly. The rain pounds steadily overhead, drowning the ticking of the old clock in the parlor, muddling the whimpers and moans of husband and dog and house. I lie in the howl and scream of the wind in the night, as the waterline rises silently up the side of the adobe.

What of the God there should be to come and retard the flood?

IT DOWNPOURS ALL night. By morning the rain slows but goes on, the weight and mass of cooling air streaming through and settling into the valley. Layers of vapor move through phases of upset and absorb before the restore. They say the skin of the globe stretches and tightens, just as the body does, fostering a drawing-together, a kind of pressure that makes for a tightening, a narrowing, a confining, from outside to inside, in a shift of blood, and a reset of set point. There are laws explaining this kind of movement of fluid—I remember the teacher teaching us this, describing laws as to the forces of boundary and density. As I'm putting the thermometer under Son's tongue, I wonder at the power of these truths, thinking they make me feel as safe as they make me feel afraid.

He drinks and asks for more, and again more, but his thirst won't be quenched. His flesh is hot and dry, and his face flushed as if burned from the sun. He's a mumble of words you've never heard, his talk coming from some lost place or a bruised piece of his mind. He won't keep the thermometer in his mouth, and I need to put it under his armpit and sit with him for the time it takes to get a measure. I hold the glass tube to the light and read the number by the marking: 105. Can't be. Such a temperature is what only a child could bear, I can hear my mother saying. Or maybe it was Rose. Or Pearl might have been the one speaking. Who knows. I shake until the mercury slides down the stem, and I put it back into Son's armpit. I hold his arm tight and plead with him when he tries to push me away. I shout his name out.

The silver line rises and stops at the same number. The ceiling fan is on as always in the room, but now I add table fans and one on a stand and I get all of them going. I pull the sheets back and I think he's shivering, but it's too violent for shivering, or even tremoring, too uneven the movement is, more spasming is what it is, first his body going all hard and bunched up and then in a sudden opened and relaxed, and then tight again, and then let go again, all of this over and over, and the shaking now become so furious the bed is shifting about over the floor, as though with a life of its own. It takes me a few breaths and just standing there, just standing not knowing what to do, until I think to look for something to put into his mouth. Rip pages from a book on the bed table, spindle them, thrust the wad between his teeth, realize now I'm shaking myself. His raspy breathing. His heaving. Who to call? No time to call. And then it comes to me to run to the bathroom and open the medicine cabinet and take from it the bottle of rubbing alcohol. When I get back to him, the fit is just-like-that stopped. He's talking now, talking about watering the roads down, talking not to me — what does he see? — but to the old man, he talks to the old man, Rose's Daddy, he needs to get up, he says, and now Son lifts himself, trying to get out of bed. He can't get his legs to move with trying — it has to be as bad as a bad dream — and he's thrashing his arms about and fending with his hands as I try to stay him, and he strikes out and sends the table lamp crashing to the ground. I take shirts from the drawer, use the sleeves of them to tie his wrists to the bedstead, first one and now the other one, his head rolling back and forth, gibberish and spit rolling from his tongue in his delirium. Run for a basin. Run for the cloths. Fill the basin with water. Add a whole bottle of rubbing alcohol. Put the soaked cloths dripping wet over Son—his legs, upper and lower, his stomach and groin and chest. Calm yourself, I tell him. Try, I say. Someone come and calm me. I fix the pillow under his head better. I talk to him. This is aspirin, I tell him. Open. Here. Drink. Please. I tell him I'm going to call someone. I tell him what everyone says, that everything is going to be fine. And then he begins shivering, really shivering, his teeth chattering. I take the warmed cloths off, rinsing each in the alcohol bath, putting them back again cool onto his body. I leave them on until they turn warm. Then I go through the routine again and again. After a while, the shivering stops. He sleeps.

By the end of whatever time has passed, the number on the thermometer is down to near what it should be. I take the wet cloths off at last, cover Son over with the sheet, but leave his arms tied until I should go into the kitchen to make the telephone calls.

I pick the receiver up, hearing nothing.

TEN

THE BREACH

The silence is what wakes me.

The old man's old dog wakes as well, seeming to know my eyes have just opened. She rises old and slow from the floor, stands there, totters, then shakes. I squint out of reflex, but not a bit of dust bursts off her fur. Only pieces of a dream scatter and drift and fade—strange rooms in a familiar place, faces belonging to another time, every picture of what might be just out of reach enough to too soon lose it.

The storm.

I arise at once, remembering, and pull the curtain away from the window, looking out to see the rain stopped. Pouches of clouds still fill the sky and reflect like pillows onto a sea of water below.

There's a feeling of a beginning coming from somewhere.

Parts of the dream. Who knows where. Could that have been me?

I put yesterday's clothes back on and go into the old man and Rose's room, where Son lies in the bed breathing soundlessly in his sleep. The room smells old. Son smells old. He smells of sweat and of urine, of things you want to turn from, of what you undertake to forget. I put a rag to his face and wipe the drool and the crust away. He rustles about and mutters something, and quiets again. His lips are cracked and blistered. I touch his skin, feel it cool and sticky.

The old dog follows me into the kitchen and heads straight to her water bowl and starts lapping. She stops and looks up, but when I open the back door to let her out, she puts her nose into the bowl and goes on drinking again. I fetch a basin from beneath the sink, squeeze a jot of dishsoap into it, and turn the faucet on, watching the iron-colored water in its slow rise to brim, the suds bubbling up and giving out to nothing in the hardness. The cover of dust is at last washed from the glass of the window. Through the panes you can see the skeleton of Rose's climbing rose, broken from its hold on the adobe wall that it had clung to for its years. Clouds beyond already begin to flatten and break into patches. Coins of turquoise appear here and there in the gray.

There was water everywhere in the dream, deliriously beautiful water. There was a boat. I wanted to get into the boat in the worst way. I wanted to be on the boat so I could jump off it and dive in, going down and deep as I could into the crystalline water. But I was made to wait, I don't know why. I waited and waited until I grew tired of waiting, for whoever or whatever it was I was waiting for, and all the time knowing I could swim easily, especially clear and pure as the water was. I couldn't stay in place anymore, and I jumped aboard the boat as it came forward just before it docked. But it doesn't dock, and now I'm on the boat and we're already pulling away from the shore and I see the water beneath suddenly become dark and thick. I'm scared, deathly scared I might fall off into the murky stench, and feel I have to hang on tightly so as not to slip overboard and be done with. The panic — it all comes flooding back to me again.

The water in the basin overflows into the sink. I shut the tap off and let go the clench I've got on the rim. I pick a sliver of soapbar out of the soapdish and take a dishcloth out of the top drawer. I carry the warm basin and the washing things into the bedroom, where I set it all up on the table by the side of the bed. Now I wash Son, beginning with his sun-coarsened face and his ruddy, chicken-fleshed neck. I rinse and soap and rub the cloth over his pale chest, the width of his rib bones like tines of drift in the sand, and then I soap his pale belly over, hairy and densely patched as saltgrass grows. I drop the cloth into the water and bring his knees to a bend, gripping the crag of his shoulder to roll him over to a side. His pale legs fall away lifeless. Rinse the cloth, soap it over, begin again. Reach for the jar of creosote cream and open the jar and rub the pungent-smelling unguent over the places reddening on Son's backside, over the ledges of his hipbones, around the mounds of his heels. By now I have roused him to some level of confused awake. He blinks and looks around, and opens his mouth when he sees me bringing a toothbrush close to his face. He lets me scrub his teeth, his tongue. His gums bleed. I put the cup to his lips and tell him to spit what's in his mouth out into the basin, but he swallows instead. I give him another drink and he coughs up the water.

Remembering the yerba buena from the Quechan woman.

I touch the scar on his forehead, shaped and welted like a centipede. I brush the hair away from his face and brush the sand that comes loose from his hair off the sheets and the pillowcase. I grasp his arms and pull him forward to get him to sit upright in the bed in order to get a square fold of clean sheet beneath him, trying to brace him like this while I straighten the sheet properly. But he won't stay—doesn't want to or can't do it—and I let him fall back again onto the pillow. He speaks in words you've never heard. He looks at me without seeing me. I wipe the brine from the creases of his eyes and apply more of the ointment to his lips. I leave the beard growing, coming in thick and red as it is.

I put an ear to his chest and hear the rapids of his heart.

I change the casing on the pillow. I gather more pillows to support him with, and I turn him once again to his side and use them to pad his back and stay him this way, using one too as a prop between his useless legs. After a while I'll come in and roll him yet the other way.

THE RIVER THAT stems into this region was once a splendid river and colored red, the old man said. And thereby the name was given, Colorado, as the desert that holds the river was also called, until the desert would be fit into a larger ordering of land gain and be given another name of Spanish favoring, the meaning of the latter tending toward diction of a harmonious nature. Yet the discourse would be turned and spoken not altogether in harmony. For the vernacular of these alluvial plains was too soon sharpened by the vanity and the avarice of the men who came. These were prophets who brought with them their visions of profit. Their wish for bounty would be promoted by promising land made desirable for selling, land that was back then called the Valley of the Dead. And hope for private reward would be spoken in the language of the public good. Talk was aimed at harnessing the river and, by doing so, claiming the melting snows of a noble northern mountain range. And these men did indeed procure the acre-feet of water needed to nourish the soil. And report of water stock and land scrip came loud from their greedy mouths.

Whereupon more prospectors came.

Whereupon the settlers came and the fields were planted and tended.

And other men came to lay and control the railways.

And the clergymen did come to rule by their means.

Teams of men came and pitched their tents, and with their stakes they marked the boundaries. Others came to dredge and excavate and scrape. Lo, numbers of miles of canals and ditches and laterals were carved into the earth, and the river was thereby captured. Thence came the day that the water did burst like a devil's tongue from out of the headgate, and it spilled red as it was and silty into the mother ditch.

And so the great diversion.

And this stretch of desert was thus claimed.

And there would be more rail lines to be laid.

And many more people did come.

And as the revenues were sown, so did man worship the work of his own hands.

And he did behold it.

Rose's Daddy took a seat on the front porch and went on.

Yet iniquity would fall upon all the inhabitants of the land. For the work of these men was done in haste and with lack of maintenance, with thinking tending toward the short and not the long of it. Indeed, the floods would come, and the violence and the spoil, the grief and the wounds thereof.

As the river cast out her waters, so did she cast out her wickedness. The Colorado rose, as did the sister river that fed into it, and the unleashed waters churned and rived away at the sides of the banks until the yokes were broken and the bands were burst and the rivers grew wider and wilder. The manmade canals and flumes and cisterns newly built were breached useless. A great torrent poured through draws and ravines, forming cataracts and rapids, and over the ledges of barrancas roiled tumbles of falls. The waters boiled and foamed, and the terrain about became a seething pot. Telegraph poles were halved, railway ties were swallowed, homes and farms and ranches were abandoned. People devised crude boats and watercraft so they might flee. Those most quick to leave were the men who had devised the concrete waterways, and they took their proceeds and vanished back east or moved to the coast for other water endeavors. Many keepers of the fields gave up in despair and went elsewhere, who knows where, but never to return to the valley. The pastors' flocks scattered. Towns were laid waste. Acres upon acres were left to become derelict, the slough and alluvium turned to fen and to pit, a choke of tamarisk thicket, a tangle of boulders and roots, a whirl of debris, the land spoiled by the washout and heap-up of gravel and sand, and thereby to go again unsown.

Rose's Daddy rose from his seat and stood looking outwardly, speaking now as if addressing the land surrounding him.

Yet the few souls who braved to remain ran to and fro and created brazen walls to contain the waters, he said. One of these men would be my father. My father and the others worked to fill the mile-wide break through which the river poured. They used boulders and gravel and clay to stanch the flow, and levees were constructed and mattress dams of piling and brush were made. Once the waters were held and had begun to recede, new headgates were built, and canals were dredged of silt, and the railways put into order. And men of ambition did again appropriate the waters. And people came and began to dwell in the gutted terrain of the valley afresh.

The old man stopped and gestured a hand at the countryside about.

Once more, man had obtained his dominion, he said. Now be it with the foresight to cage the mighty river and lessen any chance for it to again rage and take its revenge. Thence as the story goes, the great dams were erected, and with them came the reservoirs and the generators, the diversions and the aqueducts. And as the land was thus reclaimed, so were the agencies and the departments and the corps and the associations made, and too came the lobbyists and the absent landlords, and more fortunes and power were gained by speculators and those who believed water ought to be treated as property, and they might thereby wax rich. Wherefore these men called themselves practical men. Thus it came to pass that the water was tamed and it did flow river to valley accordingly. And the land was made pleasant by much of the alien labor that supported it, and was inhabited once again.

Yes, indeedy, Rose's Daddy said. Until there shall come the next great disaster, whether by nature's hand or by the violence of man. For the covet of profit is inherent in men, and the sovereignty of the economy will rank over ideals of lesser value. The monopoly of water is the goal of those who have so staked their interests in it. And yet water, to all men, is life, and thus its claim to each and every should be so justified. Would this not be right?

Yet did I not too look to water for profit?

Rose's Daddy shook his head.

Nature concerns herself not with the single mortal, but only with the species, as I have said before, he said. Is it for this reason man has taken nature for the enemy? Yet what fool would think that in this battle he might succeed?

The old man went back to his seat and spoke no more.

NATURE WOULD SURPRISE us soon enough, just as Rose's Daddy had said. The storm we got caught in caused the trenched stretch of sluggish water that still possessed a bridge overhead, and had once flowed the color red, to run hard and quick as the great river it had long ago been. The grinding waters eroded the river's banks, and the river deposited its silt and sediment and detritus in different places. Sandbars were formed anew and other channels cut, the river having reshaped itself and moved along an alternate path to take a more westerly bearing. The downpour made a mess of all the waterways, brimming over and spilling out as it did in the mother ditch, in the channels and canals, with the flood beating its way wildly through the flood-gates, chewing up bypasses, bursting through the intakes. The overflow went heaving by, at who knows how many miles per hour, carrying tangles of thicket and shrub, downed trees, jams of wood and debris, bags of feed, bales of hay, pieces of equip-ment, drowned animals, even people in the boil and the foam of it. It would take weeks to mend the wreckage and breach. It would take days to find bodies and what else mattered. So much of everything disappeared entirely.

Godwater was what the Padre always called rain that fell in this place. A word, he said, he had learned from the Mormons during a time working up north with them. What would the Padre have now to say? Was the mighty torrent a result of overpray? Was the whole mess due to some kind of extreme power of believing? Would he be of the conviction that the gathering he held before he had yet to flee this town could have produced such a deluge?

Might he truly believe these things?

Who could really believe any of it?

But people did go, as he bid them to. I wanted to see who those people were. I wanted to see what their faith looked like. Mostly I wanted to see how the Padre would do his conjuring. Because hadn't he maybe used some conjuring with me?

There were those that had come to the prayer meeting inspired by the new pastor and inspired too to bring about a change. These were the hardy kind that knew heat, knew how to live in it in the day-to-day, as anyone has got to in this place. But when the heat persisted well past its normal and barely tolerable length of stay, well, people became entirely unsettled about it. My guess is that those who came to pray did so because praying was better than doing nothing, better than waiting the weather out, just sitting around panting and sweating most of the day every day, day in and day out. And hadn't the Indians prayed for rain? If not outright danced for it? So you might say this kind of thing was in the town's history.

Still, the evening was an odd one.

The Padre was strumming his guitar when I walked into his study at the church. He was wearing a long white garment with long bell-shaped sleeves, and he was barefoot. Around his neck was a long, ropy gold chain with a Celtic cross big as a hand penduled at the end of it. His hair was grown longer and it flowed over his shoulders, Jesus-like, and his eyes had a glazed-over look to them, as if he were seeing something past the handful of people that sat about the room—this look being kind of Jesus-like too. There were a couple of the older church ladies there, perched on cushions on the floor, and their eyebrows were raised as they saw me come into the room. There was a husband who belonged to one of the ladies, and he nodded at me, and the man who worked at the tack and feed, he also nodded. Pearl was there, and Daughter Pearl—both of them came.

Everyone sat about to form a circle on the floor around the prayer rug and the Padre. The desk had been pushed against the wall and the chairs moved out for the occasion. He plucked the guitar strings softly in the middle of those convened, and I took a seat between the two men. Once I was settled, and the others resettled, the Padre began to play the instrument louder. He broke into full song. His voice was deep and surprisingly good, as if he had been schooled and knew how to use it, which likely he had. His Jesus eyes went away and his look became more searching, and as he sang he stared keenly into the eyes of those of us on the floor, one by one, as if singing to each alone. When his eyes touched mine, I couldn't help but look down. His gaze was piercing, and it was too much to have others see him seeing so hard into me. The Padre switched his melody and went directly into another song, and he soon had the whole group singing along to one of those tunes or hymns that it seems everyone who goes to church knows. I just faked it, a word here, a word there, as one does. Daughter Pearl was the whole while singing and now looking at me as well. Her stare was mean as a pinch.

After the song was over, the Padre put his guitar aside and sat down on the floor between Pearl and her daughter, so to fill the circle. He had us all join hands, which didn't please me, for I had to touch the sticky palms of the two men I sat between. The Padre had us every one close our eyes. He spoke to God for all of us. He said to God that we were assembled here for Him and we were receptive to His powers. He said to God we were His vessels and that we had come here to empty ourselves and to ready ourselves to be filled by Him and only Him.

After the holy appeal, we all opened our eyes. The older church ladies fidgeted on their floor cushions. Pearl Hart smiled at me. Daughter Pearl looked to the Padre and waited. I could imagine her yet with my garnet necklace around her neck. I could imagine, as well, the Padre rubbing her feet as he did with me.

We are not here to pray for rain, the Padre said, talking to us straight on now, and in a not-praying-for-us voice. We are here to bring a change in the weather by our visions of it. Vision is power. Do not try to will the rain, he said. Do not try to grasp it. Just imagine it. Godwater, he said. He stopped talking and got his Jesus eyes back. He reached behind himself and lit a stick of incense.

Let all of us close our eyes again, he said, his voice a coarse whispering, gone monotone. Breathe deeply and begin to imagine the clouds moving in from a distance and thickening above our heads in the heavens. See the clouds fill with spheres of water, he said. See the molecules within the spheres as they cluster and stick. Picture the forming of droplets beginning. Feel the expansion, the energy, the release. Hear the sky as it will seethe and pulse above us. Now see the rain. Godwater, he said. See the godwater falling. Feel the touch of it like love upon your skin. Feel it cool you. Feel it soothe. Faith will move mountains, Jesus tells us.

The Padre opened his eyes. Somehow knowing, I opened mine at the same time.

Do not reason, he said, looking right into me. Only believe.

When I look back to that evening, I see the whole séancelike gathering being as strange as it was ordinary. People do act this way and believe such things, they do it all the time. The stranger thing was what followed, for it was the next day that the church would burn down.

I went to the dictionary to know the word irony better.

Then I went outside to look to see what the storm had left us.

THE HIRED MAN comes slogging through the mud and stops before the door of the tackroom. He looks down at his boots, and I stop my search for another jar of creosote cream and go out to him. The bill of his cap has lost the perfect curve he had in the past kept fastidiously modeled into it. He touches the flattened lip of it in greeting, just the same. I tell him I've by now haltered the bay and the mare and have got them out to pasture. I'm about to do the same with the sorrel and the paint. The animals are all right, I say, though the whites of their eyes were showing and they were trembling like all get-out to get out when I found them. Their stalls are a mess, I say. There's more work than I can even see through here.

That's what I come for, Missus, he says.

Then he tells me the flood has all but washed away the trailer home he had been living in, a paint-blistered aluminum thing that had been settled out on a blown-over parcel of rubble and scrag. He says that all of it broke apart and was set afloat like a lot of little toy boats and that he's been sleeping in the backseat of the Ambassador ever since. I offer him the use of the toolhouse to bunk in, and after we feed and settle the horses he goes and gathers what few things there are left to him and brings the stuff on over.

The hired man begins by clearing and sweeping the toolhouse clean of the leakage and rubbish. Afterward he goes out and opens the hood of the pickup and dries the wires and resets the plugs. He borrows the vehicle to haul over an old iron-framed cot that he has fished out of the waters. He finds seat cushions from some place and dry enough, I don't know where, and I get him sheets from the house and we make a bed for him alongside the mowing-machine parts and the harrows and drags. He tidies everything in the toolroom nicely, making a home among augers and baling forks and grapples, cans of motor oil and gasoline. He sits his transistor on a bucket turned downward, and he sits himself on the cot next to it and tries dialing the music in. After a while he gives up, having found nothing but wet static to listen to. Guess I'll be having to hum a few a my own tunes, he says.

Once the hired man is settled in, I begin to feel a little bit of settle in me. He helps by driving into town to ask the man at the Centro Médico to come out and have a look at Son, returning with the message that we'll have to hold tight, as there are too many people hurt and needing care first. We can't sit around and wait, I say. We have to at least, in the meantime, try to put the place back into some kind of order.

The hired man will find spills and leaks and drafts and broken things for fixing throughout and around the old adobe house. He will change the blown fuses in the box and spackle the cracks in the walls, climb up onto the roof to straighten or replace what tiles have fallen loose or been slived, come in to inspect the rooms and corridors, fixing outlets and switches, hinges and latches, oiling the knobs and the locks on the doors, unstopping pipes and drains, untangling tangles of wires. He will help me brush the tangles and wet mats out of the old dog's old coat, help keep the horses and calves watered and bedded and fed. He will be of service in caring for Son, until more help should come, assisting with the linen changing and the bathing. His presence and his steadiness become aid enough.

Hartry, I will come to call him.

Missus, he will always say.

Together we survey the debacle. We pull rubber boots on used for irrigating and tread through the ooze and the sludge, using one a hoe, the other a rake, for walking and prodding sticks. We go out to the melon shed and point out each to the other the way the water has broken through the holes and seams of everything. We find the cement gully filled up with silty water, and all about the concrete floor there's a strew of debris. We gather the jetsam and toss it into the back of the pickup, and we motor down the road slowly, the water still half-tire high and finning out of the wheelwells in strange song as we roll along. We pass by more waste afloat, and stuff that's about dead-sunk and poked out of the muck—pieces of corrugated-tin roofing, rolls of baling wire, a section of picket fence, a downed county highway sign, stiffened birds, a bent pitchfork, a shovelhead, a tractor seat, the hipbone of a cow, a doll without a head, broken crockery, a shoe, a bit ring, even a pair of false teeth among the dunnage.

In days to follow we get out and keep at the job of hauling away the ruin and setting right what remains, all the while looking out for the man to come and check on Son. We bulldoze the flotsam and trash into heaps and cart it away. We cut up and drag out some of the spindled trees downed in the old lemon grove, clearing all the broken limbs and stumps out from it. We treat the horses' mildewed hooves, we doctor the calves, we bury drowned cats and chickens, toss limp snakes and stiff rodents and gophers into the canal. We toss everything worth nothing into the water, not wanting to leave time enough for any molder or rot of any kind to set in. We throw the junk in and stand on the bank watching it whirl and bob before whatever it is or was is sunk. We watch what doesn't sink float off like a body does. Then we go back to the old adobe house to tend again to Son.

I WAS OUT in the watertruck trying to restart it when I saw the sheriff's car motoring toward the house through still inches of water. He parked the car and got out and sloshed over to me in his rubber boots. He said something about the contacts being wet, and he opened the hood and put his head in under and fiddled around with something inside and said, Try again, and I did, and the motor turned over this time. Leave it to running, he said, and he closed the hood and came over to the passenger side and took his hat off and got in.

It needs to idle a minute, he said.

I wasn't planning on going anywhere yet, I said. I just wanted to know that I could when I wanted to.

I wasn't planning on driving all the way out here to give you a fix either, he said. I'm just checking on you and Son, is all. Ham tells me Son's laid up. Took a hard fall, did he?

Just before the rain, I said.

The sheriff stared at the inside of his hat as if looking for something inside it, a manner shared by a lot of men who have made their lives here.

Son doing okay?

I hope so. He got over a bad fever anyway. But he's not up yet. I'm waiting for that doctor's assistant in town, or whatever he is, to come out. I'm worried. I really am.

Man's got his hands full, the sheriff says. Relying on volunteers. Everybody's struggling. Everybody's doing what he or she can do.

What's Ham been doing? I said.

The sheriff looked into his hat and shook his head. Ham's in a mess, he said. He surely would've come out here to see how the two of you were doing, but he got all raveled up during the flooding. It was a disaster. The whole thing's been a disaster.

Guess that's why they call these things disasters, after all.

What makes you so smart-alecky sometimes?

I shrug.

Anyways, as to Ham. Damned flabbergasting! Jeez—I still can't reckon it, the way he and Pearl's entire house went floating away. Place slid just like that down into the water. Built right close along the riverside at the start, but who could've guessed such a thing to happen. Man, when them banks gave loose, everything fell in and all but disappeared. Wouldn't believe it to see it. Just like that. Gone. Swallowed up. Most every bit of it. They lost a lot of their stock as well. Even lost their rig.

Where's Ham at?

We got him there at the Centro Médico. He'll be kept resting a few more days. We found him bobbing down the canalbank clinging to a tractor-size inner tube he was using as a buoy. He was hollering out ahoy to get help until someone come. Nothing wrong with him really, they say. Just wore-out tired. Likely a touch of shock to boot.

There's no way to telephone with the lines still down.

It'll be a while.

I'll have to leave Son and go into town. I don't want to move him if I don't have to. Hartry can watch him for me until I'm back. Maybe I can at least get some medical advice from that man, and I can check on Ham there the same time.

Ham would appreciate a familiar face, I'm sure, he said. We're trying to get word to his wife and his girl, but they're hours away, and the road north is no good yet. Anyways, he said, you better get that husband a yours looked after.

The sheriff climbed out of the watertruck and put his hat on, raising a hand, but not looking back at me to take leave.

Later in the day I make the slow wet drive to the Centro Médico.

I'm looking to find the man that should know something here. I wander down a dank-smelling hallway, the linoleum squishy beneath my feet, and find the man in a medicine room, pouring orange juice into little paper cups. He puts the container down and looks at me and waits for me to speak. I launch right in. I tell him about Son, about how the accident happened. I tell him about the fever. I describe the fit.

He listens, not saying anything until I finish and am quiet. I look at him and wonder what he remembers of me. I wait for what he might say. He lets out a breath. He uses the word neurogenic. He uses the words tonic and clonic.

I don't know, I say.

He hurt his head, the man says, is what the case is.

That was some months back he was brought in after driving into that ditch, I say. You fixed him up all right then. He was recovered enough to work and ride again after that. He was moving about just fine.

No, the man says, I'm saying he must have hurt his head again when he took the fall off the horse. Things can go bad when a person gets hit a second time and too soon again. Yet in this instance, could instead, or in addition, be his neck.

The seizures went away, I say. They haven't since happened. It was just the one day. And there wasn't any more fever. Hasn't been. Seems to me he should be getting better with the worst being over with.

Then he ought to be up and about by now, the man says.

You don't think it just takes time for the legs to get working as they should?

The highway west is open again, he says. I suggest you and your hired man get your husband bundled up and in a truck, and then be getting on your way as soon as is possible.

The man turns away and goes back to pouring orange juice.

Where's Ham at?

Down the hall and left, he says, nudging his shoulder in a direction.

I find Ham in a common room with four other beds in it—more like cots than beds, really—with a Mexican man Ham's age, and another man across from him whose arms are swaddled and bent, and two others at the end of the room laid out flat, just kids both of them, and both looking pretty bad. Ham sits up in the bed, seeming pleased to see me. I pull a stool up to his bedside and take the hand he has out to me. He bursts into talk. He is all story, a story he has told and will tell again and again, until it is memorized and bettered.

He waggles his arms about in the air in his describing. Ye gods, when that river began to rise! he says. You could see the roiling waters beating away at the sides of the banks like there was a monster with great jaws chomping away in there. And like that came the breach—ah! holy bejesus, could not, but could not, believe my eyes. There was a couple of the hired men around left to help me. We run around like crazy men. We tried to sandbag the break as best we could, tried bundles of arrowweed brush, any kind of brush, that we'd bound with barbed wiring to stanch it, none of it working any, but we kept on trying, plugging the break with wood pilings, cut trees, rocks we'd gathered, mattresses, chairs, even a sack of dead cats and chickens, anything we could get a hold of that wasn't already washed away on us — even drove an entire disc machine into the cleave. But to no avail. The current was too strong, stronger than any man. We couldn't rein it back. No one could've. Now everthing is gone. All my stock is gone — my ponies, my beeves, my everthing. We even lost our prize, Bodacious. He turns to look out the window, breathing as though he's out of breath.

I don't know what to say, I say. Sheriff says the waters are ebbing. It won't be long. You've got to get something back. It can't all be gone. You'll see. Things just don't all up and disappear like that, I say.

Don't they? Ham says. What I'll go back and see is the outright desolation of the place, is what I'll see. He shakes his head. There won't be much left, if anything, he says. It's a free-for-all out there right now. It may even be done with. Most everthing of value that didn't die or get busted is been taken away by those who would just outright come and take it. Whatever there might've been to be found is by now sitting over on the other side of the border. And I'm too tired to start over, he says. He raises an arm and then drops it heavy as a wet towel whopped onto the bed.

That means you'll be leaving, I say, not asking a question.

There's that daughter a mine's about to give birth, he says. I ought to get up there to see her. To see it, this grandchild, when it comes. There might be something of value to the whole grand-pappy thing. People says there is, anyways.

Tell me if you see Son, I say.

See Son wheres?

In your grandbaby.

Ham shakes his head and looks down. We done the best we could with them two, he says. No one's fault, he says. Or everyone's fault, you could say. Either way you want to look at it.

Ham takes my hand again. You bring Son up and stay with us.

He's got to get better first.

The light gauzes through the cloth tacked over the window. We sit a minute in the quiet.

Ham tips his head back onto the pillow. I miss my wife, he says. I need my Pearl. Everthing here is lost to me. Lost to us. She'll tell us what we need to do. She'll hold us all together. Pearl'll know. She always does know.

The road up should be passable soon, I say.

The way is easy enough, he says.

We squeeze each the other's hand.

Go on, before you have me actin' like a weepy old man. I won't allow it, he says.

I promise Ham a visit from us, first chance there is, knowing I won't go. Then I get up from the stool and we bid our goodbyes, each waving a hand, and we say our good-lucks, as everyone does.

THERE ARE NIGHT skies that arrive clear and brilliant again. There are phases of the moon to be seen, and along with them the dim light of Andromeda, the orange ball of Mars, the cloud-shrouded Venus, and Saturn, ringed and mooned with Titan beside, and Jupiter, brightest of all. Distant suns and galaxies swing brightly above and counterwise to the clocks of our

making. There are tailed sightings of comets to behold, the orbit-
ing of manmade things, and cosmic objects that tumble and
flicker, all wondrous as lives on the earth below.

MORNING COMES WITH the warm dawn.

And the river runs whisperingly, ponderously, heavy with the
silt they say it's carried since its beginning.

I open all the shades and shutters to let the light flood inside.
Watch the drift of motes. Where can order be made?

Start with the dust. Its constant drift has been settled by
the spell of humidity, turning the dirt a covering of skin
throughout the house. Use the duster tool and wag it up high
in the air, working top to bottom, methodically, stroking over
every wall in every room, damp-ragging the baseboards, the
windowsills, the shelves. Shake draperies, beat upholstery,
whisk out insides of sideboard and cabinetry, sweep floors.
Wipe the hardwood down in a lemon-oil mix of hot water.
Mop and wax tiles and linoleum to bring to a shine once more.
Scrub stove and oven with abrasives, vinegar the inside of the
refrigerator, wash cupboards and pantry, arrange cleaning
supplies beneath sink and in broom closet, tack back anything hanging awop throughout the place. Polish appliances,
get countertops and chrome back to gleaming. Bring forth
appearances. Wash pots and dishes, leaving them dry to sparkle in the light streaming through the kitchen window. Launder and iron the linens, make the beds fresh. Finish the
ablutions.

Ready belongings for satchel and suitcase, mine and his,
accordingly. Think of the things we mostly don't need.

The old dog scratches at the doorscreen. I go outside with her and wander in the garden beds to see what might be left. There's a brittlebush down by the cattle pen that's been shocked into flowering after the storm. I cut a bunch of the hardy, baby florets and bring them back to the old adobe house and fill a vase with them.

I walk room to room in the quiet.

Rose, I say, waiting for the echo.

Rose's Daddy, I say, still hearing nothing.

WE HAD TO figure a way of carrying him out of the house and getting him lifted up into the back of the pickup. It was my idea to use the old Navajo that lay on the floor. The hired man nodded and got the rug and brought it into the old man and Rose's room, where Son still lay. We turned Son to one side, and the hired man made a face at the swelled and mottled flesh. Those sores are doubled in size every time we have to look it them, he said.

There was an odor festering. My stomach rolled at the smell of him, this man, yet my husband. My fingers left imprints in the skin in the places where I pressed. We had bathed him yesterday evening, but already we needed to bathe him again. The hired man brought in a basin filled with warm water, and I gathered towels and washcloths. Together we pivoted Son, one side to the next, and I soaped and rinsed his skin, front and back, and applied a zinc ointment to the sores while Hartry held him to stay for me. Reach me that tin of talcum if you can, I said. I powdered Son up with the stuff, putting us to coughing and sneezing in the baby-fragranced cloud of dust that rose about. The old dog went into a fit of snorting and hobbled out of the room. A cricket jumped out of a boot and skittered across the floor.

Here, spread the rug lengthwise on the bed, I said, and fold it halfways the longways. There, that's it. I had by now shaved the beard from Son's face, and we had him dressed in clean clothes and sprinkled with his old-spicey aftershave, and he smelled good and looked almost handsome again. Wait, I said. I reached for a comb and neatened Son's hair. There, I said. Ready. Now we shifted him over the lump of folded rug and turned him to face the hired man. Seeing he had a firm grasp of Son's hip and his shoulder, I could then reach for the edge of the rug and pull it from its fold so that it was full open beneath Son, and we rested him flat onto it. This is where the hard part started.

Pull the armchair up close to the bed right next to you, I said. Now we trade places.

The hired man didn't need to be told to get up onto the bed on his knees. He had the idea by now. We each of us had a good purchase on the rug edge when I gave us the one-two-three. We lifted Son enough to clear him from the bed, and we more or less heaved and pulled and reached him like this and dropped him rug and all into the armchair. The work of the lift made a sweat break on the hired man's forehead. I felt heat and color rise in me as well.

It's getting warm again, I said. You'll need all the fans going soon.

Rain don't keep us cooled for too long, he said.

Son babbled and flailed his arms at us. We had to get him from the chair to the floor, and this maneuver took less effort, as Son moved with the carry of the rug and was breeched to the boards. We could drag him along without difficulty then, over the threshold and out to the cool dark parlor and into the ticking of the old clock, across the room and over the next threshold, and out and onto the porch. The old dog stood with her nose to the screen and whimpered as we hauled Son down the steps and parked him on the ground close to the back end of the pickup.

I don't know if I've got the strength for the next big lift. I know I don't. As I was thinking what next to do, the hired man gestured toward a cleanup crew of Mexicans out on the road. He jogged over to the Ambassador and drove out to fetch the help we needed. I went into the house to see what money was left in Son's wallet.

The rest was easier. I thanked the guys who came to aid, and offered to pay them, but they wouldn't take the money I held out. The kind-eyed and ragged men just looked at Son, the way he was laid out in the bed of the pickup. They said things in Spanish that sounded like condolences or maybe snippets of prayers, and they shook their heads, surely indicating pity.

THERE WERE NOT many things to put into the satchel but for a clean shirt, a sweater hardly worn since I've been here, a change of socks and some underthings, toothpaste, toothbrush, hairbrush, comb, a book never returned to the library, the school letter welcoming me. I put the tiny leathered heart, carried so long in my pocket, into the metal keepsake box returned from Daughter Pearl, and tucked the heart in a pouch in the satchel. I put the garnet necklace around my neck. The old man's old pocketwatch I put into Son's pocket, in the fresh pair of dungarees we've dressed him in. There are clothes washed and pressed for Son and folded into the suitcase, the suitcase settled next to him in the bed of the truck. Everything else I leave in the care of the hired man. I leave it to Hartry.

Hartry will care for the old adobe house until someone should come to claim it. I leave him to care for the horses — the mare and the bay and the sorrel and the paint — the calves too, and I leave him the hotshot to poke them with, along with all the rest of it that belongs in the toolroom and the tackroom. I leave the ropes and the saddles, the bridles and reins, the spurs, the chaps, the hames and the riggings, and whatever other things — all this I leave in his care. I leave him the old man's shotgun, the old man's best hat, his boots. The pickup I will take, leaving the watertruck with Hartry. Last, but not a bit least, I leave him the old man's old dog.

This is not easy for either of us, meaning the dog and me.

You can't go, is what I say outright to the animal.

She gives a hacking cough, as if she were trying to clear something stuck in her throat, which likely she is. She watches me get into the truck and she trots alongside for a time as I drive through the stubble and tip pits of the felled lemon grove. By the time I turn onto Old Border Road, the old dog is gone from sight, and soon enough too is the old adobe house. I keep from looking back. I won't. I only check the rearview mirror to see Son laid out atop the rug, back in the bed of the truck, covered over with a dusty-colored tarpaulin.

I drive on in the polished light.

The incredible, delicate light.

How to describe it, this light? How to tell of the day? How to tell of the rarity of it, the pure aridity of it, the feeling of driving away in it? All of what had been warped in the heat and blurred in the haze stands out pristine in the day's radiance. Jets rocket in the flawless blue, leaving the yonder above us scripted with unread messages. The tracks and prints of desert creatures are etched as they once were into earth, the eskers and gametrails scrolled into foothills and riverbeds. What do the tidings bid? Where might the paths lead? Is it hope alone that pulls us forward? All about, you see emblems of truth—the heads and shoots of living things breaking through loam, birds nesting in tree limbs and cavities, small animals building their middens anew. There will be stars to see tonight, and nights ahead filled with other latitudes and longitudes, hours and degrees that spur different views.

Hold it while ye may.

Old madrone and smoke trees rustle leaves as we go. Men working along the road doff their hats, families mending homes or erecting them again turn and raise their hands, a pack of dogs runs alongside the truck for a time, barking us onward. We travel one approach of town to the next, heading out the exitway, or entryway, depending on which way you're facing, and passing the famous desert prison, deserted and ruinous as it is, a tunnel of dark cast within its sallyport. Soon the whirring of tires takes us across the bridge, throwing us over to the other side, the water below flowing again like the river it had been. We move through marshy sloughs and washes rich with ironwood and paloverde. We cross over the old railroad tracks and turn west onto highway, taking what was our honeymoon way.

As we tell of places we have been, those places we would someday go.

We traverse saltbush and greasewood, snakewood and creosote, ride over sun-varnished ground and on into barren uplands of pedregal and old lava flow. The tarpaulin billows about Son as we pick up speed, and before long the wind is tugging the tarpaulin loose from its hold under Son's head and the tuck under his boots. I'm thinking to pull over to the side of the road to fix the canvas better, but before there's a chance the thing entire gets lifted by an updraft and right like that it's spiraling up and off into the sandhills beside us. I look into the mirror and see it ghosting away, watching until it disappears.

Going on. Moving through the alone that solely the desert instills.

Up ahead are the remains of an airfield where the carcass of an old aircraft lies ablaze in full sun. The land past it turns dense with cholla and prickly pear, with organ pipe and beehive and ocotillo, with sotol, yucca, agave, with barrels of saguaro fattened by the rain, their plump arms raised in praise. The truck climbs through a gap in the foothills, where hoodoos and pulpits and spires rise above, where the road cuts through out-crops of bubbled rocks and salmon-colored cobbles and tumbles of boulders, the stones spray-painted lately with Spanish names or incised with Indian myths from centuries ago—the petro-glyphs and the intaglios—the sticked figures and ways of living carved into rock face, the gravels pecked and tamped and scraped to make hunter, lion, bison, horses with flowing manes, unnameable creatures, creeping things. The truck chugs on into higher country yet, a land of scrub pine and juniper and pinyon. I sight the turnoff to the lodge that was our honeymoon place—*just the beginning of all the places we say we have yet to get to*—and a feeling comes over me that catches under the breastbone. I fix the mirror to get a better look at Son, see him flat on his back, his boots rolled outwardly, hands at his sides. Going on. I hit the radio switch but find only crackles and buzz. I try to find a song in me and get a melody and the first line of one or two going, but nothing will stick. And on. Until arriving now to the top of the pass. We coast the rest of the way, speed through habra and gore, canyon and butte, and down into low-land, old patrol roads nudged south in the distance. I clutch and shift and touch brake when we come to where the road goes two ways.

Take the road now you have yet to take.

It's simple enough from here, with just an interchange onto a feeder road that keeps going and takes you right to the place. You know you have arrived by the arrows and signs that point the way, and by the swells in the paving that are meant to slow you, know too by the tall palms, yet anchored and pillared for support and made to stand sentry at the entrance. Dwarf roses ornament the dirt plots of the parking lot all about, and little pyramid evergreens and flowering shrubs here and there do their best to cheer, though the charm of the outside cannot disguise what the inside is. A smell of overturned earth mixed with new-sawn wood and just-laid concrete pours in through the window, all of it the smell of beginning. A piece of heavy equipment in the distance growls along a driveway being laid. I pass the many empty slots, some of them with names stenciled in paint to lay claim, but instead of putting the truck into park in a proper space, I pull up to the front of the building and stop, where here I will quit the engine and get out and let the tailgate down, with its protest of joint and hinge. Then I climb up into the bed with Son.

He looks bad. His eyes are swollen, his lips cankered, his face reddened and sweaty. No longer is he handsome to look at, and for this I can be relieved. I don't want to want him the way I did. I don't want to want him at all. I hold his head up and try to get him to take a drink of water, and he puckers his lips, but most of the water spills out of his mouth and trickles down the folds of his neck when I tip the canteen. Try again, I say, and he does, and this time he chokes and spits and curses me. I wipe his throat with a bandanna, seeing the flesh there that I have put

my lips to and loved, and a pang from an inmost place too buried
to get at becomes a reminder of what I would wish away. I wet
the bandanna more and wipe the road grime from his face, glad
he keeps his eyes closed and doesn't look at me, likely because
of the sun, or could be the crust on the lids keeps them stuck, or
maybe it's because of me, I don't know, but no matter the case,
I open the soaked cloth and use it to cover his face over. I take a
deep breath in, for me, for him, and wait for what's next, waiting
and noticing the light, how different it is here in particular and
with the season of year—a light strange as it is familiar, making
for a splendored deformity in the day that can't be explained.
What can't be explained, that which we are held in by, and what
it is that's impossible to see, simply because we're in the midst of
it and can't yet know where we are. There is no map to map the
way. No one to tell you that you're right or that you're wrong. A
big perching bird on a lamppost chucks at us from above. Son
says something, but what it is is blurred by the damp mask and
his mix-up and daze. I say something to him about time and
things getting better. I chase a fly off his chest.

There's a pounding of hammers, overlapped as irregular heart-
beats, coming from over where another part of the building is
being built, a cement mixer nearby that churns and whines, but
no voices anywhere to be heard nor anybody to be seen. After a
while I spot a couple of people through the entryway, standing inside the place looking out toward the truck at us, and I
raise my arm to gesture them toward us. The wide glass doors
open and close on their own, and two men are breathed out.
They saunter across the brand-new concrete, wearing pastel-
colored pajamas, their faces cameo'd by the sun behind them, a
slice of moon high above in the blue. They get to the truck and
see Son laid out in the back of it, looking the way he does, and

one of them nods his head and goes back in through the magic doors, this time coming back with a stretcher. The men speak in undertones, one to the other, as if knowing what is and what might be, and together they get Son out of the bed of the truck and onto the rolling cot, covering him with a clean sheet, as a heap-up of cumulus cuts in front of the sun and dims us and everything below. I stand back as they place Son's arms and legs the way they were taught to do, and they fix him snug into the sheet, and one of them unlocks the foot brake and they trolley Son along, with me following at their heels, with the cement mixer roaring more loudly in the background now, with the hammers hammering on, with the doors opening wide for us with a mechanical sigh, and Son is wheeled deep into the wondrous cool of the tiled lobby. Here I will stop at what they call Admitting, and let them go without me, watching as they move across the room to head down a long hallway, going from soil and pavement to molding and flooring, from sunlight to fluorescence, from the space they so inhabit to the emptiness that is left, as they turn the corner and are gone, with me standing and waiting, as if someone should come to put back what there had been.

Miss, a clerk behind a desk says.

A woman will hold a clipboard my way, and I will take it along with the pen attached to it that hangs from a chain, not saying anything, just filling in the blanks that need filling in, signing in all the places where the check marks have been made, and writing my full and proper name.

ABOUT THE AUTHOR

Susan Froderberg was born in Washington State. She moved east to study medical ethics and philosophy at Columbia University, where she received her doctorate. She lives with her husband in New York City.

Reading Group Guide

OLD
BORDER
ROAD

A NOVEL BY

SUSAN FRODERBERG

A CONVERSATION WITH SUSAN FRODERBERG

The author of *Old Border Road* talks with Stephenie Harrison of *BookPage*.

This is your first book to be published, so to start, congratulations! Can you tell us a little about what prompted you to write a novel and what it was like trying to get it published?

Old Border Road began as a short story, published in a literary journal and later anthologized. I went back to the story because I believed there was still more to be said. I had found a place where I could wander about, and with it a way of speaking that was coming to me pretty easily. So I wrote a first chapter, "A Home to Go Home To," which was also published as a short story. There was enough to keep me going after this, and I carried on. From there it was a matter of patience and will and discipline.

I had written a novel before but put the thing into a drawer, thinking it not worthy of publication. I was satisfied enough with *Old Border Road* to read parts of it over the telephone to a writer friend when it was finished. He encouraged me to send it out, and I took his advice and did. My agent was the first person to read the entire book.

You lived in Arizona during your high school years, and you set your novel there as well. Although you have since lived elsewhere, and now live in New York City, why did you choose to set your novel in Arizona? Did you feel you had some unfinished business there?

It was more that I still had feelings for the place. I was sixteen years old when I moved to Arizona, a time of acute memory, and with it lots of adolescent daydreaming and yearning. I wanted to be an artist at the time, more than anything. My mother advised me to think about finding a job, as mothers are wont to do. I went to nursing school, and soon after graduation left Arizona and moved back home to Seattle, where the rest of my family was living.

At times, this novel is a fairly harrowing read. As an author, do you find it difficult to put your characters through such hardships?

No, for two reasons. First, characters are words, not people. Second, human existence is filled with hardship. Every epic or dramatic poem or great novel is about a struggle of some kind; it's a striving for happiness, it's about someone trying to get something. There are endless wishes and wants. Unless we're able to strangle all desire and thereby achieve nothingness, or nirvana, there remains to us a state of being in which one desire necessarily follows another. If there is no such thing as lasting contentment or absolute happiness, how could it be a subject of art? I am with Schopenhauer here.

One piece of advice that is frequently offered to aspiring authors is that you should write about what you know. To what extent would you say you apply this principle to your own work?

Sure, it helps to be familiar with the subject matter you're delving into. Melville's experience on a whaling boat gave him the authority to write about whaling. On the other hand, I don't believe Melville necessarily threw a harpoon or survived a sinking ship, just as McCarthy did not scalp Indians or make love to dead bodies in order to write what he did. As for myself, it's true I have run barrels, and have even tried to throw a rope to heel a calf, however inexpertly. But I lay no claim to ever preparing for any role in a rodeo, except that of hollering bystander.

As an author, what is harder to write when it comes to a book: the first sentence or the last?

I would say they are equally difficult, or equally not difficult.

Trying to find a rhythm or a meter specific to the telling of a particular story, and keeping on with it from beginning to end, is the trickier thing.

Are there any particular authors who inspire you or that you feel have had a notable impact on your own writing?

Certainly Schopenhauer, as I mentioned earlier. And absolutely Emerson. Add to the list Frost and Stevens, Joyce and Beckett, O'Connor and Robinson, among others. To my mind, there is no greater American writer alive than Cormac McCarthy. All of us, as writers—as artists—come out of some petri dish, and I will admit to coming out of his. There is no such thing as the innocent eye, or the innocent ear, no matter what anybody tells you. On the other hand, we are each of us necessarily what no one else can possibly be.

Do you find your philosophy background has enriched your writing?

Probably, because the opportunity to study philosophy has enriched my life. But I'm happier being a writer than I would have been if I were doing philosophy work, as writing has set me free in a way that philosophy—specifically, Western philosophy—could not have. In Western philosophy, you must follow formal logic—if A, then not B. In fiction, you may have both A *and* B, if you so choose. You can be exhausted and you can be exhilarated at the same time: one state need not negate the other. Or you can be derived and you can be unique, without contradiction. This is not to say we can do away with logic—there would be no language without it. But in writing, it's possible to bend language toward a more Eastern way of thinking.

Also, I would say my background—both practical and educational—has been so varied that philosophy is only a part of it. My time as a critical care nurse enriched my life: sometimes, I consider it the most important work I've done, though at the time I was too busy to realize it. My undergraduate degree (after nursing school) was in economics; that too opened me up to a better way of understanding the world. And my PhD was a joint degree: I was in Columbia's School of Public Health as well as in the philosophy department. It was the era of interdisciplinary studies, and I was fortunate to have been able to design the course of my study—no one there before had formally done anything in medical ethics.

What are you working on next?

Another novel, this one also inspired by a particular landscape, though it isn't set in the desert. I know where I am, but I have no idea where I'll end up. It's a voyage of discovery. I'm setting forth, trying to leave things behind.

Adapted from an interview that originally appeared at BookPage.com.

QUESTIONS AND TOPICS FOR DISCUSSION

1. Many of the characters in *Old Border Road* are not called by their given names—Girl, Rose's Daddy (the old man), the Padre, Pearl's daughter, and Son, for instance. At the end of the novel, Katherine writes "her full and proper name." What do you think this is meant to convey about her future?

2. The Kirkus review for *Old Border Road* called it a "highly stylized, uniquely voiced first novel." In what ways did both the colloquial diction and the more elevated, almost biblical language help or hinder your pleasure in reading?

3. "For if not striving, what might there be but tedium?" says Katherine. How does this thought, also expressed by Rose's Daddy, separate her from Son? Is Son a cipher, or is there power in his silence?

4. Both Rose and Pearl Hart advise Katherine to overlook the philandering nature of men. How do the two women differ from each other in conducting their lives? Which is Katherine more responsive to, and what does this reveal about her own character?

5. Do you think that Rose's Daddy's suicide was justified? Did his "sermon" influence your thinking about this question?

6. How does the natural world—the landscape and weather of the Southwest—intensify or determine the human events recounted in *Old Border Road*? How have the landscape and climate where you live affected your life?

7. What was your reaction to Katherine taking refuge with the Padre? Aside from Son's infidelity, what do you think were the strongest immediate causes of her desire for another companion?

8. How are Hartry, the hired hand, and Ham able to provide support for Katherine when the other men in her life have abandoned her? Do these characters serve to banish gender stereotypes in the novel? How do Pearl's daughter and Katherine differ in their relationships with men?

9. Ranching and rodeo require manual work and dexterity, as well as a willingness to take risks. In what

ways do these efforts mirror your own work and outside interests? How do they differ?

10. At the beginning of *Old Border Road*, Katherine is
alone, and she is alone again at the end of the story.
In what ways has she gained the fortitude and inde-
pendence to move forward? What impact do you
imagine the receipt of "some letter from some
school" will have on her life?

THE BRAVE
A novel by Nicholas Evans

"Well written, thought provoking.... Nicholas Evans now brings readers *The Brave,* another first-rate story but with a decidedly different twist." —Sybil Downing, *Denver Post*

"In his first novel in five years Evans displays a sure hand at drawing characters and their motivations and settings as diverse as a gloomy boarding school, glamorous Hollywood, and the wide-open spaces of the West. This should appeal to all lovers of good storytelling." —Dan Forrest, *Library Journal*

THE TERROR OF LIVING
A novel by Urban Waite

"Phil Hunt is a decent guy who supplements his living by muling hard drugs in the Pacific Northwest. Bobby Drake is the deputy sheriff who's trying to hunt him down. The resulting chase is pure dynamite. This is one of those books you start at one in the afternoon and put down, winded, after midnight." —Stephen King, *Entertainment Weekly*

"This formidable fiction debut by Urban Waite unfolds in short and often all too memorably violent sequences, yet the author also allows his characters room to wrestle with private demons as the intense, often gruesome tale races toward its satisfying resolution." —Tom Nolan, *Wall Street Journal*

Also available from Back Bay Books

SAINTS AND SINNERS
Stories by Edna O'Brien

"Edna O'Brien writes the most beautiful, aching stories of any writer, anywhere."   —Alice Munro

"There is no Irish writer who compares in terms of style, stamina, depth, or meaning."
—Colum McCann, author of *Let the Great World Spin*

ROOM
A novel by Emma Donoghue

"An astounding, terrifying novel....It's a testament to Donoghue's imagination and empathy that she is able to fashion radiance from such horror."   —*The New Yorker*

"Donoghue brings her story to a powerful close that feels exactly right. This is a truly memorable novel....It presents an utterly unique way to talk about love."
—Aimee Bender, *New York Times Book Review*

Back Bay Books
Available wherever paperbacks are sold

Also available from Back Bay Books

BEING POLITE TO HITLER
A novel by Robb Forman Dew

"Dew has captured, beautifully, the poetry of the every-day.... With lush, graceful language, she reminds us that much of what we consider to be ordinary in our lives, in the end, turns out to be quite extraordinary."
— Jim Carmin, *Minneapolis Star Tribune*

"Highly original.... Robb Forman Dew covers both the cosmic and the quotidian as she follows a formidably intermingled group of people in the town of Washburn, Ohio.... Dew's novels iden-tify and describe not just a town and its people but the Ameri-can mind-set at particular moments in time."
— Meg Wolitzer, *New York Times Book Review*

THE WIFE'S TALE
A novel by Lori Lansens

"Mary's odyssey of heartache and hope is not so much about finding her husband as it is about rediscovering herself."
— Lisa Kay Greissinger, *People*

"Heartbreakingly funny and sad.... Lansens — who lived so memorably inside the heads of conjoined twins in *The Girls* — sketches another indelible female character here."
— Tina Jordan, *Entertainment Weekly*

Back Bay Books
Available wherever paperbacks are sold

Available from Mulholland Books

THE BAYOU TRILOGY

Under the Bright Lights • *Muscle for the Wing*
The Ones You Do

by Daniel Woodrell

Collected for the first time in a single volume—three early works of crime fiction by a major American novelist.

"A backcountry Shakespeare.... The inhabitants of Daniel Woodrell's fiction often have a streak that's not just mean but savage; yet physical violence does not dominate his books. What does dominate is a seasoned fatalism.... Woodrell has tapped into a novelist's honesty, and lucky for us, he's remorseless that way."
—*Los Angeles Times*

"Daniel Woodrell writes with an insistent rhythm and an evocative and poetic regional flavor." —*The New Yorker*

"Woodrell writes books so good they make me clench my fists in jealousy and wonder." —*Esquire*

"What people say about Cormac McCarthy goes double for Daniel Woodrell. Possibly more." —*New York*

Mulholland Books
Available wherever books are sold